Book Two

◆

Flight to the Citadel

By

Laura L. Comfort

Essence of Galenia: Flight to the Citadel

By Laura L. Comfort

Copyright 2014 by Laura L. Comfort
Cover Design & Photos by Laura L. Comfort
Images by CanStock: Design West, W20R

ISBN: 978-0-9920792-3-9

"I am enough of an artist to draw freely upon my imagination. Imagination is more important than knowledge. Knowledge is limited. Imagination encircles the world."

— Albert Einstein

Lexis,
Thanks for being my fan!

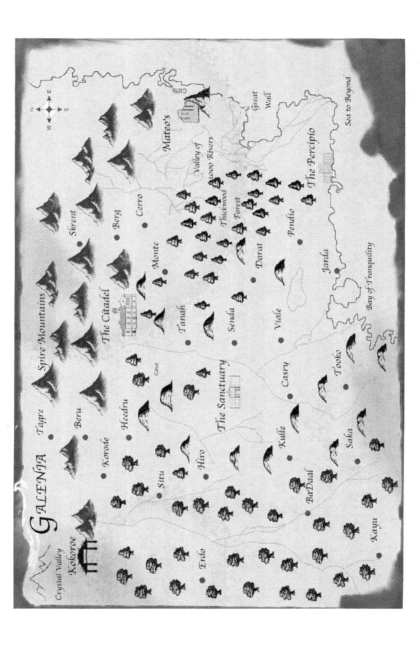

For Sydney and Keaton

◆

Thank you for your patience; a year is a long time to

wait to find out how a story ends!

Table of Contents

Prologue

THE DUST BILLOWED.

Thrown to the ground for the tenth time, Hanna lay winded. She groaned in pain as the world spun out of control around her.

"Up!" Tahtay Biatach bellowed, also for the tenth time.

Hanna propped herself up on her elbows.

"I can't!" she whined. "I think I'm going to be sick."

Tahtay Biatach knelt down beside her.

"Why is that, do you suppose?" he asked, not unkindly.

Hanna sat up further and rubbed her face with her hands.

"I'm just so dizzy. And banging my head on this so-called matt over and over isn't helping either."

"Hmmm. That suggests you're not falling right."

"Falling right! It's a little thing called gravity. I don't think there's any other way to fall but down."

Biatach laughed in spite of himself.

"Yes, I suppose I should rephrase that. You need to improve how you land."

Hanna opened her mouth to snipe off another derogatory comment, but Biatach raised his hand.

"Yes, Hanna. There is a right way and wrong way to land. That is if you consider preventing injury the *right way*. As for being dizzy, there are ways to help with that too. Perhaps we will take a break from this exercise and work on finding your centre."

"Does it involve keeping both my feet planted firmly on the ground?"

Without answering, Biatach stood up and offered his hand to Hanna. She reached for it, grateful for the help, but when she lent her weight to him, he released his grip and she tumbled back to the ground.

"Ouch!" she cried. "Why did you do that?"

With no hint of humour Biatach replied, "This is serious training Hanna. You will be surrounded by heartless, cruel people. Right now you are too trusting. It is my responsibility to make you tougher, not just physically, but mentally. From now on you need to be wary of those around you, for you never know when they will try to throw you to the ground."

He walked a few paces away before he turned back and added, "...or try to kill you."

Hanna shivered. What had she gotten herself into?

* * *

Leaning against a tree in an isolated part of one of the gardens at Kokoroe, Hanna recounted her lesson to Kazi. She paused to guzzle her mint water that she had picked up from the main hall.

"I don't get it," Kazi said, "You were the best in Biatach's class — you barely broke a sweat, but now you're always telling me how completely exhausted you are. What's going on?"

2

"Well, before he would give us a couple laps around the field or a trip through the obstacle course, which I had no problem with. Now he tells me *'ten laps Hanna'* and if I do ten laps without much effort he says *okay, let's have another five*. Then, if I'm still upright, he'll give me a few more until I actually collapse on the ground."

Kazi smirked, "Well that's easy, just collapse on the ground sooner."

She rolled her eyes and groaned. "I tried that once, but he knew I was faking. He said *while your down there, let's have fifty push-ups*. If my butt was too high, he'd place his foot on it and give it a push and then he started to measure how low I got to the ground. By the end my arms were shaking like crazy. To say he was lenient by letting me rest after would be deceiving — what choice did he have? I couldn't move."

"I'd be lucky to do ten. Fifty pushups is really good."

Hanna considered a moment and recalled that not too long ago she had dreaded pushups.

"Back home ten would have been my max. I'm not sure why, but I feel stronger here. Maybe it's something to do with the Essence." Since coming to Galenia, Hanna discovered she was capable of many things that she couldn't do back on Earth. In addition to having greater endurance and strength, she was also able to see and manipulate the Essence, an essential element contained in all life and even the very air on Galenia.

"Have you ever asked Master Juro about it?" Kazi asked.

She chortled. "Perhaps if I had asked him a few weeks ago I would have gotten an answer, but ever since I offered to help with this Mateo business he barely tells me anything. Mostly he tells me to *observe, concentrate, focus*. It's all about trying to manipulate the Essence."

"I guess that makes sense. Being able to use Essence saved your life when that wolcott attacked."

"I suppose," she conceded. "It's just that I can't help but think maybe he doesn't want me to know too much. You know? In case when I'm in enemy territory I might say too much or something?"

Kazi nodded. "True, you can't tell them what you don't know. Still, you'd think Master Juro and Biatach would be a bit easier on you. I mean, you've only been at this for a short time."

"Right?" Hanna was grateful to have a sympathetic ear. It helped to alleviate her misery. And by the end of their conversations, Kazi always had her laughing.

The next day, when Hanna arrived at the site of her training session with Tahtay Biatach, she was surprised to find someone else instead. As she approached she recognized the tall, slim figure of Karn.

"Hey Karn. What are you doing here? Please don't tell me it's to gather more stories for dinner conversation. I'm afraid I'd provide you with far too much material." Every time she saw Karn, Hanna was reminded that when they first met she made a fool of herself at the river crossing. She had climbed up on the log bridge and discovered too late she was backwards. In an attempt to make up for her blunder, she chose to do a flip off the end like a gymnast, which resulted in a scolding. Karn delighted in sharing her prideful moment with all her friends at supper that night.

4

Karn laughed. "I believe I get to join in with your training. I understand you're learning a form of weaponless defence?"

Hanna raised her eyebrows. "Is that what I'm doing? I thought I was just being thrown around a lot and being pushed to utter exhaustion."

"Sounds fun, can't wait to be part of it."

She couldn't tell if he was being sarcastic or not.

"Glad to hear," she said, "as they say back home: misery loves company."

Just then, Tahtay Biatach arrived.

"Let's have ten laps today and from this point on, if I'm not here when you arrive, just start doing laps."

Karn nodded and took off. Apparently he knew Biatach's methods well enough not to argue. Hanna had learned the hard way — whenever she questioned Biatach's instructions, he often tagged on extra work. She quickened her pace so she could catch up to Karn; she'd hate to find out there was also a penalty for coming in last.

* * *

"Well?" Master Juro sat cross-legged in his usual chair in his domicile facing Tahtay Biatach.

"She's improving. It was slow at first, but I brought Karn in to train with her two weeks ago, and now she's pushing harder. And complaining less."

"Good. I too have noticed a change. She seems more focused. How long do you suppose?"

Biatach sat quietly contemplating the question for a moment.

"I think by spring she will be ready. Of course, I'd prefer to have a couple years to train her."

Master Juro nodded.

"It would be preferable. I think that it would be unwise to wait. Spring will have to do. That gives us around nine months." He paused then added, "Yes, I think that she will progress far in that time."

Biatach crossed his arms and leaned back.

"It's only a month before semester change. That's going to be hard on her."

"In what way?" Master Juro asked.

"Kazi will be leaving, as will all her other classmates, aside from the Juro that is."

They both knew that the Juro did not leave after one semester since they had years worth of studying to do at Kokoroe. Master Juro considered Biatach's statement for a moment trying to assess the effect the semester change would have on Hanna. True, she no longer attended lessons with her original classmates, but she did spend her off-hours with them. Her Essence training was introspective and didn't provide much in the way of socializing. Perhaps he would have to devise a way to allow Hanna to connect with the new batch of students when they arrived.

"Of course," Biatach continued, "She'll still have Karn for awhile longer." Karn had already completed his training at all three schools. He had returned to Kokoroe for specialized training with Biatach.

"That's something. Do they get on well?"

Biatach chuckled. "Yes, I think so. They do seem to enjoy trying to outdo each other."

"Thank you for bringing this issue to my attention. I will give it some further thought."

By that he meant he would take the matter up with Tahtay Etai; she was better suited to dealing with the emotional side of the students. Empathy was an ability Master Juro was not proficient with.

CHAPTER ONE

Cryptic Codes

THE FLAME FLICKERED.

Sitting on her mat on the floor in the candle-lit room, Hanna looked at the relatively empty space around her. The room consisted only of a low bed, rug and some shelves that, up until a few moments ago, contained all her personal possessions along with her school uniform. It was somewhat disquieting to think everything that she had acquired while living on Galenia for the last year, fit into one bag.

Two sets of clothes, some mittens and a hat that Cardea had knitted, and a wooden box containing all her most valuable treasures. Inside were trinkets and letters from her new friends. Messengers arrived every week with letters, packages and greetings from the world outside the school, Kokoroe.

The first few weeks no letters had come for her. Hanna didn't think much of it as she had no family on Galenia. Besides, she told herself, she was only visiting and would be going home soon. But then, she began to feel a pang in her heart. She was reminded of how far away she was from her own family. When the mail was delivered, she would leave the Long Hall and wander alone as she couldn't bare to watch her fellow students excitement as they poured over their letters and unwrapped their packages.

She fondly remembered the day the Messenger came with something for her. She was slipping her shoes on at the door when the Messenger called her name. He handed her a bundle wrapped in burlap and tied with string, and her name delicately painted on a ribbon. She held the bundle gingerly, but was too stunned to move. Not only had she never expected to receive anything, but her name was on it. She had learned that the people of Galenia had developed a pictorial writing system. Even the names of the people were written in symbols. While at school, she showed her teachers and her friends what her writing looked like and she kept a journal in her own writing. To help her learn the language, she had begun a translation book as well, with the help of Tahtay Jillian. But in all that time she had never seen anyone write her name.

She finally remembered to thank the Messenger and asked him who this gift was from. He informed her it came from the village of Kayu and Cardea sends her love. With glee, she skipped back through the grounds and made her way to her room. She wanted to be alone when she opened it; she wasn't ready to share it with anyone else just yet. Hanna hadn't seen Cardea since she left Kayu. She was a guest at Cardea's home for the two weeks she had been there.

She made herself comfortable on her bed, then carefully untied the string. Inside she found a delicate cloth with something wrapped in it sitting on top of a letter. As she unwrapped the cloth, she noticed the beautiful embroidery work that she assumed Cardea had done. There were little flowers and leaves stitched throughout the piece. Inside the cloth, Hanna discovered a small figurine carved out of wood. It was a cute whimsical character and she was sure it was the handiwork of Hamlin, Cardea's husband. She gently placed the gifts aside then opened the letter.

She wondered how Cardea had learned how to print her name, as she repeated it again at the top of the page. Referring to her translation book she was able to get the gist of the letter, but later she had Kazi help her decode the rest. She felt that what the note specifically said was trivial; it's what it meant that really mattered. It meant Hanna had a home, a family, somewhere to go if she couldn't actually get back to Earth. It meant Hanna was loved.

After that, Hanna, with Kazi's help, began corresponding with Cardea on a regular basis. She never asked how Cardea had learned to write her name because it felt magical and she wanted to keep it that way; learning that it was simply copied from a paper the Master Juro had sent or something would ruin the moment. Sometimes Cardea would include some herbs or a small figurine Hamlin carved out of wood. Whenever Hanna felt particularly homesick she would open the box where she kept the letters and reread each one. She even rewrote the letters into English so she would never forget what all the symbols meant and to make them easier to reread.

When Kazi and the other students she had started school with finished their three month semester and moved to the Citadel six months ago, her stack of letters increased until the lid of the box barely closed. Tahtay Jillian was kind enough to help her translate them once Kazi had left. It was a comfort to receive correspondence from her classmates, but her favourite were always the ones from Cardea and Kazi. Cardea brought the comfort of home and Kazi helped relieve the loneliness that she felt. It wasn't that she was alone, she had one-on-one training with Tahtay Biatach, classes with the Juro and had taken on the role of mentor to new students who arrived at the school.

At Kokoroe, everyone learned how the Juro had survived before the races came together. Come the end of the semester, all but the Juro moved on to other schools as further studies at Kokoroe required being able to manipulate the Essence. Her classmates were kind enough to her, but being Juro, they were long-lived and studied at Kokoroe for many years, meaning most of them were much older than her - hundreds of years even. Hanna had proven to be talented with her Juro-like skills so the few Juro that were her age weren't even in her class. She had made friends with the other races, the Jagare and the Jivan, but since every three months there was a semester change, they would leave for the Citadel making it difficult to build friendships. Even Karn, a talented Jagare who had returned to Kokoroe for specialized training with Tahtay Biatach and joined Hanna in her defensive fighting lessons, had moved away a few months back. They had laughed as they compared bruises and strived to surpass each other and she thoroughly enjoyed his companionship, but Karn being four years older felt more like a big brother than the kindred spirit that Kazi was.

She told herself that it was better this way. Eventually she would be going home, leaving Galenia and all its people behind, so it wasn't a good idea to get too close to anyone anyway; it would be hard enough to leave behind the friends she had already made. Instead, she delved into her training.

Now, as she tightened the buckle on her bag, a wave of excitement ran through her. Tomorrow she was leaving Kokoroe. Eventually she would be sent on a mission to infiltrate the Kameil, a sickly race that terrorized the villages and were in league with someone known as Mateo. Mateo was considered the most likely culprit for causing tears that were destroying the planet. The tears were how Hanna arrived on Galenia in the first place. Her hope was that if she discovered how Mateo caused them, Master Juro would be able to reverse the effects and send her home. Right now her initial destination was the Citadel to finish her training and it meant she would get to see Kazi and all her friends again.

The letters that Kazi had sent in the last few months had become more vague. He mentioned that he was taking some music lessons and was doing really well, but he alluded to spending much of his time in other studies. What the other studies were, he didn't say. Kazi always refrained from answering her direct questions and filled his letters with trivial things.

He wrote about his father's visit one time and how he felt bad about keeping things from him. She felt Kazi was oblivious to the irony of that sentiment since he was keeping things from her too. She hoped once they were reunited he would be more forthcoming.

After ensuring her bag was shut, she slid into bed, extinguished the candle, and attempted to shut off her mind. She needed her last night at Kokoroe to be a restful one as she was likely to get little sleep on the journey.

CHAPTER TWO

Soul Enterprise

THE AIR WAS STALE.

Nandin sat at the table in the empty command tent, reading over a scroll and rubbing his tired eyes. When he had been appointed Commander some eight months back, he didn't really know what to expect. In addition to continuing as the Yarus' morale officer, urging the men to excel and giving rousing speeches about what they could offer the Kameil and people of Galenia, he met with Mateo to discuss the Yaru missions and to go over his reports. What had taken him by complete surprise was his extended education and the amount of paperwork involved in his new role.

Since he had left school at sixteen to work the farmlands of his village, he never attended the Percipio where he would have learned higher math, geography and practiced his penmanship. Mateo felt it was crucial for Nandin to increase his knowledge in order to be successful in his current position.

He didn't mind learning these things; in fact, he was pleased to discover he was rather a good student. Sim had been assigned to him to help with his studies; however, Nandin was often required to go it alone as Sim would delve into a book, his face hidden by his hair that refused to stay tucked behind his ear, and then, he'd suddenly pop up to rush from the room mumbling that he had to go "check something out." Nandin admire the Yarus' love of learning, but he made for an unreliable teacher. When Sim would return, he'd give that tentative smile that meant something between *sorry-I-forgot-about-you* and *you-won't-believe-what-I-found-out*. It didn't take Nandin long to realize the amazing things that Sim discovered tended to be less than exciting facts on plants or a new breed of bug. He endured Sim's quiet, but excited retellings of these facts and was glad when his studies were deemed complete.

Nandin preferred the physical training sessions he was given. He wasn't the climber that Nean was, but he could hold his own. He didn't mind Nean's need to taunt him as he climbed as it gave him extra incentive to reach the top faster. His desire to retort with a witty response had to wait until he then — a lesson he learned the hard way. Once he lost his focus on climbing because he was trying to come up with his reply: he forgot to check he had a firm handhold before moving up and the rock he grabbed came loose; if it wasn't for the safety line he would have been a pile of mush on the ground far below. The mistake gave Nean a whole new range of derogatory banter to send Nandin's way. Instead of getting upset though, Nandin waited for the opportunity to return in kind. Considering Nandin was extremely skilled at most things, more often than not, it was Nean who was at the receiving end of Nandin's gibes. They always knew when to draw the line though and when the junior Yaru, Kameil or new recruits were around they showed each other their due respect.

At first, Nandin thought it odd he was no longer considered a junior Yaru even though he arrived at the same time as the other junior Yaru did. His promotion to Commander put him on the same level, if not a notch higher, than the five Yaru captains. Most of the captains didn't mind Nandin's quick rise in status. Blades was the exception.

Blades had an intimidating presence to begin with: tall, muscular to the extreme, hair shaved so short you could see the scars on his head, the constant five o'clock shadow on his jaw and his cold black eyes that glared under furrowed brows. He always stood, legs shoulder-width apart and his arms folded like he was angry with the world…and he was. A bit of a drunk and brawler in his youth had caused him his sentence of banishment. He complained bitterly of the unjust society that would toss out a kid for having a bit of fun on a day off. The facts painted a different picture. The then twenty-year-old's idea of fun was not only on every day off, it was also most evenings. It included drinking, gambling, and fighting, which was not limited to men or even those who picked fights with him. Bystanders were often in the way of his rampages. When he belted the elderly wife of the innkeeper, the residents of Cerro decided enough was enough and cast him out. Cerro, located in the northeastern quadrant of Galenia, meant it was close to the rumoured valley of Mateo and so he sought it out. He had no desire to spend the rest of his life roughing it in the wilderness alone.

When Mayon, as he was known then, arrived at the valley, the first thing Mateo did was curb the man's drinking. It didn't take long to discover that he drank out of boredom rather than any form of addiction, so Mateo wasn't required to refuse Mayon alcohol altogether. When he gave him the treatment and he successfully became Yaru, Mayon's new abilities gave him plenty of motivation to train. As his skills with the sword became an exceptional display of speed and accuracy, his new name "Blades" made his transformation complete.

Mateo put Blades desire for violence to good use and had him hunt the Addicts who raided Essence sources and killed anyone in their way. Blades mission was to destroy them, preserve the Essence and try to leave no evidence of the existence of Addicts or Yaru. Unfortunately for Blades, who really enjoyed these missions, there were not that many Addicts and therefore he only went on these missions once or twice a year. Mateo had other tasks for Blades to perform though: some of them were to his liking, others he barely tolerated. Gathering Kameil or seeking out potentials were not high on his preference list and over time his lack of patience and brutish ways caused him to be less than sympathetic to the Kameil and rather heavy-handed in their retrieval. Mateo made it very clear that he would not tolerate Blades abuse of the Kameil. The other four Yaru that existed at the time, were surprised that being beaten by Mateo didn't make Blades angrier. Instead, Blades became an even more dedicated Yaru. He figured anyone who could pummel him so thoroughly deserved his devotion.

Nandin knew very little of Blades background. He understood the man was driven by anger and the missions he was given often seemed to appease him for a time.

When Nandin became Commander and those cold eyes turned on him as though by glaring hard enough he could cause Nandin's insides to explode, Nandin did his best not to do anything to irritate Blades any further. Sometimes he wondered at Nean's sanity as Nean often went out of his way to provoke Blades.

Thanlin seemed to be the only one who Blades actually connected with. They were constant companions. Thanlin was not driven by the rage that Blades was, but that didn't make him less of a concern. He always seemed like he had something to prove. It sickened Nandin as he watched Thanlin catch a baby rabbit and break its neck. He laughed when Nandin asked why he'd done it. His explanation was simply: to show that he could.

Unlike Blades, Thanlin preferred to keep his hair short, not shaved and his chiselled jaw was always kept clean. Although he wasn't mean and angry like Blades, his lack of compassion, or in truth any emotion at all, kept Nandin from becoming too friendly with him as well.

Aside from Nean, Plyral was the other Yaru captain that Nandin considered a friend, not just a fellow comrade. Plyral was enthusiastic and full of energy. His eyes were always darting about as if he was searching for action. His wild, dark hair with its sun-kissed tips suited him; it was as if he was too busy to bother with it. He accepted his missions of seeking out potentials and gathering Kameil with pleasure, excited by the challenge. Plyral explained it was the same as tracking when he went hunting, but instead of having to kill his prey, he brought them home as new recruits. Plyral and Jon, Nandin's closest friend and also the Huntmaster, would spend hours recounting their hunting stories, which Nandin could barely stay awake for let alone find exciting — it was only Plyral's need to jump up and demonstrate his moves that kept Nandin from nodding off.

Plyral's energy meant he didn't loiter around anywhere too long. Sure, he'd gladly share a drink with his fellow Yaru and take in a game or two, but a short time would pass before he was off again. If there was no mission, he'd seek out something else to stalk.

Nandin sometimes envied Plyral's freedom. Although he wasn't a fan of hunting, he would have liked less time behind his desk and more time on missions. But being at base camp did have its perks. Camp was located in a clearing in the middle of Thickwood Forest so it was far from the conveniences of castle life, but there was always a handful of Kameil who kept the place running. They provided him with all his meals and popped into his tent for a brief visit between their shifts. The command tent had decent cots for sleeping in and he was privileged to have his own horse for carrying messages between the camp and the valley.

Although carrying messages between the two locations was hardly an exciting adventure and also required him to make detailed records of all that occurred, he did enjoy his dealings with Mateo, plotting and planning the missions. When he handed them out to the captains, he watched with quiet contentment as they lit up when receiving the ones they liked best.

One thing above all others outweighed any of the downsides to his post. When the Kameil and the potentials were brought back to the camp it was Nandin's job to win them over. Often times they came to the camp out of curiosity or desperation, but by the time Nandin had a chance to talk with them, they were committed to the cause; they were anxious to be part of the family. And family is what it was for Nandin. Everyone had a role to play and they were there for each other. His charm and enthusiasm won over the most skeptic of guests. They were in awe of him. He didn't realize he had their commitment personally; he assumed they were devoted to the dream of a better, more equal Galenia.

When the days or weeks between new arrivals began to drag on, Nandin made sure to keep in shape — he knew he wouldn't always be behind a desk. In the tent, he did a routine of push-ups and sit-ups, stretches and such, but he preferred stealing away into the woods to climb trees, do chin-ups and practice jumping from one tree to another. He would return to his desk to continue writing up his reports content for the time being.

He read over the current report he had just finished, making sure he hadn't left out any details. When he was satisfied, he set it down and stretched. The day was still early and before he started the next report, he thought another run through the woods would do him some good. As he stood, the tent flap was pulled back as someone entered. Nandin knew the man coming in was currently the Kameil on lookout duty.

"Commander," he said with a bow, "Captain Nean is returning with a new potential. They should be entering the clearing shortly."

Nandin clapped and rubbed his hands together.

"Excellent! Thank-you Thais, please order the men to have some food prepared while I get ready."

"Yes, Commander." Thais bobbed his head again and backed out of the tent.

Nandin practically skipped over to his trunk to don his black Yaru apparel. There was no point wearing it to sit at his desk or to work out in the woods, but when greeting new guests it was exactly the right thing wear. He felt it gave the Yaru a look of authority and a mysterious air that people were drawn to. He wore it with pride.

Once he was dressed he pulled up an extra chair for his guest, tidied his desk and waited eagerly for his arrival. It was turning out to be a great day.

CHAPTER THREE

Less Travelled

IT WAS TIME.

Hanna could hardly contain herself as she made her way to the main gate carrying her bag, with a bounce in her step. She was pleased to discover a small group had gathered to see her off. She had expected to see Master Juro there and knew her guide would also be present. She didn't expect to find her Tahtays Biatach, Etai, and Jillian, as well as a few of her fellow students.

As she made her way through the crowd she was met with enough hugs and farewells to give her pause in leaving. This had been her home for most of her time on Galenia, was she really ready to walk away? When she saw Krigare on the edge of the crowd any doubts quickly disappeared. Seeing the same acorn brown hair and freckles as his son Kazi, gave Hanna a renewed sense of urgency.

"Krigare! It's so nice to see you. I'm glad you arrived before I left."

Krigare chuckled in a familiar way.

"His arrival is not by chance," Master Juro said as he emerged from the crowd. "Krigare is to be your guide to the Citadel."

"Wonderful!" Hanna exclaimed.

As a Messenger, Krigare had been back to Kokoroe every six to eight weeks since he first escorted Hanna and Kazi. He always brought a parcel or letter for Hanna. Often they were messages from her friends who'd moved onto the Citadel or from Cardea and Hamlin, but on the occasions he had not encountered any of them on his route, he would give her something he himself had picked up for her.

She had met many Messengers since being at Kokoroe, but was glad that it would be Krigare who would be her guide. She was sure he would have news of Kayu, the village she had first come to on Galenia and he also had plenty of good stories, some of which would most certainly include Kazi. She wondered if, now that she knew so much more about Galenia and its people, the stories she'd already heard would have new meaning.

As Master Juro passed on messages to Krigare, Hanna continued with her farewells. Tahtay Etai gave her a long hug. "Now you take care and remember," she whispered, "don't give up hope."

Tahtay Etai had been the one who brought Hanna back from the brink of despair when Master Juro told her she would not be going home. She told Hanna that even though it may take awhile, she believed one day Hanna would go home. As Hanna became better acquainted with Etai, she knew her to be sincere. Hope, like a candle in the darkness, was enough to keep Hanna from utter despair — it gave light enough to see the choices that lay before her. She had come to accept that there was always a choice, limited though it may be. She could choose to allow depression and defeat to consume her or hold onto hope and take action to try to change her fate.

Tahtay Biatach stood beside Etai. Hanna had spent most of her time with Biatach. He was tall and intimidating, a hard taskmaster and constantly increased his expectations for Hanna. Many nights, as she soaked her aching muscles in a hot bath, she cursed him. It wasn't until this moment, faced with saying goodbye that she came to realize how much she'd miss him. He had become like a father to her and she knew, beneath his bear-like demeanour, he really was a gentle soul.

At a loss for words, Hanna flung her arms around him. A little startled at her display at first, he picked her up and hugged her back, then whispered in her ear.

"I'm coming with you."

"What? How can you do that? What about your other students and Kokoroe's defence?"

As he replaced her on the ground, Master Juro answered her questions.

"Tahtay Biatach's apprentice can oversee the classes for the time being and Gatekeeper Jaylin will see to Kokoroe's security. Right now it is your security that is the priority."

Hanna was about to object, but realized he had a point. It was not as if she felt she was any more valuable than anyone else, but after all the time and effort they had dedicated to her training, it would be tragic if something happened to her before she even went on her mission. As confident as she was in her defensive abilities, she was not in a hurry to put them to use. Tahtay Biatach was definitely a welcome addition to the upcoming journey.

As Biatach and Krigare mounted their horses, the crowd began to disperse wishing them all well as they left. Master Juro pulled Hanna aside.

"It may be some time before we meet again, but at the Citadel you will find others who will help you with your future venture."

Hanna bowed. "Thank you Master Juro...for everything. My training, a place to live...I've always felt so welcome here."

"No Hanna, thank you. You have offered your help at great risk and for this I am in your debt. It has been an honour to get to know you."

Master Juro returned Hanna's bow. She was touched by his kind words, yet felt a sense of foreboding, like this was not just a goodbye for now, but a farewell forever. On the upside that could mean he thought she'd be going home. Then again, maybe he didn't think she would survive the upcoming assignment.

Shivers went down her spine. She swung up onto her horse and waved. With one last look at the immense Kokoroe gate, Hanna prepared herself for whatever may lie ahead.

* * *

Hanna was initially concerned what the ride would be like. She had spent some time grooming the horses while at Kokoroe and taking them for rides on day trips when they went into the woods for some 'hands-on' lessons, but she hadn't ridden for hours at a time since the two-week journey she made when she first came to Kokoroe. She remembered how sore she was and how long it took her to get use to riding. Now that she had once again been in the saddle for several hours, she was glad to discover her previous experience, as well as all the physical training she had been doing, seemed to be making the journey easier this time around.

As they rode, Biatach quizzed her about the animals and plants they saw. She wasn't sure if it was because of Kazi's absence or the fact that Biatach took this as another instructional opportunity, but the trip took on a much more somber tone than her first one.

That evening when they stopped to make camp, a chill went through her. As she gazed into the darkening woods, she was worried that a wolcott might emerge. The attack that she had experienced when Master Juro and her were observing a tear still haunted her. Each rustling of the bushes and flickering of the shadows had her looking over her shoulder.

"So," she said hesitantly, "we are planning to sleep outside then?"

Krigare smiled at the reluctance he detected in her voice. "Getting a bit pampered up at that school were you?"

"No, no, it's not that. I just wondered how safe it is. I mean, how would we know if a wolcott came up on us while we are sleeping?"

In all seriousness Biatach replied, "We'd know because we'd be screaming as it trampled us."

Seeing Hanna turn pale and eyes widen with fear he added, "But that's why we will take precautions."

"Like what?" she asked. "I don't recall any special precautions last year when we went to Kokoroe."

Krigare said, "There was much less chance of encountering a wolcott in the woods to the south. They tend to stay closer to the mountains."

"I don't think I will be able to sleep tonight. What can we do to be safe?" she asked feeling more nervous with each comment they made.

"Well," Biatach said, "wolcotts may be big, fast and vicious, but they have limits. For example, they don't climb trees."

"Does that mean…we'll be sleeping in trees?"

Biatach nodded. "That we will. Krigare, do you mind starting the fire while Hanna and I set up our sleeping areas?"

"I'm on it," he replied with enthusiasm.

Biatach unwrapped a bundle that he had unloaded from his horse earlier. He removed a roll of canvas, rope, a small sandbag and some odd shaped leather with metal rings and hooks.

"Before we climb any trees let me first show you what the beds look like and how to attach them. It's much easier to do this on the ground than hanging in a tree."

He unrolled the canvas and handed one of the three to Hanna. She noticed it had metal grommets at each end.

"Those sort of look like hammocks," she said mostly to herself.

"We call these pico wraps after the small animal that swings from the tree branches. We need to thread these shorter ropes through the grommets and tie a knot. Here, take this one and copy what I do."

He handed her two ropes, each as long as Hanna was tall. He showed Hanna how to tie a knot so it wouldn't slip out of the grommet and then repeated it again with the other rope at the head of the wrap.

"When we get up there, we will wrap each rope around a branch, slip the rope through the other grommet and tie another knot. The key is finding the right tree with branches far enough apart that the pico wrap is stretched out. Otherwise when you lay in it, you will be kissing your knees, not a very comfortable position to be in all night."

Hanna laughed at the image of the hulking figure of Biatach bent in two hanging from a tree. He attempted to smile in return, but as she began to shake and tears came to her eyes, he sensed he was the butt of a joke.

"Here," he snapped, tossing her a large bundle of rope.

Hanna staggered as she tried to catch it, but was unprepared and it slipped through her arms to the ground.

"Alright, come on chuckles. We need to find the right trees."

He picked up the remaining items and headed to the trees. They didn't have far to go since, as Biatach explained, Krigare had picked a place to camp in the ideal setting. Having often travelled this way as he carried messages across Galenia, he knew where the best places to camp would be.

Once they chose the three best locations to hang the pico wraps, they gathered them up along with the other gear. Biatach attached the sandbag to the end of a long rope.

"Stand back, I'd hate to knock you over while I do this."

Hanna thought that he didn't sound very sincere, but she heeded his warning without comment and stepped back. He swung the end of the rope round and round a few times before he released it. It sailed up and over the targeted branch and then descended towards the ground as Biatach loosened his grip on the other end of the rope. He undid the bag and handed it to Hanna.

"Now it's your turn. Attach the bag to your rope the same as I did and toss it over that branch there."

He pointed to the next tree over from where his rope now dangled. Once she felt the sandbag was secure, she began to wind up and then released the bag. She missed.

"Again." He demanded.

And she missed again. On her third try, she actually hit the branch, but the bag still didn't get high enough.

"Underhand Hanna." Biatach instructed. "And step into it as you throw."

Hanna shook her head in frustration. Why did he always wait until she struggled to give her his good advice? It felt like everything was a test and she didn't feel like she was passing. Some months back she had mentioned this to Karn who agreed wholeheartedly. Thinking of Karn reminded her that it wasn't personal; it was just Biatach's way.

She swung her rope and took the step as per his instructions and viola! The bag was finally hanging from the branch, but only briefly as she had forgotten to hold onto the other end of the rope so the bag quickly began to plummet to the ground. Before it hit, Biatach reached out and caught it along with the other end of the rope.

Hanna's gratitude at his catch was short lived as he grunted, "I only brought the one bag, and I'd hate for it to rip open." And then, as if she needed to be told, he added "next time, hold onto the other end of the rope before you throw the bag."

Checking her frustration, she just smiled and nodded. He handed Hanna the rope and untied the sand bag.

"Okay, next step is to tie the two knots. The first you wrap around like this," he demonstrated, "and it should leave you a loop like so. This end will be attached to your pouch. Now you try."

Hanna attempted to do as shown and her knot did look right, but her loop ended up being too small. Her second try produced the results Biatach was looking for.

"Good," he said. "Now try this one. This knot allows you to pull the rope up or down or hold you in place."

Hanna successfully tied the slipknot correctly the first time.

"Excellent."

He reached for the leather that he had assembled and slipped his legs into. Then he rolled up a pica wrap and secured it to his chest with a leather strap that was attached to the shoulder straps of the contraption.

"This is the pouch. It gives you something to attach the ropes to and sit in as you ascend." He said holding up one for Hanna. "Notice the shoulder straps are adjustable so make sure to tighten them so you won't slip out of it."

He helped Hanna put on her pouch making sure to point out each step of the way. Hanna recognized the significance of his assistance; she knew it meant that doing it wrong would be hazardous. After the final step of attaching the pico wrap he walked over to his rope.

"I will show you the next steps on my rope, then I'll descend so I can come spot you on yours."

He attached the pouch with a metal hook to the rope and then put one foot on the tree. He tested his weight, pulled the rope and placed the other foot on the tree. He slid the slipknot up the rope and then walked up the side of the tree. He repeated this step a few times, stopped to make eye contact with Hanna and then did the whole thing in reverse until he was again standing at the bottom of the tree.

"Now, your turn."

Suddenly, the idea of climbing made Hanna excited. All thoughts of the wolcott gone from her mind, she skipped over to her rope, anxious to climb up the tree. Biatach watched as she attached herself to the rope, practiced moving the rope up and down through the slipknot and then tested her weight. When she finally felt ready, she placed one foot on the tree then proceeded to do exactly as Biatach showed her.

It was slow at first, but she eventually found her rhythm.

"I think I'm getting the hang of this," she called down.

She heard Biatach chuckle and was surprised he sounded further away than she expected. For the first time, she looked down and instantly regretted it. As the world began to spin around her, she focused her gaze on the tree trunk in front of her until she felt steady again.

"You're almost there, Hanna. Once you can reach the branch, swing your leg around it. Just make sure you have your back to the tree's trunk and not the other way around."

She could hear the snide remark Karn would make about her being backwards on the branch, like she was when she had first taken the crossing at the river on the field trip to the Demi Geode. Having no intention of being found backwards again, she finished her ascent and confidently swung her leg around the branch with her back firmly pressed against the tree. As soon as she caught her breath and was secure in her position, she chanced looking back down at the ground. Biatach was looking back up at her.

"Well done! Now just sit tight while I make my way up."

Contentedly, Hanna watched as he reattached himself to his rope and began his ascent. Once he was comfortably situated on his branch he undid the pico wrap from his chest and unfolded it.

"Now open up the wrap and circle the rope around the branch a few times, slip the end through the other metal ring and tie the knot I showed you. Make sure to keep clear of your climbing rope. You may need to slide the pico wrap further out so it doesn't become entangled."

As Hanna followed his instructions, he continued speaking.

"We are fortunate with these trees as the branches are thick and well placed. Keep in mind that for some trees you may have to climb higher or use a different branch to attach your pico wrap to than the one you used for climbing." He finished tying his wrap then said, "Once you've got the first part of your wrap in place, you'll need to climb over to the other branch to attach the other end. Let out a bit of your climbing rope so you have some room to move. Don't panic if you slip and fall; your knot will hold tight. It won't loosen until you pull it the right way."

True as that may be, she wasn't about to test out that theory. Taking care to have firm hand and foot holds, she climbed to the other branch just like she witnessed Biatach doing. After she had completed attaching the other side of her wrap, she was happy to see a comfy looking hammock attached to her tree.

"Can I try it?" she asked.

"Just give your knots a good pull first to make sure everything is tight then go right ahead."

Once she tested that everything would hold, she gingerly manoeuvred herself onto the bed. She eased herself back into a horizontal position.

"This is awesome!" she yelled.

Gazing up into the greenery above she was giddy with excitement.

"This will be so neat to be up here at night...but uh, what if I roll off in my sleep?"

"Oh sorry," Biatach said, "I meant to show you that on the ground. Notice all the ties along one side of the wrap?"

"Yes," she replied.

"Tonight, at bedtime, you will undo a few of them to open up the wrap. Then you can slip yourself in and retie them. If you slide yourself down a bit, your head will be completely covered. Aside from keeping you warm it will keep you dry if it rains. The canvas has been treated to keep it waterproof."

"Cool. So its like a waterproof sleeping bag that hangs from a tree."

"Sleeping bag?" he asked.

"Oh, its what we used for camping back home, but they were made of much softer and fluffier material. This stuff doesn't look to be very warm."

"By itself it wouldn't be, but there are warm blankets inside the wrap," he explained. Once he finished and tested his own wrap he carefully moved back to his climbing branch. "Well, let's make our decent. We still have to do up one more wrap for Krigare. Then I'll show you how to hang our food supplies to keep them out of any animals reach."

When Hanna reached the ground she found her legs were trembling.

"That was a rush!"

"I'm glad you enjoyed it. Now you can do Krigare's. That tree there will do." He pointed across the small clearing.

"Tahtay Biatach, I was wondering, what about the horses? I can't imagine you'd hang them up in a tree."

Biatach snorted, "No, certainly not."

"Well, wouldn't the wolcotts attack them?"

"Yes they would; very good observation. The horses can sense the danger and would alert me before a wolcott could attack. I should be able to get myself into position to defend them. I'll pepper the beast with arrows and since the wolcott won't be able to tell where the attack was coming from it would most likely run away. If it doesn't, I will free the horses so they can run to safety."

"What would happen to them? Wouldn't they get lost?"

Biatach shook his head.

"The horses know these woods better than I do. They travel between the towns and cities constantly. They'd head for the nearest one."

"How do you know that?"

"That's where the food is. As well as a safe haven away from the wolcotts. Although, once they have encountered one they may be a bit too squeamish to go back into the woods."

She sighed. "Ya, I know how that feels."

"Okay, enough chatter. Hang Krigare's pico wrap up so we can move onto our next task."

After setting up camp, they finally sat down at the fire for dinner. It wasn't long before they finished their meal, put out the fire and ascended into the trees for the night. Hanna was too excited to be scared and once she was firmly tied into her pico wrap, she was completely content. She had left one tie open, allowing her a view of the sky above. Not for the first time she wished she had paid more attention to the skies back home. The only constellations she knew were the Big and Little Dippers and there was no sign of them out here. She wondered if any of the stars she saw now were the same as the ones she could see from Earth. With that thought in mind, she decided she would start a star chart so she could compare it to the skies when she got back. As sleep beckoned to her, she slid further down her wrap, did up the last of the ties and peacefully drifted off to sleep.

CHAPTER FOUR

Temporary Tourist

LIGHT PENETRATED THE WRAP.

The sounds of the night creatures faded away as the day broke and the musical awakenings of the day began. Birds squawked and called to each other, pico's nattered as they swung from branch to branch. Even the trees seemed to shake themselves as if preparing for the new day. She opened her eyes and had a brief moment of claustrophobia. As she started to fidget and gasp for breath she heard Biatach's calm, commanding voice coming from below her.

"Easy Hanna. You are up in a tree."

Hanna froze and slowly exhaled. *Right, I'm up in a tree.*

"Take your time," he continued, "Give yourself a chance to wake up before you undo your wrap and make the climb down. Please remember to put your safety harness on first. I am here whenever you're ready."

After the initial shock had passed, she carefully opened up her hammock and admired the view around her. Aside from the inconvenience of the climb to get in and out of bed and the confined space, she decided she quite liked sleeping in a tree, being rocked between the branches and having a green canopy overhead.

Once firmly on the ground, they ate breakfast, packed up and were on their way. Less than half an hour passed before they came across an Inn.

"Krigare, you must have known there was an Inn this close by," Hanna stated.

Krigare nodded. "Of course I did."

She rolled her eyes. "Then why did we bother sleeping in the trees? The Inn would've been a little bit more convenient, don't you think?"

Biatach spoke up. "This is not a pleasure trip Hanna. Kameil don't sleep at Inns. You need to learn how to survive like a Kameil."

"So you're saying the Kameil sleep in trees?"

Biatach shrugged. "Of that I can't be sure, but when you are on your own it will be the safest place for you to be and much easier for you to conceal yourself."

She swallowed and tried to clear her throat. Something about that comment didn't sound too good.

"What do you mean *when I'm on my own?*"

"Tonight we will arrive in Heedru. You can sleep in a bed there," he replied ignoring her question.

Krigare said, "Yes, we can get a few more supplies while we are there. This will be your first visit to a city, won't it Hanna?"

Hanna thought about it a moment. She had been to a few villages of varying sizes since she came to Galenia. Kokoroe was large and there were more than just students that lived there, but it was predominately a school, not a city.

"Yes, actually," she said. "I'm curious. Does it resemble any of the towns we went through last year or is it more like Kokoroe?"

Krigare laughed. "None of the above. You're just going to have to wait and see."

"I'm scouting ahead." Biatach gave his horse a nudge and quickly took off.

The day carried on with Biatach returning for a while then took off again to scout never encountering anything major to report. They came across a few travellers on the road, some heading for Kokoroe others returning to their villages for a break. Hanna recalled that students were able to take off any semester and return at the start of the next one since the lessons went on all year long. She sighed knowing she would not get to enjoy a three-month break from learning. In fact, for her, it seemed to be quite the opposite. Her studies were compacted so she could learn as much as possible as soon as possible. Of course that suited her fine since she didn't plan on spending a lifetime on Galenia. She enjoyed learning about their history and their ways through her tailored lessons, which provided her with what she needed to know for when she encountered the Kameil. Unfortunately, much was conjecture and speculation since the entire Kameil population were outcasts and the little anyone knew of them usually came from raids. In fact, the general consensus was to stay away from the Kameil. There were even rumours that the Kameil were diseased, but her teachers never gave credence to them. Hanna wondered how she would ever manage to convince anyone she was Kameil given her lack of knowledge.

When they finally cleared the trees and rounded a bend in the road, Heedru came into view. She gawked at the city before her, It was a mountain: literally. Cobblestone roads lined with closely packed buildings zigzagged back and forth up the side of the mountain. The rust-coloured roofs dominated the scene as plush green trees attempted to peak out above them.

"Wow," she exclaimed. "What is it with you guys and mountains?"

Krigare laughed. "That's where we find the largest deposits of crystal Essence. Smaller pockets can only sustain the villages."

Not quiet ready to accept that explanation, Hanna couldn't help but point out that Kokoroe, which was also nestled in the mountains, didn't have much need for Essence since the only hatchlings that were there were the rare ones the teachers and their families had.

"Yes, but Korode is the city of Kokoroe, like Heedru is the city of the Citadel. Both are only a days ride from the schools and each city is vast."

Biatach chimed in, "Plus the schools' locations are also a tactical advantage. It's easier to protect."

"True, true." Krigare nodded his agreement. "Definitely a reassuring benefit for us concerned parents sending our children away from home."

"No city gate." Hanna pointed out.

"No real need. There's only one road in and that first building is the city watch. Anyone not permitted in would be stopped within moments of treading up the road." Biatach explained.

"You mean the Kameil?"

"Yes and any one who has been banished."

She thought a moment. "What about animals? I seem to recall the fence around Kokoroe was mostly to keep them out."

The corners of Biatach's mouth twitched as if he was attempting to prevent anyone from seeing him smile.

"Yes, that is correct. Kokoroe is a rather quiet place built in the heart of the wilderness whereas Heedru is a loud bustling city with brick buildings carved out of the mountain itself leaving little in the way of its original form and, therefore, function. Animals typically shy away from such places."

"That sounds a bit...I don't know, destructive?"

Biatach shrugged. "Not really. The mountain still stands."

"You don't seem to approve," Hanna ventured.

"Kokoroe was built more in harmony with the nature around it. I like it better."

Thinking of the streams and tree-lined paths that she had spent many hours strolling through, she could understand his view.

"I agree. What did you mean animals 'typically shy away from'?" Still carrying the fear she'd experienced from her chase with the wolcott, she didn't think 'typically' was a strong enough word to make her feel safe.

Not picking up on Hanna's concern, Biatach waved off the issue. "Oh you know, there's always small creatures that hover close by. They live off the scraps that are left lying about and that sort of thing."

He turned to Krigare. "Which Inn were you planning on staying at? The Rock Bottom Inn or The Jolly Jongleur?"

Krigare gave a knowing smile. "Well, actually I thought we'd stay at the Messenger's Haven."

"Oh, right. Of course."

Hanna wrinkled her brow. Obviously she had missed something. "What do you mean 'of course'?"

Krigare replied, "The other Inns are nice, but we will receive perks at the Messengers Haven."

"Such as?"

"Well, first of all, we won't have to pay."

"Good perk." Hanna agreed.

Krigare continued, "We will be guaranteed rooms, the food is delicious and I have a few supplies they keep for me."

"Wait a second," she said as something dawned on her, "I don't recall ever paying to stay at the Inns on the way to Kokoroe. In fact, I didn't think there was such a thing as money here."

"I suppose you wouldn't have encountered coins since this is your first time to a city. In the smaller towns people typically use credits. For every job you do or goods you produce you receive credits that you can then trade for other goods or services. That works just fine in a small village. In the cities, that is inconvenient because you must go to the Distributor to claim your credits in order to use them. Also, it's easier to falsify credits. In a small town everyone knows each other and what they do, in the city, not so much."

"You mean people try to give themselves credits they haven't earned? Like stealing?"

Krigare nodded. "I suppose you could put it that way. It would be too easy and far too tempting I guess. That's why they created coins."

He went on to explain how they use coins in exchange for goods. Hanna, being very familiar with the system, listened patiently trying not to interrupt.

She peppered him with questions and he obligingly answered. Their system intrigued her; the similarities and the differences to what she was familiar with back home. Credits were like credit cards, but they didn't have banks instead they had Distributers in every town. Messengers received privileges since they travelled between villages and cities and their salaries came from Sanctuary.

Hanna tried to wrap her head around his enthusiastic explanation. It was more detailed than she had bargained for. Some of his information though stuck in her mind. She thought it interesting how the Messengers each had their own insignia they would leave wherever they went so that their expenses would be compensated by, what she thought of as, their form of government.

Biatach cleared his throat. "This is all very fascinating," not sounding the least bit fascinated, "but as we are about to enter the city, I'm suggesting you lead the way. I'm not familiar with the where the Inn is located."

Krigare winked at Hanna and then gave his horse a kick to take the lead. The streets were crowded with people: some selling wares others buying them. Most were on foot, but a few travelled on horses. It didn't take long before she was assaulted by the smell. Between the sweat, horse manure, spices and various foods being cooked at vendor stalls, her stomach started to turn. She was relieved to discover the Inn was fairly close by, and yet was concerned to be staying at a place in the middle of the overwhelming aroma.

They left their horses with a stable boy and made their way inside. The Inn was a most agreeable haven. Once the doors were shut, the noise and the smell were trapped outside, much to her relief. The windows at the front let in enough light for most of the place, but left the back tables in relative shadow. The fire was unlit as were the candles that were placed on the tables. Not overly extravagant, the Inn still had a feeling of opulence compared to the other Inns she'd been in. The chairs were covered in fabric, the tables were polished, rugs covered the floor and one side of the room looked like a men's club complete with leather-like couches, armchairs, throws, footstools and a bookcase. Pictures lined the walls showing landscapes, buildings and cities. Before they took more than a few steps, a stocky Jivan with salt and pepper hair came through a back door.

"Krigare!" he exclaimed arms open wide as he embraced Hanna's travel companion.

"Nice to see you Jock! The place looks a little quiet tonight."

"Ah yes. We just had a few Messengers leave this morning. You have the place to yourself my friend," he said eyeing Biatach and Hanna.

Krigare replied, "Let me introduce you to Hanna and Tahtay Biatach."

Without missing a beat, Biatach stepped forward and bowed. A little slow on the uptake, Hanna followed suit.

"Tahtay Biatach! I am honoured!" Jock bowed longer and lower than was most likely required and Hanna suddenly felt that perhaps she had grown complacent with the level of respect she had shown Biatach.

"Hanna," Jock continued, "I have the perfect room for you. I think you will enjoy your stay at Messenger's Haven."

She returned his warm smile. "I'm sure I will. Thank you."

"Come in, come in." He waved them through. "Please make yourselves comfortable while I fix you something to eat. Krigare will you be needing your locker?"

"Yes thank you, but it can wait until later."

"Very good." Jock replied as he rushed out of the room.

"You have a locker?" Hanna asked.

Krigare nodded. "All the cities have Inns set up strictly for the use by Messengers...and their guests, of course. One room is dedicated for lockers that we can leave extra items in. It comes in very handy. I keep different seasonal clothes and extra pens, ink, paper and such in mine. That way I don't have to carry it all on me. When you're a Messenger, you are always in a rush."

They quietly enjoyed a delicious meal: steamed vegetables, freshly baked biscuits and some sort of roasted bird that Hanna was unfamiliar with. It had a somewhat tangy flavour to it.

It didn't take long before she felt herself beginning to drift off so she made an early exit and collapsed on the bed in her 'perfect room.' She barely had the chance to notice the fresh flowers on the table, lace curtains trimming the window and the beautiful quilt with its own colourful, repeating floral design before sleep claimed her completely.

* * *

The knock came early the next morning. Last to bed, first to rise, Hanna wondered if Biatach ever actually slept. Surprised to find a bowl of warm water on her bedside table, she grabbed a facecloth and washed away the road dirt as best she could. When she saw how dirty the water was, she quickly checked the bed to see if there would be a dirt impression of where she had lain. With relief, she noted, it remained fairly clean. After a quick, but satisfying breakfast, she found Biatach, Krigare and the horses waiting for her outside the front door.

"Do we get to walk around town a bit?" she asked. The morning, being much less busy, seemed to be lacking the smells and crowds that had nauseated her the previous evening.

Biatach spoke reluctantly, "I think, Hanna, we should leave the sightseeing for another day."

Biatach and Krigare exchanged glances and some unspoken communication seemed to occur since Biatach suddenly changed his mind.

"Okay, I'll scout ahead and Krigare can take you on a quick tour. I'll meet you outside the city in an hour."

Krigare nodded and began leading Hanna further into the city while Biatach headed east.

"What is his obsession about scouting?" she asked. "Does he really expect to come across Kameil on the road this close to a city?"

Krigare replied, "It's been known to happen, but not only the Kameil can set an ambush. There are a few who choose less than honourable ways to survive."

"Really?" From everything she had learned so far it seemed that the Kameil were the only ones to cause trouble.

"Don't get me wrong, it usually is the Kameil, but there are other bandits. I've even heard tell some have been known to join up with the Kameil." Krigare shook his head. "But those are just rumours."

Hanna was disappointed. The people she had met had been so kind and giving, to think there was a darker element to Galenia shattered the image she had conjured.

"Where are we off to?" she asked changing the subject. "And why did Biatach have such a sudden change of heart?"

"Hmm. 'Change of heart,' I like that. Well, I think he realized that you've never been here before and it may be a long time before you get a chance to come back."

"You mean, he realized I may not come back."

Seeing Krigare's face fall she quickly added, "In case I find my way home or something. Where are we going?"

"Up," he said. "Only way to go. This level has mostly just market and trade stalls."

He pointed out a blacksmith shop that was flanked by a tack and feed shop and a tanner. Across the street were bake houses, a dressmaker and a weaver. When they reached the end of the street the road made a sharp right-hand turn heading further up the mountain.

Krigare gestured. "Up this street, there are a few more inns as well as apartments. At the end of this street, it turns back again and is lined with more shops. It continues winding like this all the way up the mountain. There are some unique shops on the various streets, but you will find many trades repeat. Do you wish to continue up?"

She looked at the street ahead and the street they had just came from.

"I think this is far enough," she replied. "If each street looks more the same, we may as well start moving on to the Citadel."

Krigare nodded.

"There are some more interesting buildings further up and the view is quite spectacular, but it would take the better part of an hour to get there. Maybe there will be another opportunity for you to return and you can stay for a longer visit."

Hanna nodded as they turned their horses around and headed back they way they came. Krigare stopped at a few of the shops along the way adding to his other provisions for the trip. They met Biatach just outside the city shortly before their allotted hour was up.

The rest of the day continued on, uneventful, very much like the first part of their journey. Again, Biatach insisted they sleep in the trees, but this time he decided that Hanna should set up the pico wraps on her own. He explained that it was important that she could do it without any help. As much as she didn't like to think about that, she was grateful she was becoming more skilled at being self-sufficient.

Aside from the pleasure that she would have sleeping in the trees, there were other perks to staying in the woods again. It would give her a chance to play with fire. Master Juro had demonstrated how even fire contained Essence and could, therefore, be manipulated. With the flick of his hand, he caused the flames to mould into various shapes as if he had pressed a cookie cutter into them.

When Hanna tried she was only able to cause the flames to split like a forked tongue. Master Juro had pointed out that she had manipulated the Essence in the air around the flames, not the fire itself. He assured her this was still impressive for someone so early in her Essence training, but that didn't dissolve the disappointment she felt. There hadn't been many opportunities to practice this technique, as it wasn't deemed a high priority in her training. Now, with nothing much to do but watch the fire die out before they settled into their wraps for the night, Hanna smoothed a patch on the ground as close to the fire as she could manage without being scorched and set her mind to the task of creating a circle of flame.

It took a great deal of concentration. Krigare and Biatach sensed this and remained quiet as they watched her work the flames. After ten minutes of focusing her attention, she was able to feel the Essence, but again a split in the light was all she could achieve.

"Well done!" Krigare exclaimed. He didn't know what task she was trying to perform, but moving flames by some controlled, invisible force was impressive to him.

She sighed. "It's no better than what I did the first time."

Sensing the frustration in her voice, Biatach said, "I understand fire is particularly difficult to manipulate."

"Yes," she confirmed. "There isn't much Essence in it and it burns up almost as quickly as the flame is created, but it's there. I should be able to do something more with it."

Biatach reached over and placed a hand on her shoulder. "I'm sure in time you will."

She nodded and went back to concentrating. Another thirty minutes passed before the fire was barely more than burning coals and Hanna stood brushing herself off. Trying not to be disgusted at her lack of progress, she yawned and stretched.

"I think I will call it a night," she said and headed to the tree where her pico wrap hung.

Contentedly, she snuggled in her wrap pushing thoughts of the fire behind her and instead looked forward to arriving at the Citadel the next day. As she did up the last of the ties, she wondered what type of bed she would sleep in the next night.

CHAPTER FIVE

Fighter Flight

THE MORNING WAS TEDIOUS.

It wasn't until mid-afternoon the following day that they met any travellers on the road. Biatach had scouted ahead and reported back that there was a family of Jivan accompanied by a Jagare heading toward the Citadel.

"They are on foot so it won't be long before we overtake them," he explained.

When they first came into view, it was easy to distinguish the towering form of the Jagare amongst the Jivan. They were currently resting on the side of the road, the mother fussing over the children while the father chatted with the Jagare. Greeting them as they passed, Hanna felt a chill run up her spine. She acknowledged each of them in turn, but when her eyes met the Jagare's, her words stuck in her throat. The man was intimidating with his shaved head and massive frame, but there were other reasons that caused her to stare, a smile frozen on her face. The man returned her gaze with cold, unblinking eyes. Forcing herself to turn away, she resisted the urge flee.

The continued down the road and after she figured they were out of earshot, she spoke to her companions, attempting to keep the fear out of her voice.

"Tahtay Biatach, they were not Jivan. And he was not a Jagare."

Biatach's gaze narrowed. "What do you mean?"

"Well," she hesitated; worried that perhaps she was wrong. "The family looked normal enough, but the Essence…it didn't sit in them right. It wasn't a part of them. I'm not sure if I can explain it."

"What about the Jagare?" he asked sternly.

"He was something else. He had more Essence than anyone I've seen and it was part of him. It was almost like he was both Jagare and Jivan."

Biatach and Krigare exchanged worried glances.

"Hanna, do you think you can ride faster?"

"I thought you'd never ask," she said relieved.

They quickened their pace. Hanna urged her horse to a gallop, grateful to put some distance between them and the strangers.

* * *

Blades watched intently as the travellers made their way by. They had met a few people on the road, but hadn't encountered any problems so far. He was a little shocked at first when he recognized Tahtay Biatach. Knowing the amount of students Biatach had over the years, and the little time Blades had spent at Kokoroe, he was sure Biatach wouldn't recognized him. He had been cast out from his home some six years earlier, his sudden reappearance would warrant questioning. He held his breath as he passed. When Biatach didn't give him a second glance he thought they were in the clear, but then he noticed the girl. She was looking at him like she could see into him. He knew that look — it was the way Mateo looked at him after his treatment. His jaw clenched as he waited for her to speak; she continued on in silence.

The Kameil that he was leading sensed his distress and began to inquire after the group had gone, but he shushed them as he strained to hear the other travellers. He couldn't make out what the girl was saying, but he heard the horses pick up speed. *She knew!* He didn't know how, but she knew.

Fearing for their safety, he decided they would need to leave the road.

"It will take longer," he explained, "but the road is not safe for us anymore. We must hurry."

He nudged the smallest child, urging her on and led them into the woods.

* * *

The school finally came into view. After the initial sprint away from the unusual party they had encountered, Krigare insisted they keep the horses at a steady trot as they would tire out too quickly if they continued at a gallop. After two hours of bouncing along, Hanna was quite relieved to be arriving at their destination.

She gawked at the colossal structure before her. It appeared to be a castle, as it was a large stone structure with high walls and arched windows. The building, however, lacked the battlements and towers typical in all the movies, storybooks and toys she'd ever seen. They slowed their horses down to a walk making conversation much more manageable.

"It's so different than Kokoroe. And much larger than I thought it would be."

Krigare said, "It wasn't always this stone behemoth that you see now. It used to be a wooden fortress–the high walls kept out the wolcotts, Draka, and other beasts that inhabit the area."

Automatically, Hanna looked over her shoulder as if the very mention of a wolcott would bring one out of the forest.

"The Great Fire in the year 867 destroyed most of the old fort." Krigare explained breaking into his storytelling mode. "Vowing never to let that tragedy happen again, the people rebuilt it out of stone. It was an epic tragedy, more than just lives were lost. You see, the Citadel is also our library. It holds the greatest collection of all the written documents on Galenia. The building you see is only a portion of the Citadel."

She raised her eyebrows. The road they were on led them up the side of the mountain toward the castle, which was nestled against the rock face on one side and on the other side the land dropped away. What more could there be? Krigare smiled as he watched her attempting to understand.

"There are caves in the mountain. Some scrolls managed to survive the fire as they had stored many works in the caves since they were better preserved there. After the fire, greater precautions were taken. The mountain itself has become an extension of the castle. The library now completely resides inside the mountain. The castle is its gateway as well as home to those who keep it. Based on

54

the amount of people, The Citadel is sort of a city unto itself."

"A city?" she asked. "I thought all the cities had to be close to a crystal pocket."

Biatach raised his hand.

"Sorry to interrupt what I'm sure would be a long and pleasant conversation, but we do have an urgent matter we need to deal with. Hanna will have plenty of time to learn about the Citadel."

"Yes, yes you're right, of course. My apologies." Krigare said, turning and winking at Hanna.

They followed the curved, cobbled roadway around to the front of the castle. As they approached the immense, wooden door with black wrought iron hinges, Hanna noticed a tower attached on this side of the castle, just slightly taller than the building. Hanna thought whoever stood up there would have an extraordinary view. Before she could ask what the purpose of this lone tower was, a smaller door within the larger one opened up.

"Krigare, I thought it was you I spied, but I doubted myself since it is rare to see you with travel companions."

"Good day Gatekeeper Talyn." Krigare dismounted and bowed, then the two clasped elbows in greeting.

Biatach dismounted and began to bow.

"Tahtay Biatach, as I live and breath! A most welcome guest! It's been many years since you have honoured us with your presence. Shall I send word to Master Jagare of your arrival?"

Biatach nodded. "That would appreciated as I have pressing news that must reach him at once."

The Gatekeeper gave a quick bow. "I will see to it. Krigare do you mind leading your companions to the main meeting room while I alert Master Jagare?"

Krigare led the others through the gateway and into a small courtyard on the other side. Two young students hurried to greet them.

"We will see to your horses," said the Jagare girl who took Hanna reigns while the Jivan male took the others.

Hanna noticed the reverence in their eyes as they watched Tahtay Biatach who strode to the entrance of the keep, Krigare a step behind. Taking a moment, Hanna bid her horse goodbye. She was not as attached to this horse as she was to Jade, the horse she rode from Kayu to Kokoroe, but after so many days together there was still the beginning of a friendship that she would miss. As she hurried to catch up to the others, she discovered her legs felt like jelly after riding so fast for so long. Catching herself as she tripped up the stairs, she took a moment to get her balance before continuing. Inside the doorway, she saw a large foyer with multiple doorways and three separate stairwells, but no Krigare or Biatach in sight. Nervously, she looked around. The stairway straight ahead was empty as was the one to her left. When she glanced at the one to the right, panic began to bubble to the surface. But then Krigare poked his head out of a doorway at the top of the stairwell. She waved and eagerly ascended the stairs to catch up.

Her legs ached as she climbed and she groaned when it suddenly dawned on her that she had finally made it to her destination, which meant tonight a warm bed, bath and soon, a reunion with Kazi. Krigare patiently waited for her on the landing, then led her down a corridor lit with torches. They passed through a set of double doors into, what she assumed must be, the main meeting room.

Large arched windows dominated one wall letting in a rainbow of colours as light penetrated the mosaic of stained glass. The opposite wall held painted portraits of various proportions, the largest of which was life-sized. One side of the room was covered with beautiful rugs topped with club chairs circling a marble fireplace large enough for Hanna to stand in. But the most dominating feature was the thick, polished, wooden table with fifteen chairs to a side and two large unlit, candled chandeliers hanging above it. Currently, enough light poured through the windows making the candles unnecessary.

Tahtay Biatach stood motionless, like a great stone statue, clasping one wrist in the other hand behind his back and wearing a severe expression. If not for the somber look on Krigare's face, Hanna may have broken out giggling, although the very air in the room gave her a sense of foreboding. She closed her eyes and focused her thoughts, bringing the image of the strangers to the forefront of her mind. She knew she would need to explain what she saw and she wanted to make sure she was as accurate as possible.

Moments later the doors opened and a bear of a man walked in. Taller than Biatach and broader of shoulder, he indeed was the perfect image for the master of the castle. He walked straight to Biatach and they clasped arms. Hanna wondered if this was the formal greeting at the Citadel like bowing was at Kokoroe.

"Biatach!" he bellowed, "It has been too long my friend."

"Master Jagare, it is an honour to see you again."

"Ha! So formal," he barked. "Shall I call you Tahtay then?"

Biatach glanced at Hanna. "May I introduce you to the Seer?"

Hanna shot a puzzled look at Biatach, as she had never heard him refer to her as "The Seer" before. In fact, it was a term she had not heard since the first week she had been at Kokoroe. She wondered why he would use it now.

"Ah, the legendary Hanna," he said clasping her arm and bowing his head. She blushed at his attention.

"Krigare, it is wonderful to see you as well."

"I'm sorry to cut the introductions short, but we have a pressing matter to discuss. Hanna thinks we've encountered Kameil on the road and they were not alone."

"Let us sit and discuss this further." Master Jagare motioned to the seating area.

They each took a seat on one of the leather club chairs. Hanna felt like a child as she slid back into the enormous claw-footed chair, her legs dangling off the floor and her arms unable to reach both arm rests at once. She scooted to one side trying to appear more at ease, but it left enough room for another whole person to sit next to her. She thought she must look extremely silly. How would Master Juro, being much smaller than she, be able to look dignified in this situation, she wondered.

"I have summoned Tahtay Puto, shall we wait for his arrival?"

Biatach nodded. "Probably a good idea. He will want to hear this."

At that precise moment, Tahtay Puto entered the room. Clearly a Juro, he was less than half the height of the average Jagare, wore a white robe with silver embroidery down the front seam and a shiny, silver sash tide around his waist. A large ring of keys dangling from the sash, jingled as he moved.

"Tahtay Puto your timing is perfect as always. Please join us." Master Jagare said motioning to one of the empty chairs. "Biatach was about to share something of importance."

Everyone nodded their heads in a semi-bow in greeting to the newest arrival who competently leapt into one of the chairs. He sat cross-legged with his hands resting on his lap. Hanna thought he almost looked to be hovering on the chair, which became a throne to his meditative, dignified looking state.

Well, I guess that answers my question.

Biatach began to explain their seemingly innocent encounter. "But Hanna believes," he concluded, "they were not what they appeared to be."

Feeling a little flushed as everyone's eyes turned to her, she explained how the Essence didn't sit in the travellers naturally. When she explained what the leader of the party looked like, Tahtay Puto gasped.

"Shadowman...the Yaru!" Tahtay Puto said in an agitated whispered.

"Shadowman?" Hanna asked.

"There have been raids by these black-clad figures. Rarely do they leave any witnesses, but one who survived said they appeared like shadows, killed everyone else and vanished without a trace. The dying Kameil called them Yaru. There have been whisperings. Mateo has created these Yaru who look like Jagare, but are something more."

Master Jagare stood up. "I will assemble a patrol at once. Biatach, I will need you to lead it. Come with me."

The two withdrew in haste, leaving the others to continue the discussion.

"Tell me child," Puto said more forcefully, "how certain are you that the others were Kameil? You say they didn't appear to be ill."

"Well, I've never seen a Kameil before, but they definitely weren't Jivan. Their Essence was all wrong."

Puto studied Hanna for a moment then turned his attention to Krigare.

"We will need to get messages out to the Sanctuary and I'm sure Master Juro will want to hear of this."

Krigare nodded. "I'm due at the Sanctuary, so I will go there first thing tomorrow. Is there another Messenger on hand to go to Kokoroe?"

"I'm sure Biatach will take him the news when he returns."

"Of course," Krigare said.

Puto placed a gentle hand on Hanna's shoulder. "I'm sorry Hanna, but we need to leave you for now. I will send someone in to show you to your room. I'm sure you could use some rest after such a journey."

She smiled wearily. She was more than happy to leave these concerns for others to deal with; rest definitely sounded appealing.

CHAPTER SIX

Rest Assured

SHADOWS WERE EVERYWHERE.

After a brief wait, someone arrived to lead Hanna through the dimly lit castle. Most corridors lacked windows and wall sconces were the only source of light. Climbing many more flights of stairs, followed by several twists and turns down various hallways, left her feeling disoriented. Her guide was a middle-aged Jivan woman who explained her chief responsibility was guest services. Exhausted from the journey and the stressful past few hours, Hanna didn't make small talk and barely took notice of the women's comments or the various tapestries that hung on the walls.

When they arrived at her room, the woman showed Hanna the door, bowed and quickly disappeared down the hall. Decorative area rugs covered the stone floor of the room; heavy drapes flanked the window where the shutters were currently opened. A small table with two chairs was placed to provide an excellent view while seated. A modest fireplace was on one wall and on the other was the most lovely four-poster bed. The large posts were carved in a twisted pattern and had curtains matching the ones for the windows. A heavy down duvet covered the mattress and two pillows were propped against the headboard. Hanna had always wanted a bed like that.

In the middle of the room was a large wooden tub. Kicking off her dirty shoes, she entered the room and discovered the tub was full of hot water. Noticing towels and a clean robe lying on a stool, she happily stripped off her clothes and sunk into the bath, surprised it had been prepared for her.

Once she was clean, but before the water became too cool, she stepped out, dried off, wrapped herself in the robe and jumped onto the bed. She gave a little giggle, feeling like she was in some sort of dream. Burrowing under the quilt, she contentedly fell asleep.

An urgent knock at the door interrupted her brief rest. She wasn't sure how much time had passed, but she knew it couldn't have been too long as there was still light in the sky. She slid out of bed securing her robe and opened the door.

"Hanna!" Kazi cried as he bounded into the room and swooped her up in a big hug twirling her around before placing her back on the floor.

"It's so good to see you," she said looking up at him. "Kazi you're a giant! You're almost a full-head taller than me now!"

He laughed in his carefree way, which she had missed so much.

"Hardly a giant. Have you seen Master Jagare? Now there's a giant."

"Tell me about it."

Looking down at her he said, "You haven't changed a bit though! Not one bit. You look exactly like you did when I met you a year ago - even your hair is the same."

"I know," she sighed. "It's like I'm frozen in time. Master Juro thinks I am aging, just really, really slowly. Another side effect the Essence is having on me."

"That's great!" he replied.

Hanna groaned. "How is that great? I'm stuck at fourteen!"

"You won't always be. Think of it this way, when you're forty you'll still look twenty."

Hanna shook her head. "You and your silver lining. Enough about me, tell me what's been going on with you and what was all that cryptic stuff you said you couldn't tell me in your letters?"

Kazi had the good grace to look sheepish.

"Sorry about that. I really wanted to tell you, but I was told I wasn't to say a thing. I'm not sure if I was allowed to explain about becoming a Minstrel or if I just wasn't suppose to mention being part of your team. Of course, no one was going to read my letters except you but still, I suppose a Kameil could intercept it and then there goes the whole thing, right?"

Hanna shook her head trying to clear it.

"I have no idea what you're talking about. Start from the beginning."

Kazi grinned. "I'm learning to be a Minstrel. I started learning the viol, although the kettledrum is a bit easier to pick up if I'm really going to convince anyone I've been a minstrel for some time. My instructor thinks I've got natural talent, which will really help. I'll carry a viol with me when we're travelling anyway, so I can keep practicing it at least—"

"Whoa. Hold on," she interrupted. "What are you talking about?"

"Oh, right. A viol is a six string instrument that you play with a bow."

Hanna held up her hands.

"That's good to know, but not what I'm asking about. What do you mean 'when we're travelling' and convincing people you're a Minstrel?"

Before he managed to get another word out, a knock came at the door. Hanna gritted her teeth as she went to answer it; the suspense was making her edgy.

"Evening, my lady. I thought you might like something to eat."

The lady who had shown her to her room came in carrying a tray of food. She crossed the room and placed it on the small table.

"Shall I have someone clear out this bath now or would you prefer to wait a bit?" she inquired glancing at Kazi.

Anxious to finish her conversation, she hastily replied, "Can it wait for a bit?"

"Yes ma'am." The lady bowed and left, closing the door behind her.

Hanna turned to Kazi. "Now talk," she commanded.

Kazi laughed as he stuffed a piece of fruit into his mouth.

"I did get ahead of myself, didn't I? I've been asked to be part of your team! Isn't it great?"

Still perplexed, feeling like she'd walked in during the middle of someone else's conversation, she slumped over the table holding her head up with her hand.

"What team?" she asked.

"They really didn't tell you anything? *Geez!* And I thought I was kept out of the loop. Master Jagare has assembled a team to go with you on your mission, whatever that may entail, and I'm on it," he added seeming very pleased with himself.

Hanna felt relieved. Every time Biatach hinted at her being out on her own, fear gripped her. Maybe she didn't have to be alone after all.

Smiling, she sat back in her chair feeling lighter, as if a great weight had been taken off her shoulders.

"That's really great Kazi," she finally replied, "but why would I need a Minstrel? No offence."

Grinning wider he said, "No offence taken, but why is the question, isn't it? I have no clue. I told Karn a while ago that I wasn't about to let you just waltz into a pack of Kameil. I said one way or another I was going with you. And I meant it! Shortly after that, I was asked to be part of the team, but I have no idea how he convinced anyone a Minstrel would be able to help. Maybe to keep the mood light or so I can write an epic tale telling of your great adventure! Either way, I have been part of the training sessions too." Thoughtfully scratching his chin, a smirk came across his face. "Maybe it's so the Kameil will think I'm just a wimpy minstrel and then: *Wham! Pow!* I'll knock them out."

Laughing hysterically, Hanna almost fell out of her chair. "Now this I've got to see! Or perhaps you are to play a rocking beat while I kick the crap out of them."

Not altogether pleased with Hanna's hysterics he pouted, "I could kick some crap."

This, however, caused her to begin a whole new round of laughter. Tears streamed down her face.

"Oh, ha ha." Kazi said. "If you are quite finished I'll take you on a tour."

They scarfed down the last of the fruit and bread before heading to the door.

"Um Kazi, I don't suppose there's something else for me to wear other than a bathrobe?"

Kazi shrugged, "It's a good look for you."

Her expression was less than pleased so he gave in and pointed to the wardrobe that stood unobtrusively in the corner. She pulled out a pair of taupe pants with the familiar drawstring top and matching, loose fitting, long shirt. Unlike the typical uniform at Kokoroe, Hanna noticed the top was intricately embroidered with gold and silver thread. She laid the clothes on the bed along with a silver-coloured sash.

"I'll just wait outside for you." He winked as he walked out the door.

Hanna clapped her hands as she bounced over to the bed. She had been at the Citadel for less than a day and she was already having more fun than she had in months, she couldn't remember the last time she had laughed that hard. Smiling to herself, she slipped into the outfit on the bed all the while thinking that the tour was bound to be exciting— life with Kazi had never been dull.

CHAPTER SEVEN

Mountainous Feat

HANNA BLINKED.

Lacking windows, the hallway was much darker than her room and it took her a moment to adjust. Now that she had a little bit of rest and had eaten, she took the time to admire the statues, paintings and tapestries as they walked by. She couldn't help but drag her hand along the cool, stonewall as she went and she felt each of the woven tapestries. Some of the art depicted people and landscapes; others were strange, mythical-looking images.

"What is this?" she asked as she touched one of the stone carvings.

"That is the work of someone's imagination. Some of the stones are actual animals, but mostly students like to be creative."

Hanna started. "These were made by students?"

Kazi smiled. "A bunch of them are. These are the better ones. The Tahtays prefer to have the best ones in their hall. Who can blame them when they have to walk by them day after day and year after year?"

"What do you mean the Tahtay's hall?"

"That's where we are."

"So, you mean, you don't have a room up here?"

"Ha, I wish! No, I have the good fortune to bunk with my fellow students ten floors below."

"Oh, does that mean this is just a temporary room for me? It's too bad, I really like that room," she sighed.

Kazi placed his hand on her shoulder as he continued guiding her down the hall.

"Well then, I'm happy to report that the room is yours. You are part of the elite now Hanna, but don't worry, I'll be up to visit you often so you won't forget who your friends are."

Normally she would have had a witty response, but she was still rather confused.

"Why would I be up here? I'm sure they didn't run out of space everywhere else."

"They probably spent a good deal of time discussing where to put you. They tend to like their routines around here and you don't quite fit into them." Seeing her perplexed expression he continued, "You won't be attending the regular classes so you're not really a regular student. My guess is that they decided to treat you like a visiting Juro. Everyone knows you're a Seer so giving you that room ensures you the respect and perks any visiting Juro would receive. And if you're a guest, it won't seem strange when you leave and come back."

"I guess that makes sense, but why do I need the extra respect and perks?"

Kazi nodded, "The perks include not having to do any chores or other student-like routines; those would really cut into your training schedule. Besides, I doubt it will be long before we go on our mission. As for the respect, that's a given, you are the Seer after all."

"Why does everyone keep saying that? Biatach called me the Seer today too and I've never heard him say that before." She held up her hand as he opened his mouth to reply. "And don't say it's because I can see the Essence, I figured that much out for myself."

Kazi shrugged. "My guess is that they want to ensure everyone knows your special, so they don't question your...situation."

She rolled her eyes. "I would have thought they'd want to keep me and my 'situation' hush, hush. Nothing like announcing to the world 'here is someone who doesn't belong. Keep an eye out for her.'"

"They may have intended to keep it secret, but you've met too many people at Kokoroe who are now here. You're famous Hanna," he said clapping her on the back. "Believe it or not, people knowing you're the Seer will cause less questions. If you were to pretend to be a normal Jivan then everyone would be wanting to know why your aren't doing what every other Jivan student is doing. Announcing that you're special, people are more likely to be content to hold you in awe and expect that Master Jagare knows what he's doing."

She shook her head at the absurdity of it all. Kazi just shrugged as he led the way. As they continued wandering through the castle exploring classrooms, the kitchen and eventually the students quarters, she explained her encounter on the road and everyone's concern.

"What did they do?" he asked.

"Tahtay Biatach and some other Jagare's went off in search of them. I have no idea what they'll do if they find them."

They discussed the possibilities. Kazi was sure that they would be brought back to the Citadel for questioning and maybe even spend the night in the dungeons.

"There are dungeons here? That doesn't sound very *Galenian*. I mean, I thought it was a peaceful place." She recalled what Krigare said about the bandits and knew she was still being naive. "Besides, isn't this supposed to be a school? Do they use the dungeons for some sort of medieval punishment if you act out in class?"

Kazi shrugged. "It is a school, but there are tons of people who live here who aren't students. This place is pretty much a city. And with that many people around, someone's bound to get into trouble. As I understand it, the dungeons don't get used very often. I think it's more of a nice-to-have than something they need."

As they descended another set of stairs she suddenly felt concerned.

"You're not taking me to the dungeons now are you? Cause I really have no desire to see them, thank you very much."

He smiled. "No we're not heading there. But there is one more thing I have to show you before we go for supper. I saved the best for last, believe me."

They reached the end of the stairs and walked down a dimly lit hall; Hanna shivered.

"Is it me or did it just drop in temperature?" she asked.

"Yep it did. Don't worry, that has been taken into consideration."

They came to a corridor with a heavy wooden doorway set in a rock wall.

"Is that the mountain?" she asked with excitement.

"Right again. You're really on a roll!" he exclaimed sarcastically.

She swatted at him, but he jumped out of the way nearly falling in the process and laughing the whole time.

"So what are we going to do about the cold?"

He led her to the far side of the room where rows of hooks held heavy cloaks. An open chest revealed hats and mitts, some of which had the tips cut off.

"That's kind of strange," she said holding up a pair.

"Not really, you'll see. But you won't need those. Take a pair that isn't cut open and grab a hat too."

She found a pair of mittens, slipped on a hat then perused the cloaks, looking for the best fit.

"Just how cold is it in there?"

"It's not that bad, like a cool fall day. The plus side is, that it stays the same temperature all year long so it doesn't get any colder. We'll be moving around a bunch so it won't feel too bad. It's for those that have to sit for hours on end that the cloaks really come in handy since the cold has a way of seeping into your bones. Here, this one should be your size."

He draped a heavy, grey cloak around Hanna's shoulders and then found one for himself. Kazi grabbed one of the unlit lanterns from a shelf and lifting the heavy latch, they pulled the door open revealing a dark tunnel and a cool draft rushed passed them. Even though there were lit torches on the walls, they were far enough apart that much of the tunnel was left in darkness. They closed the door behind them and began walking into the mountain. With the door closed, the air was still and musty.

"Aren't you going to light the lantern?" she asked in a hushed tone which seemed appropriate as they walked among the dancing shadows.

"Not yet," he replied equally quietly. "We won't need it until further ahead."

They continued for a short time until they came to a door set in the left-hand wall. Just before Kazi opened it he advised Hanna not to talk, as people were working. They entered a room full of tables and stools. The tables were slightly slanted and on each stool sat a Jivan or Juro wearing the half mittens and diligently writing in large books with quill pens. Hanna realized wearing full mittens would have made it difficult to write. Piles of rolled paper sat in crates on a larger table. The room was lit by an overhead candled chandelier and multiple wall sconces. As Kazi led Hanna through the maze of tables and chairs, not one person looked up. She wondered if they had even noticed their arrival.

At the far side of the room was another door, which Kazi opened and led them through. This room was again lit by a chandelier and one wall sconce. In the centre of the room sat a lone table with a few empty chairs. It was the walls, however, that grabbed Hanna's interest. There were no pictures, statues, wall hangings or windows. These walls contained honeycombed cavities and each were filled with scrolls. Hanna ran her hand over the wall.

"This is so cool. It's like they dug right into the wall."

"They did," Kazi said as he lit his lantern. "Let me show you the next room."

The next room was dark aside from the glow of Kazi's light, but she could still tell the room was identical. Without pausing Kazi passed through the room and into the next, ensuring he closed the door behind them.

"They're all the same!" Hanna exclaimed as she followed Kazi.

"Yes, on this side they are, but these are different."

He pointed to some markings carved into the rock shelves. Hanna recognized the dot and line markings as numbers, but she was unsure of what the other carvings were.

"Years and...something?" she asked.

"As good a guess as any. I really have no clue. The workings of the library are not something junior students are informed of."

"How many rooms are there?"

Kazi shrugged, "I have no idea. Hundreds probably. There are more rooms on the other side of the corridor, but those have artifacts and such from the old days. I've only been in one, most of them are locked."

"But the scroll rooms aren't?"

"Lots of them are, but I haven't tried too many to know which ones, I've only been here a couple of times. Come on, there's one more thing I want to show you."

Hidden in the shadows in the corner of the room was another door she hadn't noticed before.

"Watch your step." Kazi advised as he opened the door, crossed the raised threshold and stepped out onto a ledge that ran along the side of the mountain. Hanna joined him, pressing her back against the rock wall as she looked up. A crack in the mountain high above let in enough light to reveal a vast cavern, but she still couldn't make out the ceiling. The drop off was hidden in shadow giving no hint to its depths. The ledge was empty except for a set of rail tracks leading off into the distance.

Kazi hung his lantern on a hook on the wall, closed the door and pointed to some markings carved into it.

"Remember those in case our light goes out so we know where we came out. We'll be passing many doors, but most are locked and I'd rather not have to try them all."

Hanna brushed the carvings gently with her hand.

"So these dots mean three, but I'm not sure about this sign. It looks like a backwards 'S' but the ends are spiralling."

"Imagine there was a line here across the top then down the side with another spiral here," he said using his finger to draw and imaginary line. "What would it look like?"

She thought for a moment then retraced his lines herself.

"A scroll!" she declared.

He nodded. "Yup, that's it. This is door three of the scroll rooms. Some of the doors have different symbols such as the first one we entered. It has the symbol for scribe on it since that's where they do all the writing."

"What is it that they're writing?" she asked.

"Let's walk and talk," he replied leading her along the ledge. "Did you notice they were writing in books?"

"Yes, and there were a bunch of scrolls on the table."

He nodded. "Correct. Their job is to transfer all the scrolls into books. And not just any book, they're combining scrolls with the same subject."

"That sounds like a huge task."

"To say the least. There are thousands of them and new ones coming in every day."

"Where did they all come from?"

"The oldest ones are copies of the writings from cave walls and messages between the early tribes. Then there are the writings of everything we know from medicine to farming, censuses to songs and ballads. Those are being added to daily and arrive mostly from the other schools and the Sanctuary, but there are others who contribute as well."

"Why don't they just write in books? Seems like a whole bunch of extra work to have it all rewritten."

"There are lots of reasons. The first one I can think of is to make delivery a lot easier. Books are big and heavy – not the easiest thing for Messengers to be carrying all over the place. And then, of course, there's the amount of information any one person has to contribute. There may be a few who have a books worth of information to share, but usually they are just adding to what someone else has started or updating what we know. Plus, if they're writing about several topics, it could become rather confusing. The scribes take all this random stuff and organize it so it's easier to find."

Once again Hanna was struck by how much she had taken for granted back home. Books here were still a novelty. She had her own bookcase full of stories, textbooks and the like. She recalled the stacks in the public library reaching to the ceiling, row upon row. When did it all start? At what point did books become so readily available? Picturing the library brought her back to her current situation.

"Where are all the books then? We just saw scrolls."

"There are rooms further along for the books. They're the same as the scroll rooms, just filled with books instead. Ah, here we are. I figured we'd find one soon. Help me move this to the tracks would you?"

She grabbed one side of a flat wooden cart with wheels. In the centre was a teeter-totter looking device with handles on each end. They pushed the heavy cart over to the tracks and then together lifted one side at a time until the wheels were in place.

"Okay, here's where the fun begins. Hop on."

Reluctantly Hanna stepped onto the cart. Together they began to pump the handle up and down and the cart began to move down the track. They passed scroll room three and then several more before Hanna could no longer make out the door markings as momentum picked up.

"We're getting faster!" she stated with just a hint of concern in her voice.

Kazi laughed. "Of course we are. That's why it's fun! The tracks lead down, right to the bottom of the chasm. Wahoo!" he shouted as the air rushed past and the cart sped up.

As they raced onward, the cold breeze bit at her face. The pump handle was moving all on its own now. Hanna needed to steady herself so she sat down and grabbed onto the handles support structure. Kazi, oblivious to Hanna's mounting anxiety, was leaning back against it, his arms in the air, relying on gravity to hold him in place. He showed little concern of falling.

"This is great Kazi," Hanna hollered, "but how do we slow down, I mean, before we hit whatever's at the bottom?"

Kazi made an attempt at grabbing the handle, but it was moving too fast and almost knocked him off the cart. He began looking around and shot Hanna a nervous look.

"You don't know how to stop?!" she shrieked now giving way to fear as their predicament became clear.

"Of course I do," he replied thoroughly unconvincingly. Carefully holding onto the centre support, he turned himself around to face Hanna. He began to feel around the structure, obviously unclear as to what he was searching for.

The cavern was growing darker and darker the further they descended; only the occasional flicker of light was given off by random lanterns lit along the way. There was just enough light for Hanna to make out a gravel pit ahead with the tracks ending at a rock face where large boulders lined its base. And they raced towards it.

Kazi was now panicking as he desperately searched for a way to slow the cart and continued his attempt at grabbing the handle as it violently pumped up and down. Hanna closed her eyes and slowed her breathing to calm herself. She removed the mittens and tucked them under her legs.

"Kazi sit down and hang on," she commanded calmly.

Keeping her eyes closed, she reached out in front of her and felt the air rushing through her fingers. Then, she felt something more. Her hands became rigid as she began to gather Essence. To Kazi it looked as though an invisible weight was pushing down on her. Hanna leaned back slightly and then thrust forward with all her might pushing the invisible Essence towards their dead end.

WHAM! The Essence ricocheted off the rock and hit the cart. The force of the Essence rushed past them and they felt themselves being lifted off the cart before they plopped back down. The cart itself responded as though they had ridden through an elastic sheet that gave in a little then pushed them, causing the cart to slow, then slide backwards before it came to a complete stop — barely an arms length away from the rocks. Kazi leapt off the cart and danced around.

"That was so great!" he hollered. "Fantastic! Absolutely unbelievable! Hanna…*how did you do that?!*"

Hanna slowly lifted herself off the cart and stretched her legs. Calmly she walked over to Kazi, placed a hand on him to stop his bouncing and then punched him on the shoulder.

"Geez Kazi," she shouted angrily, "One minute you have me in tears from laughing, the next I'm fearing for my life! What are you trying to do to me?"

Rubbing his sore shoulder, Kazi couldn't help but grin.

"I'm sure you needed a little excitement after all those months at Kokoroe."

"What were you thinking?!" she scolded.

"Some of the senior students were telling us how much fun they had taking the cart to the bottom. I've been wanting to try it for months."

"And you didn't bother asking how to stop the cart?"

"I just assumed it would level off or something."

She shook her head, "Well I think that's enough excitement to last me a few more months. Now if you're quiet done putting me in mortal danger...."

She turned away abruptly and began picking her way through the rubble.

"What is all this?" she motioned to the piles of dirt and rocks.

"This is where they dump all the debris from the rooms. They carve it all out and fill those carts there," he said pointing to a row of carts lined up in a clearing they had passed, "then empty them here and repeat until the room is done."

"Why bother?"

Kazi looked at her puzzled.

"I mean, why not just empty them into the chasm. What's the point of coming all the way down here?"

"Well it's not really 'way down here' anymore. The last room is not that far back up. As for the chasm, well just come and take a look."

He stepped around the rocks and over the tracks offering a helping hand to Hanna.

"Careful not to trip," he said.

"Oh now you're worried about my safety?"

Undeterred, he continued walking into the shadows. Once through the gloom Kazi gestured dramatically.

"Ta-da," he said cheerily. "The Citadel's greatest treasure."

A pool of water held a small island of crystal stalagmites. A large, rose-coloured crystal stood at its centre and was surrounded by many more of varying sizes and shades. A soft glow on the other side of the pool hinted at the presence of others. Hanna was reminded of Crystal Valley that she had visited last year. She had been sworn to secrecy about its existence so she didn't share her thoughts. Instead she asked,

"What's that light over there?"

"It's for those working at the nesting grounds."

"Do they live down here?"

He shook his head. "Too dangerous. As it is, they have to keep well back in the tunnels to prevent absorbing too much Essence."

"Can we go closer?" she asked, cautiously creeping to the waters edge.

"Well…" he stuttered grabbing her sleeve, "we should probably be getting back. It's almost supper."

Hanna, catching the hesitation in his voice, turned and squinted, trying to see him better in the shadows.

"What aren't you telling me?"

"It's just, we're not exactly suppose to be down here."

Before she could respond, he prattled on.

"I've been here for months and I haven't been down here yet. They let us take the handcart to get books that we may need, but we always have an escort. Of course we've all heard what's down here, but I just wanted to take a look."

"Kazi," she inhaled deeply.

"Come on Hanna, who knows if I'll get another chance? It's only because you're here that I'm given a free pass to go wherever—"

"And the first thing you do is go into a restricted area? That'll be the end of your free passes."

Kazi got on his knees, "Oh please don't tell anyone. I'm begging you! I have all sorts of perks because I'm part of your team. If anyone hears of this I'm sure to lose them or maybe even get kicked out completely!"

Hanna grunted. "Oh get up you twit. Let's get out of here before we get caught."

He hurried back to the cart and jumped into position this time facing the way they had come.

"Look Hanna, the brake."

Kazi pointed to a foot peddle on the side of the cart. Hanna just rolled her eyes. She picked up her mitts and put them on. Once she was on board, he began to pump.

"Aren't you going to help?" he asked.

She smirked, "I think you can do the work for now. You owe me that much at least."

"Yes, of course," he quickly agreed. "Whatever you want."

"Good. I plan to hold you to that."

Kazi was rather pleased; their adventure had almost ended in catastrophe, but Hanna had prevented it and instead it had been fantastic! He knew she wouldn't stay mad at him, especially after what he had planned next. He just hoped she didn't really mean that she'd had enough excitement.

CHAPTER EIGHT

Stage Sight

THE WARM AIR ENVELOPED THEM.

After exiting the mountain, they returned their
cloaks, mittens and the lantern to the entrance. As Kazi led
her back through the castle, Hanna was completely turned
around and doubted if she would be able to find her way if
left on her own. They entered a narrow corridor that led to
a large, brightly lit, crowded room. Before she could get
her bearings, Kazi held his arms above his head and began
yelling.

"She has arrived! Welcome to Hanna, the Seer!"

"The Seer!" the crowd repeated raising their
glasses and cheering.

Hanna blushed as all eyes turned to her. To make
matters worse, she realized that Kazi had led her out onto a
raised platform so that she was clearly visible to everyone
in the room. Before she died of embarrassment though, a
familiar voice spoke up.

"Oh, Kazi your so melodramatic! Come on Hanna,
let's get you something to drink." Celine extended her
hand and helped her jump down from the stage. She gave
Hanna a hug and led her through the crowd. Celine was
one of her first fellow students at Kokoroe and had often
written to Hanna over the last few months. She was a most

welcome sight now. As Hanna squeezed through the crowd, which consisted of familiar faces, she was patted on the back or tugged and pulled in greeting.

"Thanks Celine, Kazi is really pushing his luck today."

Hanna shot Kazi a look over her shoulder and shook her head to see he was still on stage now brandishing what she assumed was a viol.

"Let the festivities begin!" She heard him holler as he struck up a tune accompanied by a few more musicians who had joined him on stage. The tune was boisterous and obviously a popular one among the crowd who began to clap their hands to the beat as Kazi began to sing.

> *Doyle saw the biggest beast*
> *That ever plagued the land,*
> *As it scrounged for mushrooms,*
> *Doyle decided to take a stand.*
> *He snuck up right behind it*
> *And took his mighty spear*
> *With just one, hell-of-a shove*
> *He stuck it up its rear!*

The whole crowd joined in for the chorus and Hanna couldn't help but take up the clapping.

> *Oh! The great deeds done*
> *By Dolye and his mighty spear*
> *He's bold! (Clap, clap) He's brave! (Clap, clap)*
> *And he laughs in the face of fear.*

Completely taken by the song, Hanna and Celine stopped working their way through the crowd to stomp and clap with everyone else.

> *Now the mighty wolcott,*
> *It had him on the run.*
> *But Doyle didn't worry,*
> *Cause it was all good fun.*
> *There was no escape so*
> *He had to use his wits,*
> *But Doyle just disappeared*
> *Down into the pit.*

This time when the course repeated the crowd began shouting *He's bold!* (*Clap, clap*) *He's brave!* (*Clap, clap*) while shaking their hands in the air; others began doing a energetic little jig.

> *Hurrying to the scene*
> *The clan gathered round,*
> *Worried for their comrade*
> *They saw go under ground.*
> *When they came to the pit*
> *It was to their surprise,*
> *Doyle was sitting on his kill*
> *A twinkle in his eyes!*

As the song repeated the chorus for the last time, Hanna was able to join in. Watching the dancers and the crowd, she was surprised to realize she knew everyone in the room. They were all students whom she'd met at Kokoroe at some point during her stay there. It was startling to see how many people she had encountered. She knew, of course, that the Citadel housed a lot more people than those in attendance. As the song wrapped up, Celine and Hanna continued walking to the back of the room.

"Celine, where are the other Citadel students?" she asked.

"Kazi just invited the people you knew, he thought you'd prefer it that way. Want some punch?"

They reached the buffet table that was loaded with breads, fruits, vegetables, pies and sliced meat. A large bowl surrounded by mugs held fruit punch, a rarity, prepared on special occasions. After she filled her mug, Hanna scanned the room. Every now and then she would make eye contact with someone, smile a greeting and continue looking around. After all this time it still felt surreal to her, standing in this great room with stone walls covered in tapestries and lit by giant candled chandeliers, and filled with people she knew, but instead of the typical jeans and t-shirts her classmates back home preferred, the guests were wearing cotton-like pants and tunics tied in place with coloured sashes similar to what Hanna herself was wearing. The variations came in the embroidery work stitched into the tunics and the colour of the sashes. Hanna's own top was rather detailed with stitching scrolling its' entire length in silver and gold. She was thankful they had worn cloaks on their little adventure or she was sure it would be covered in dust like the bottom of her pants were. When she noticed Celine's embroidery was pale blue and consisted of a simple pattern just below her left collarbone, she wondered if there was some relevance to the stitching.

"Celine, I noticed everyone's tunic is slightly different, unlike our uniforms at Kokoroe."

"Yes, it's nice hey? These are our dress clothes. We don't have many opportunities to wear them. The embroidery work indicates the student's level as well as the trade they have chosen. I really need to spend time putting in a few more rows, but stitching just isn't my strong suit."

"You mean...everyone has to do their own?" Hanna asked.

"Of course. Unlike our day-to-day uniforms, we get to keep these ones."

Hanna thought for a moment before it dawned on her. "So whose clothes am I wearing?"

Celine giggled, "Yours silly."

"Yes, but...look at all this stitching. I certainly didn't do it. Plus it's obviously for a senior student, the whole thing is embroidered."

Celine's smile broadened. "It's the typical tunic of a visiting Juro. It makes sense that's what they'd provide for you since you have Juro status, not to mention you're The Seer."

"Oh I wish you wouldn't," Hanna sighed, "This Seer business is starting to make me nervous. It feels like I'm being put up on this imaginary pedestal and I'm just waiting for someone to realize there's no reason for it and I'll come crashing down."

"Nonsense!" out of nowhere, Kazi appeared and wrapped his arm around Hanna's shoulders. "Only just today you showed how amazing you are! Your pedestal is absolutely solid."

Hanna rolled her eyes. "That was just a fluke."

"What's this? Hanna, are you being amazing again?" Biatach said as he and Krigare approached her growing group of admirers.

Kazi turned slightly pale as Hanna replied. "Not really, just trying to keep Kazi out of trouble, as usual."

"Good," Krigare said, "I know only too well how easily trouble seems to find him. He could use someone to keep him in line. It appears he's enjoying himself far too much — that's a good indication that mischief is just around the corner."

Recovering his wits, Kazi piped up, "No it isn't, it was just a bit of fun. Hanna could use some fun after the monotony of Kokoroe. They seriously need to liven things up a little."

Biatach crossed his arms. "Oh really?"

Hanna suppressed a snicker behind her hand and Celine suddenly became very interested in her shoes. Kazi had the common sense to blush, "Aw, come on, you have to admit it's a little on the dull side."

Biatach raised his eyebrows looking unimpressed with Kazi's observation. Kazi, realizing he may have gone too far, changed the subject.

"I thought you were out chasing Kameil, Tahtay Biatach?"

Quite aware that Kazi was attempting to get out of a lecture, Biatach hesitated, but seeing how the others attention was focused on him, clearly interested in his answer, he let the matter slide.

"I was charged with showing the scouts where we spotted the travellers. I don't have time for a manhunt. I need to return to Kokoroe, and the sooner the better."

"Agreed." Master Jagare joined the conversation. "We need to meet first thing tomorrow morning and then you can be on your way. Kazi, please do remember that this gathering needs to finish up within the hour. Some of you have an early start in the morning." To Hanna he added, "And I'm afraid that includes you." Hanna nodded as Master Jagare continued. "I apologize, but I need to steal away Tahtay Biatach."

Master Jagare gave them a quick bow and headed back out the main door. Biatach shot Kazi a stern look before briskly turning and following. Krigare just shook his head.

"Son," he said, "you need to learn when to hold your tongue. I'm sure I can find a Tahtay who could assist you with that."

Kazi hung his head, "Sorry dad. I'm just a little wound up today, not thinking clearly."

Krigare gave him a warm smile. "Well, that's a start, at least you know you're not thinking straight. Now, why not play us a few more tunes before we have to turn in for the night?"

Kazi instantly brightened, turned and bounded across the room and back up on stage.

"Hanna," Krigare spoke in a soft but serious voice, "you will look after him, won't you?"

"Of course," she replied. The responsibilities were beginning to pile up, the weight on her shoulders got just a little bit heavier.

Within the hour, the students had their fill of food, drink and socializing and began drifting back to their rooms. Hanna diligently stayed until the end to thank all of the people who came to greet her, but she could barely keep her eyes open. When the last student left, Kazi showed Hanna the way back to her room.

"I'm so glad you're here Hanna."

"Me too. It hasn't been the same without you." She gave him a hug, and then retired into her room, grateful to kick off her shoes, remove her clothes and slip into bed.

Finally tucked up under her heavy duvet, Hanna was able to relax, physically at least; her mind was still buzzing. She thought about her action packed day and hoped the morning would bring something a little less dramatic.

CHAPTER NINE

Scheme Team

Morning came early.

Hanna browsed through her wardrobe and discovered that in addition to the dress outfit, there were a variety of leather pants, vests and cotton-like shirts. She had never pegged herself as a hunting type, but she soon discovered that the snug fitting clothes had a much more familiar feel to her. Aside from the fabric, it felt similar to wearing jeans and a t-shirt. She thought it odd at first that this was the school uniform until she recalled that the Citadel was focused on learning the skills of the Jagare, it only made sense that they would wear the hunters' style of clothing.

Once she was dressed, she was unsure what to do. Thinking she would attempt to learn her way around the castle, she ventured out into the hall only to be greeted by Krigare.

"Good morning Hanna! I was just on my way to wake you. We have an early meeting we need to get to. Let's see if Biatach is still lingering."

He knocked on the door across the hall. There was a thump and groan. Krigare opened the door to see what was the matter. From the shadows Biatach snapped, "I'll be right out. Close the door already."

They patiently waited for Biatach. It was so unusual for him to be the last one awake and ready to go, Hanna was concerned.

"These blasted rooms are pitch black without windows. How's anyone suppose to be able to tell the time?" he complained bitterly as he emerged from his room.

She realized that Biatach's punctuality relied on his ability to see the sun. In Kokoroe, daylight could penetrate every bedroom. Even the pico wraps didn't block out light completely. In the solid stone of the Citadel, with the heavy wooden doors, rooms without windows would be in utter darkness. Hanna's concern for her mentor turned to amusement, as she finally discovered Biatach's Achilles heel. She refrained from commenting though, as he seemed to be in no mood for ridiculing.

In silence, they made their way back to the main meeting room where they had met Master Jagare the day before. Hanna was surprised to find that there was already a group of people sitting around the food-laden table topped. She recognized Master Jagare at the head of the table and the Juro, Tahtay Puto, but not the Jivan and the Jagare on his left.

Master Jagare waved them over. "Good morning Hanna, let me introduce you to Tahtay Shanti and Tahtay Magnus, and I'm sure you remember Tahtay Puto."

Puto greeted Hanna with a smile while both Shanti the Jivan, and Magnus the Jagare, bowed their heads. Hanna marvelled at the detailed embroidery work on Tahtay Shanti's tunic. It was full of bright colours, flowers and exotic looking birds. In addition to this lavish design,

Shanti's almond skin and silky black hair gave her a rather exotic look. Hanna thought she was quite stunning and was amazed at the contrast between her and the teachers from Kokoroe who seemed rather plain in comparison. Tahtay Magnus was fairly typical of what Hanna had come to expect from a Jagare: lean, tall and muscular. His grizzled beard, scruffy grey hair and his lazy smile reminded her of her grandfather. Magnus appeared to be more of an easy-going figure than the strict disciplinarian that most Jagare seemed to aspire to.

"Please sit," Master Jagare said, "and help yourselves to some food."

Hanna, feeling famished, filled a plate before taking the offered seat as did Krigare and Biatach. Again the door opened and Kazi scrambled in followed by three others.

"Sorry for our tardiness, some of us had a hard time getting out of bed." Hanna grinned broadly as she recognized Karn who was scowling meaningfully at Kazi. She wondered why he wasn't at the party the previous night.

Master Jagare waved them in. "Yes, I figured as much," he said. "Well, come sit, so we can get started. Hanna, I understand you are acquainted with Karn and, obviously Kazi. This is Tasha and Dylan." Tasha was a rather plain-looking Jagare with her hair pulled back in a braid and a serious look on her face. She was in her early twenties, yet she had the look of someone who had seen her fair share of action. Dylan was shorter than Kazi, but looked to be much closer to Karn's age. His eyes darted around the room, taking it all in without moving his head. With a nod from Master Jagare, Kazi and Dylan eagerly loaded their plates with food followed by the more reserved Karn and Tasha.

Master Jagare cleared his throat. "Okay, let's get on with it," he said impatiently. "As most of you know, I have trackers out hunting a party of what we believe are Kameil and, potentially, a Yaru. They have orders to follow them, but nothing more. Hopefully they can provide us with some useful information. Hanna, while you were at Kokoroe, Karn has been assembling your team."

"My team? I didn't realize there would be others." Hanna asked hoping he would explain more than Kazi had.

"Of course," he replied, "you didn't think we'd just send you out alone, did you?"

Hanna hesitated, casting a quick glance Biatach. Aside from how young her team turned out to be there was something more pertinent on her mind. "I thought I was the only one who could, uh, blend in with the Kameil."

Master Jagare nodded. "True enough, so it has to look like you are on your own. If I could, I would have you surrounded with guards, but you'd never be able to infiltrate the Kameil that way, so you will have to get in alone. But I still want to have eyes and ears on you at all times. The plan is to get you in and out as quickly, and as safely, as possible. Dylan is skilled at being able to move with silence and stealth," he explained to everyone at the table. "We hope he'll be able to observe Hanna at all times. If she's in trouble, he'll know. Tasha is an excellent marksman, she'll have Hanna covered if there is a need for it. Karn is our strategist — he'll plan the actual event, plus he is valuable asset if anyone should run into trouble." He inclined his head to make eye contact with Karn and gave him a knowing smile.

"So," Hanna said, "that just leaves Kazi. What's his part in all this?"

Master Jagare smiled. "That was one of Karn's ideas. Care to explain?" he added turning towards Karn.

Karn sat back and crossed his arms. "We need the Kameil to find you, but not us. Also, you have to be found hiding since a young Kameil, all alone, would hardly be out in plain site. If we all hide, then it's a matter of luck that they won't find the rest of us. So the best way for us to be covert is to be overt."

He looked around the table seeming to enjoy the confusion he saw there. "As you know, Minstrels travel all over the world, usually accompanied by at least one Jagare, if not an entire group of people. Typically, word has been sent ahead to let towns or cities know the Minstrel is coming as the Performers Guild has prearranged his or her destinations. It is known when they will arrive and when they will leave. None of them have ever gone missing — no kidnappings or strange disappearances. Aside from this being great for Kazi's safety, it also allows him to be loud and carefree and, thusly, attract as much attention to himself as possible. Sure enough, the Kameil will know he's around, but they won't do anything about it, other than keep an eye on him. At some point they are bound to notice Hanna lurking about, attempt to rescue her and then she can get into the camp to get the information she needs. Meanwhile, Kazi's companions can discreetly follow Hanna, ready to help her escape when the time is right."

Hanna noticed Biatach's crooked smile, which she knew meant that he was impressed. Krigare looked at little less than convinced, as did Tahtay Shanti. Kazi's grin showed that he was thrilled to be part of the operation. For her part, Hanna smiled; hoping that she looked like she too, thought this was a brilliant and fail-safe plan. A tightening in her gut told her otherwise.

Krigare cleared his throat. "Not that I doubt anyone's abilities, but isn't there older, more experienced people that could be assisting Hanna?"

Karn smiled, not insulted in the least. "Our being young also has a purpose. Older, more experienced people would be more guarded while travelling. It's part of our disguise."

After a few moments of silence, Tahtay Biatach looked puzzled. "What's Hanna's story for being out on her own? And why would she be lurking about?"

"Well," Karn replied, "it's plausible, that if a Kameil of Hanna's age was suddenly abandoned by her family she may have to scrounge a living off of others. I haven't worked out the actual back story as of yet."

"We have time," Master Jagare interjected. "I want Hanna to start practicing with the team and work out some exit strategies before I send any of you out there. Plus, I want to know if the Kameil have some sort of base camp outside that valley of theirs, and if they do where it is, how long they stay there and what their security is like. This will give Karn the ability to have a detailed plan drawn up before you head out."

Krigare shifted in his seat. With a note of concern in his voice he asked, "Are you sure that the five of them on there own is still the best plan? What if—"

Master Jagare raised his hand interrupting Krigare's next question. "I plan on having the Vaktare assembled and in position as closely as possible without being noticed so they will have plenty of backup."

"The Vaktare?" Hanna asked before she could stop herself.

"They are a group of specially trained Jagare. If the Kameil, or any of those Yaru, try to stop you from leaving, they'll have a very nasty surprise waiting for them."

Hanna attempted to look reassured at this statement, but she couldn't help but wonder what the Vaktare were specially trained to do. The image of fully armed Jagares storming into a group of weak, sickly Kameil was disturbing. Hanna counted herself lucky that the Vaktare were on her side.

CHAPTER TEN

Temper Mettle

THE MEETING CONCLUDED.

Once the general plan had been discussed, the conversation became more casual. The teachers and leaders broke off in discussion about messages being sent, and more mundane matters that Krigare and Biatach needed to pass on once they reached their destinations. Hanna absently nibbled on a biscuit as she considered the plan that Karn discussed. Most of her teammates seemed to be of similar mind, except for Kazi, who could no longer handle the silence of his team and the rather dull conversation of the others.

"So Karn, why didn't you join our festivities last night?" he said with mock hurt in his voice, "Is this whole *leader* thing going to your head? You don't want to be seen hanging around with us lowly students?"

Karn chuckled. "Yeah right. I would have loved to join you. Sorry I wasn't there Hanna. Master Jagare asked me to take a few students out hunting yesterday. We didn't get back until late."

"You'll just have to make it up to her," Kazi said winking at Hanna.

Karn raised one of his eyebrows. "And just how do you propose that I do that?"

Kazi shrugged. "Oh, I'm sure we'll think of something."

At that moment Master Jagare stood. "I think it's time we get on with our day. Thank you all for coming. Karn, please include Hanna in your morning training schedule. Tahtay Puto will meet her here after lunch for her afternoon lessons."

As everyone made their way to the door, Krigare pulled Kazi aside as Tahtay Biatach did similarly with Hanna.

Biatach placed his large, muscular hands on Hanna's shoulders.

"You will do well, Hanna. I trust Karn and Master Jagare to provide you with everything else you need to be successful with your mission. And when you're done, we will meet again."

Hanna wasn't sure if he was trying to convince himself or reassure her, but she was a little unsettled by his comments and wondered if she really would see him again. Without hesitation, she leapt forward and wrapped her arms around her mentor.

Biatach patted her on the back, suddenly aware of the tightness in his throat and the tears forming in his eyes. He sighed; wondering at what point Hanna started meaning so much to him. Never one who considered having children of his own, he realized that this was what it must feel like to be a father. He broke their embrace and bowed slightly, then quickly left the room without a backwards glance. He hoped that, one-day, he really would get to see her again.

* * *

Karn led the group into the courtyard where most of their training sessions were to take place.

"Okay, let's do some warm-ups and then let's see what Hanna has been working on these last few months."

They ran through a quick routine of lunges, jumping jacks and arm stretches and then spread out for the much-anticipated demonstration. Without warning, Karn lunged at Hanna in an attempt to knock her off her feet. Instinctively, Hanna stepped sideways grabbing Karn's wrist and pushed down on his elbow forcing him to his knees. When he tried to straighten up, she pushed harder causing him to buckle.

"Excellent," he yelped. "You can let me up now."

"Good reflexes, Hanna," Tasha said approvingly.

Dylan whispered, ensuring only Tasha would hear, "It's nice to see Karn taken down for a change. It'll keep him humble."

After brushing the dirt off his knees, Karn looked up and noticed Kazi looking far too pleased.

"Kazi," he said, "I think you can be our next volunteer." If he had heard Dylan's comment, Karn may have chosen him for the next demonstration instead.

Without giving Kazi a chance to consider, Karn pulled him into the centre of the group.

"Okay Kazi, just run straight at Hanna and try to tackle her to the ground." He gave him a little nudge of encouragement.

"Don't worry Kazi," Hanna said, "I won't hurt you."

Kazi nodded and then ran towards her. This time, when Kazi got close, she knelt down and proceeded to flip him over top of her. He landed with a ***WHOMP***, flat on his back.

"Owww," Kazi groaned.

Hanna grimaced. "Opps, sorry. I guess I won't hurt you…much."

"No, no," Karn interjected, "that was fantastic. I think that would be a great thing for us to practice." He reached over and gave Kazi a hand up.

"So far," he continued, "we've been working on general drills: running laps, pushups, mostly building up muscle and working on endurance. Now I want to refine our skills. Over the next week, we will do some individual fine-tuning. For example, Tasha is very skilled in archery, but I want to give her some more challenging practice in that area. Now let's get warmed up."

After running a few laps, they spent the rest of the morning practicing tossing each other to the ground. At first Kazi was looking forward to the training — after Hanna had thrown him to the ground with such ease, he thought it would be great to know how to do that. Once they had spent the better part of an hour learning to fall properly, and then were tossed to the ground a few times, he decided that maybe watching someone else doing it was better than participating.

Lying on the ground, feeling a little winded from the last throw, he voiced his complaint. "Why do I need to learn this anyway?" he grumbled. "I'm just supposed to sing and be a distraction remember?"

Karn helped Kazi to his feet once again. "Just because a Minstrel has never been attacked doesn't mean it can't happen. Besides, once Hanna's with the Kameil, you can drop your act and be part of the rescue team."

"But…what? Really?" Kazi had been about to protest again, but liked the idea that his role would be more substantial.

"Absolutely." Karn replied, "The more help we have the better."

Kazi grinned. "How come you didn't mention that at the meeting this morning?"

"Well," Karn hesitated while looking around at his team who were all intently listening, "I didn't want your father to worry." Seeing the concerned looks of his team, he added, "I plan on preparing you the best I can. If you plan on finishing your Minstrel apprenticeship when this is all over, you will often be on your own anyway, so these are good skills to have. For now, we have the Vaktare available if we need them, so this will probably be the most secure you'll ever be."

Kazi nodded. He knew if Karn had disclosed this part of the plan, his father would have fought harder to keep him out of it. If Hanna was willing to take the risk to walk right into the hands of the Kameil, Kazi could be brave enough to be there to help get her out. He appreciated Karn's discretion.

"Thanks Karn. I won't let you down." He resumed the guard position and prepared himself to be thrown to the ground once again.

Hanna and Karn, who had spent many hours at Biatach's tender mercies, were quiet pleased with the mornings activities, as they had mastered the art of landing. The others, who were utterly spent and sore, were grateful when the session was over.

Watching the team limp back inside the castle, Hanna whispered to Karn, "Perhaps next time we should provide some mats, after all, they are on our side."

Karn chuckled. "Good point."

He decided that tomorrow he'd take a different approach and give his team a chance to recover from the bruises they undoubtedly received today. Tahtay Biatach taught him how to be a skillful fighter, but after many exhausting hours of drills, Karn felt that there needed to be a little fun thrown in. He grinned as he realized he knew just the thing.

* * *

Dylan glared at Karn. He was decidedly unhappy about today's exercise. Karn wanted Tasha to work on her archery skills, but the wooden targets set around the grounds were way too easy for her. Apparently what she needed was a moving target and being the fastest runner in the group, Karn decided that Dylan was the one for the job. Karn assured him it was perfectly safe as the arrow tips were blunted and Dylan was provided with extra padding. The fluffy batting stuffed under the typical leather gear had Dylan feeling incredibly foolish, especially as it was made for the Jagare. Dylan was short, even for a Jivan, meaning the vest sagged below his bottom and the calf pads were past his knees. In addition, since he was running away from Tasha, he had all the gear on backwards.

"You know," Dylan said, " being made to run across the grounds while arrows are shot at me is bad enough, but this is ridiculous."

"You're fine," Karn said remaining expressionless.

The rest of the group attempted to suppress their amusement except Kazi who just roared with laughter.

"Keep laughing Kazi," Dylan snapped, "it'll be your turn next."

Kazi quieted at that. Still, a huge grin lingered across his face.

"Come on Dylan," Karn encouraged, "get going. Your head start lasts until you pass the first target and then she gets to open fire. Remember to swerve as if you were really being fired upon."

Dylan mumbled as he took off, "I am being fired upon."

The team was hard pressed to keep from laughing as Dylan attempted run, barely able to bend his legs with the backwards gear.

Tasha slung the quiver over her shoulder, withdrew one arrow and notched it. When Dylan approached the first target, she raised the bow and took aim.

"Are you sure about this?" she asked, glancing at Karn.

"It'll be fun," he replied.

Tasha smiled. "For me anyway."

Dylan picked up the pace and began to dodge. Tasha waited half a moment and then loosed her first arrow.

SMACK!

"*Youch!*" they heard Dylan's cry in the distance as the arrow bounced off his back, but he kept running. The others couldn't help but wince. Dylan feigned left and right, ducked and jumped, but time and again Tasha's arrows found purchase. When one arrow thumped Dylan right on his buttocks, Tasha lowered the bow. Kazi howled with laughter; Tasha just shook her head.

"Karn, I think Dylan's going to be pretty annoyed with you," she said.

Karn nodded. "I think maybe you're right. From now on miss him on purpose, but just. Let's see the arrows go between his legs or past his arm."

Tasha agreed and continued shooting, this time aiming to miss. On her third arrow she accidentally caught Dylan on the back of an exposed part of his arm. Even from this distance, they could hear him curse.

Karn rested his hand on Tasha's shoulder. "I think that'll do." Tasha nodded and unstrung her bow. Karn cupped his hands to his mouth and hollered for Dylan to come back. "And pick up the arrows on the way!" he added.

Hanna couldn't help but chuckle. "Good idea Karn, that'll cheer him up."

Karn waved the comment aside. "Dylan knows it's all for the benefit of the team. He'll be fine."

When Dylan finally made his way back, arrows in hand, Hanna and Kazi helped him get his gear off. He was remarkably quiet, aside from a few grunts as they peeled off the layers, and he had a glazed look about him. Karn slapped him on the back.

"Great job Dylan! I think Tasha's proved she's quiet capable of covering us if need be. Why don't you take a break while Hanna and I demonstrate more defensive techniques?" He handed Dylan a water skin. Dylan took it without a word.

Karn felt a little uneasy about Dylan's silence, he usually had a witty remark to add to any discussion. Karn was sure the Jivan would be back to his usual quick retorts once he'd had a rest.

Again Hanna showed the group the wrist and lock arm movement she had done on Karn the previous day, but this time she did it in slow motion so they could see how to do it. Together, Karn and Hanna showed a few more moves disarming an opponent, what to do if they were grabbed from behind or pinned to a wall. After the demonstration the group spent the rest of the morning practicing the techniques that Hanna and Karn had shown them.

"Good work everyone," Karn said with enthusiasm. "We'll be working on the same stuff tomorrow...except for the archery. I think we're okay there." He chuckled, but seeing Dylan's glare, Karn cleared his throat and added, "Next week we'll work on Dylan's area of expertise. He can give us some tips about unseen movement as well as moving without being heard. Once he figures we're ready, we'll be going into the woods to test our skills." He hoped this would brighten Dylan's mood and was pleased to see a smile on Dylan's face, but he was a little unnerved by the sinister look in his eyes. A chill went down Karn's spine. Maybe target practice on his team members wasn't the best plan after all.

* * *

Hanna was caught off guard when they entered the main hall for lunch. There were far more people in attendance than she had anticipated. Not only did the number of bodies in the vast space catch her unawares, but also the noise that echoed throughout the space was totally unexpected. She was reminded of the school cafeteria or the food court at a mall back on Earth. It made perfect sense when she thought about it; although, she had become accustomed to the hushed tones and mild atmosphere of Kokoroe. She did not expect the laughing and hollering that was currently filling the room.

Kazi led her by the elbow to the front where multiple tables stretched out as a buffet where they could fill their bread bowls with soup and help themselves to a variety of vegetables. Kazi explained that meat would be available at the evening meal. With so many people to feed at the Citadel, they were lucky if they had enough meat even then. Working their way through the maze of haphazard tables and people milling about, they found a few empty chairs and settled down to eat. Large mugs were on the table as were pitchers of a green liquid Hanna never seen before.

"What is it?" she asked Kazi.

"Boco juice. They add it to the water. It makes it safe to drink."

"You mean the water isn't safe to drink?"

Kazi shrugged. "It's just a precaution I think. There are a lot of people living here, so it's just a precaution."

"You said that,"

Kazi shrugged again then reached for the pitcher. "It's good though. Try some."

When she reached for a mug Kazi stopped her. "Grab a mug that's upside down. The other ones have already been used."

Hanna shook her head. Compared to Kokoroe this place felt chaotic and just slightly uncivilized. As she flipped a mug over for Kazi to fill, she noticed Master Jagare at a table close by.

"What's Master Jagare doing here?"

Kazi gave her that infectious grin of his. "He always eats with the students. Well, almost always. If he has meetings or something, like this morning, he isn't here, but that's not too often. Take a look around. Pretty much everyone eats here. Tahtays, students, the castle staff — it's just one of those things I love about this place."

As she watched, Kazi lifted his bread bowl and begin downing his soup, then tore off a corner of his bread to wipe the contents off his chin. She started to wonder where she fit in. Kokoroe was too quite and tame, the Citadel was a too loud and wild. Back home, it would have been a trigger for a migraine, but for some reason she wasn't getting one. She was tempted to ask to take her meals in her room. For now she decided just to eat quickly and attempt to find her way back to the main meeting room where she was suppose to rendezvous with Tahtay Puto.

Sitting in a quiet corner of the garden, Tahtay Puto observed as Hanna focused her energy on the Essence inside herself. He could tell her concentration was wavering.

"You can not focus. What is distracting you?" he asked.

The pointy pine needles sticking into her butt, she thought. Or perhaps it was the ache in her legs after sitting with them crossed for the last half hour. Then again it could be the fact that she had her eyes closed but was keenly aware she was being watched. None of these seemed to be reasons she could voice, nor were they anything new to her. She had endured her fair share of these types of sessions while at Kokoroe; they just never got any easier.

"I just feel the need to move," she contented herself with saying.

"Yes, I sense the Essence in you seems active. Your attempt at relaxing seems more akin to forcing a lid on a boiling pot of water to keep it from overflowing. This is fascinating to me."

Hanna opened her eyes. "Why?"

"I have only encountered a few Kameil in my time, but I witnessed how the Essence passes through them. They are only able to absorb enough to let them survive. I would have expected the same of you, but that does not appear to be the case. The Essence you receive from the stone you wear pulses through you. You seem to latch on to it and it vibrates throughout your entire being."

He nodded as his eyes scanned her. "Yes, this exercise will not do. You need to move with your Essence, not try to fight it. Stand up."

Hanna was relieved. She had learned a lot about manipulating the Essence over the last year, but she still hated trying to sit still.

"Feet shoulder width apart. Eyes closed. And now, just sway, ever so slightly, no big movements. You are the breeze in the trees." He paused. "Can you feel it now?"

Breathing in deeply and slowly, Hanna felt a tingling in her fingers. As the feeling grew, so did her awareness of it, until her whole body was covered in the prickling sensation. It was as if she had been numb and now everything was waking up. This was the most aware of her Essence she had ever been. She smiled.

"How did you know?" she asked, as she opened her eyes again. "How did you figure it out when they haven't at Kokoroe?"

Puto chuckled softly. "Kokoroe trains the Juro using traditional methods that have worked for hundreds of years. You might share our abilities, but you are not Juro. It made sense to me that perhaps you required a fresh approach. When you spend as many years as I have living the life of a Jagare, you learn to appreciate different perspectives. The Jagare do not like to sit still much either, even though they have learned to master the need not to move. Being successful hunters requires that skill."

"Who would have thought sitting still was a skill?"

"Indeed, but it is one that just may save your life. We will work to calm your boiling waters so you will no longer have a need for the lid."

"Oh goody, more riddles. At least, you explained what you meant. Master Juro would have said the one liner and I'd have to wait to understand."

Puto chuckled again. "I remember," he said. "I will endeavour to be less of an enigma than Master Juro. Let us practice for a little longer and then I will dismiss you for the day. We will continue again tomorrow afternoon."

Hanna nodded and closed her eyes; she was the breeze.

CHAPTER ELEVEN

Omission Control

THE CAPTAINS RETURNED.

The five Yaru clustered around the table studying the map that dominated it. Thanlin tapped on a stretch of land between the towns Viale and Darat. Commander Nandin marked the spot with an X.

"Another six?" Nandin asked. When Thanlin nodded, Nandin continued, "So all together we have fifteen new Kameil in the camp and two more potentials. Has anyone heard from Blades?" Nandin asked using Mayon's nickname.

Nean said, "Yes, where is he? Blades always prides himself on being punctual. He planned on being here two days ago."

"And I would have been," a voice grumbled. All eyes turned to the entrance as Blades entered the command tent, "but we had to leave the road and cut through woods. We were being tracked."

Shock quickly rippled throughout the room. The Yaru always took precautions when gathering new potentials and the Kameil that were spread throughout Galenia. With the Essence capsules that Mateo had supplied, it was relatively easy for the Kameil to pass as Jivan. The Yaru

113

were easily mistaken for the tall, muscular Jagare and therefore, moving the Kameil throughout the land was relatively safe. The risk lay in the possible encounter with a Juro, as only they would be able to recognize what the Kameil and Yaru truly were. However, this was a small risk as the Juro rarely left the town or city they were appointed to, aside from the random pilgrimage or a graduate from Kokoroe moving to their new placement. Juro students studied for decades so even those placements were few and far between. Mateo was familiar with the pilgrimage sites so the Yaru knew which areas to avoid or, at the very least, be more cautious of. For all these reasons, the Yaru had managed to move throughout Galenia unobserved—being tracked had never occurred. Blade's assignment to bring in the Kameil family rumoured to live west of Tanah should have kept him clear of the riskier locations.

It was Nean that broke the silence. "What did you do Blades, stop by Kokoroe for tea?"

In no mood for joking, Blades glared at Nean. "Thanks *Captain Nean*," he replied with a hint of mockery in his tone, "I think I'm a little more discreet than that."

Nandin waved him over. "Blades, tell us everything."

Blades described his journey, glossing over the unremarkable parts of convincing the Kameil family to come with him and giving them the Essence capsules. When he explained how Tahtay Biatach was escorting a student and a Jivan garbed like a Messenger, even Nean's casual manner turned humourless.

"Did Biatach recognize you?" Thanlin inquired knitting his eyebrows together in concern.

114

Blades shook his head. "I don't think so. He seemed fairly indifferent when he passed. I'm sure he thought he should know me, since every Jagare passes through his school."

Plyral added, "Every student suffers his teaching at some point, but even so, it would be a slim chance he'd remember every student."

"Nor would he be able to tell you were Yaru," Thanlin added.

"Yes," Nean agreed, "he may live like a Juro, but he doesn't have their gifts."

Nandin nodded. "So why then do you think they bothered tracking you? Did the Kameil still look ill?"

Again Blades shook his head. "It was nothing like that. I think it was the girl."

He held up his hand to prevent any further interruptions.

"She was young, I'd say thirteen or fourteen and she appeared to be Jivan, but there was something…different about her. I can't really put my finger on it, but the way she looked at me…she looked," he paused struggling for the right words, "she looked into me. It was like Mateo did, after the treatment. As if she was reading my Essence."

He looked into each of their eyes and saw understanding—no one would forget those first few days recovering from the treatment, despite the fact that most of them wanted to.

Sim, broke the silence that had fallen over the men. "Did she say anything?"

"No. They just passed by without a word. Once they rounded a bend in the road, I heard them speaking and then they picked up the pace and raced away. Right away I was concerned, so we left the road and made our way through the woods instead. Every few hours I doubled back just in case and sure enough there was a small scouting party on our trail. They seemed more intent on finding us than hiding themselves. I had to leave a bunch of false trails and take the Kameil on a very roundabout path in order to get here, but I'm confident we lost them."

"Well done," Nandin said, "after I hand out orders, we will break camp and move base camp to the other site, just to be on the safe side. Blades, would you point out where you found these Kameil please?"

Blades studied the map for a moment then pointed to the location where he had picked up the family. "Four," he said anticipating Nandin's next question.

Again Nandin marked the map. "First off, I still want one member from each team to stay and patrol the camp. That leaves two Yaru per team. Kal," Nandin said referring to the Yaru he had befriend when first meeting Nean and was now his second-in-command, "will escort the newest arrivals back to the valley and return to our new location to wait for the next bunch. If I'm not there, send any messages for Mateo with Kal." He glanced around at the men to ensure they understood.

"Before you arrived Blades, Thanlin was telling us about a group of Addicts heading north of Darat." Blades cracked a rare smile as Nandin explained. "He figures they're planning on attacking the nesting grounds in that area. I want the two of you to take your teams and deal with them. If you take the horses and leave today you might catch them before they get there. Mateo wanted me to remind you when dealing with the Addicts, make it quick and clean. Avoid killing the locals and try not to be seen."

Blades and Thanlin exchanged knowing glances; they doubted Commander Nandin knew what they *were* instructed to do if they were seen; Mateo didn't leave witnesses.

"Sim," Nandin continued, "your team is to resume your collection of the Gelei plants you found in the north and check out those caves we heard about in the area. Plyral, your team is to continue scouting for Kameil in the west, but due to this latest development, stick to the southern roads."

Nandin took a moment to observe the Captains; giving them their favourite assignments was one of the highlights of his position. Finally, he turned to Nean. "Your task is a bit more challenging."

Nean stood up straight, challenging sounded like fun.

"I've learned that there is a group of Kameil living in Senda. I can't imagine how they've managed to survive in the city since Senda's supply of Essence is heavily guarded. As I'm sure you know, the city itself is surrounded by a towering brick wall with two gates leading into the city, both of which are guarded by Jagare and monitored by at least one Juro at all times. Which means — "

"I get to climb." Nean finished Nandin's sentence with a grin. Nandin would have found his friends enthusiasm amusing except for the last assignment he had to share. "Yes, you and your team are to head there and seek out this group. And I will be joining you, but first, I think I need to get the news of this girl to Mateo. We'll plan to meet in about a week's time."

Nean slapped Nandin on the back. "Excellent. Now we're going to have some real fun."

Nandin rolled his eyes. If he had known that Nean's idea of fun included suicide missions, he may not have chanced leaving the safe, quiet life he'd been living. Noticing the intensity of Nean's excited anticipation, Nandin realized, he too was exhilarated by a sense of purpose and he had to admit he'd never felt so alive. Perhaps, he reflected, he would have taken the chance after all.

CHAPTER TWELVE

Exhaustive Account

MATEO PACED.

It had taken Nandin just over two days to reach the valley as he travelled alone and on horseback, anxious to deliver his news. As Nandin watched Mateo, he knew he made the right choice in returning to the castle before proceeding to Senda. Watching Mateo's expression, he didn't know whether or not Mateo was pleased or worried about what he had said.

"Mayon said she definitely looked like a Jivan?" Mateo asked using Blades real name.

"Yes. She was school-aged and clearly larger than any Juro."

"If she can see the Essence, Master Juro would know about it," Mateo said thinking aloud. "But why send her to the Citadel? Surely he'd want her at Kokoroe for training, unless," he stopped and looked at Nandin. "Was it possible she was a prisoner?"

Nandin thought for a moment. "I don't think so. Blades didn't mention anything like that. She was being escorted by Tahtay Biatach though."

Mateo nodded. "Yes, that is very peculiar. My bet is that he was her protector. There are few Jagare based at Kokoroe that could fill that role and I suppose if she was a prisoner they would have been heading south, to the Sanctuary."

Mateo clucked his tongue as he thought over the mysterious girl. A Jivan with Juro abilities was just the sort of person he'd want to get his hands on. The possibility opened up too many questions for him to guess at.

"Nandin, I want you to keep an eye out for this girl. If you find her, try to persuade her to come here. She would be an indispensable addition to our cause, another person to help with the Essence. Just think of the Kameil we could help."

"How would she be helpful?"

Mateo replied. "I'm only one man Nandin, and I'm the only one able to create the Essence capsules. If I had someone who could see the Essence, they would be able to share the work and help with my research. The two of us could come up with a permanent cure for the Kameil, perhaps without resorting to liquid Essence. And a Jivan would be way more sympathetic to our cause than a Juro — they are not brainwashed by Master Juro for as long and the Jivan race have experienced life without Juro abilities."

Nandin scratched his head. "Well then, I'd better find her. Do you want me to go to the Citadel?"

Mateo resumed his pacing. "No, not yet. Meet up with Nean as planned, but find out what you can about this *Seer* — if that's what she is. I don't want you risking yourself if it turns out to be nothing; if she truly is a Seer there will be rumours I'm sure. Something like that would spread like wildfire."

Thinking of the rumours that arose around the Three and even about Mateo himself he added, "Just make sure you don't believe them."

"What do you mean?" Nandin asked puzzled.

"The stories may ring of truth, but may not be completely factual. When you have the facts, you will know if it's worth the risk."

For the first time since Nandin joined Mateo in his study, Mateo noticed his clothes and frazzled appearance.

"Nandin, you look exhausted. Have a rest and get cleaned up. Would you mind taking the time to do up your report before you go to Senda?"

"Of course, I will work on it in the morning. Thank you, sir."

Nandin bowed, relieved to return to his room as he could barely keep his eyes open. As Mateo watched him go, he thought again of the news of the girl. He rubbed his hands together. *A Jivan with the Sight, imagine if she had other Juro abilities.*

CHAPTER THIRTEEN

Forbidden Fruit

THE KNOCKING REPEATED.

It echoed somewhere deep in Nandin's unconscious mind as he allowed himself to drift back to sleep. Suddenly, he was being roughly shaken awake. He groaned, opened one eye and mumbled a greeting to Jon who was hovering over him.

"Glad you're back," Jon said. "Are you here for awhile this time?"

Nandin stretched and then finally pushed himself into an upright position. "Nope, just until tomorrow. Thought I'd catch a quick nap before I started working on my reports."

Nandin noticed his friend's crestfallen expression as he whispered, "Oh."

"What is it, Jon?"

Jon slumped his shoulders. "I was just hoping we could talk."

"Of course we can," Nandin said, "I've still got time. Actually, I had every intention of seeking you out after my snooze. But I'm awake now, what's on your mind?"

"Do you think we could speak somewhere else? Outside maybe?"

"Sure, let's head down to the gardens. It's been awhile since I've been there."

Nandin hopped out of bed and briefed Jon about his last excursion as they made their way through the castle and into the gardens. Jon gave a concerned look when Nandin mentioned his upcoming mission to the city.

"I'm not too worried," Nandin said with confidence, "Nean's got a head start, so I'm sure I will be in good hands when I get there. Now tell me, what's this all about?"

Jon nervously peered around the gardens, making sure they were alone. Nandin knew that even though it had been almost a year since coming to the valley, Jon still had trust issues. Whenever he wanted to talk to Nandin about something he felt would be controversial, he waited until they were out hunting or in the gardens before discussing it. Today the gardens were empty, aside from the birds that were busy building their new nests and the insects that were finding their way to the newly opened flowers. Content they were on their own, Jon finally confided.

"It's Sarah, I don't know what to do."

"What's happened? Did she get hurt?" Nandin asked suddenly concerned.

Jon shook his head. "No, no, nothing like that."

"Did the two of you break up?" He interrupted again. He knew that Jon had been growing steadily fonder of Sarah and had been coming up with more and more excuses to go into the valley to see her. On feast day, she was guaranteed to visit the castle and when the two weren't dancing, they could often be found huddled in a quiet corner talking. At first, Nandin had felt a bit jealous

123

that Jon had found someone he could so easily connect with, but seeing the happiness it brought him, Nandin became one of the couple's biggest supporters.

As they wound their way along the gravel path through the chest high shrubs they came upon a bench. Jon collapsed on it, leaning on his knees and holding his head in his hands. He began rocking back and forth; Nandin's concern doubled.

Finally Jon looked up. "I think I'm in love with her," he managed to say.

"Well, of course you are, why is that a problem?"

"We were suppose to be just friends. Nandin, she's a Kameil!"

Shocked by his friend's statement, Nandin hesitated. "But...I didn't think that bothered you. We've become friends with the Kameil after all this time, haven't we?"

Jon sat back. "But Nandin, I'm *in love* with her." Seeing his friend's puzzled expression, Jon asked, "Nandin, what do people do when they are in love?"

"I suppose they get married."

"Right. They get married and have kids."

Nandin smiled. "I'm sure Mateo would approve."

Jon felt frustrated at Nandin's lack of understanding. "All my life I've been raised knowing one day I would marry a Jagare. And I was taught of the tragedy of the Kameil. Don't you see? If I married Sarah our kids would be Kameil, which means they'd be sick and without Essence. How could I ever knowingly do that to a child?"

Nandin, finally catching on to Jon's concern said, "You don't know that Jon. Because of the treatment, your kids might be stronger and healthier than any child born on Galenia. Beside, you don't have to have kids."

"Sarah has already told me she wants a family and *might be* is still a risk. How could I take that chance?"

"Think of it this way, if Sarah had never met you, she would have most likely married a Kameil. Her kids would definitely be born as a Kameil and therefore, without Essence and sickly. But she did meet you and now any child she has with you has a greater chance of being healthy than ever before."

Jon's eyes brightened. "I…I never thought of it that way."

Warming to his theme, Nandin continued, "You are the best thing that has ever happened to her. Not only is she more likely to have strong children, she would have one of the best protectors on the world and a great provider. And Sarah is one of the prettiest girls in the village. If you don't want her, then step aside and let someone else have a go."

Even though Nandin was smiling, Jon darkened at the jibe. "But she's Kameil!" Jon contested again. Unable to contain his frustration, he got up and started pacing back and forth, grinding his fist into his palm. "Juro marry Juro, Jivan marry Jivan and Jagare marry Jagare — that's they way it's suppose to be."

"That's all well and good Jon, but who do the Yaru marry? In case you've forgotten, you're not a Jagare anymore."

Jon stumbled in mid-stride. Of course he had undergone the treatment and even though he knew he was technically a Yaru, he realized he still saw himself as a Jagare. Seeing Jon hesitate, Nandin continued.

"So far, all the Yaru are men. I like you well enough, but I'd take a female Kameil over your hand in marriage." Nandin smiled. Seeing his friend's serious expression, he added, "Since you're no longer a Jagare, the rules and traditions you grew up with no longer apply. This is one of those choices Mateo always talks about and here's your chance to make it."

He joined Nandin on the bench once again. Nandin watched the transformation come over his friend as his words sunk in. The shadows that had loomed over his features disappeared as he lifted his chin, the tension in his shoulders let loose and he sat a little straighter.

"Do you thing Mateo would approve?" he asked. "Not that I need his permission or anything, but if he doesn't like the idea we'd probably have to leave the valley."

Nandin waved his concern away. "I'm positive he'd be all for it. He's seen you two together. I'm sure he would have stepped in long before now if he had a problem with it. In fact, if I was you, I would go and find Sarah and ask her straight away," he said. "I'd like to know what she says before I have to go tomorrow."

Jon abruptly stood up. Sensing their conversation was coming to an end, Nandin joined him.

"Where will I find you?" Jon asked.

Nandin laughed. It was one of the things he had always admired about Jon: once he made his mind up, he acted.

"I'll be in the library, filling out my reports."

Jon grabbed his friend in a hug and then quickly strode out of the gardens. Nandin sighed. One day, he thought, love would be his priority.

CHAPTER FOURTEEN

Hostile Engagement

NANDIN STUDIED THE PARCHMENT.

Over the last few weeks, out in Thickwood Forest, he diligently marked all the locations the men had found Kameil, Essence plants or sources, and Potentials on a map that he carried with him. He knew that once he returned to the castle he would need to update the wall maps that dominated one side of the library.

He sat at a large, wooden desk making final notes in a heavy, leather bound book. When he decided to become a Yaru he hardly expected to be reading and writing, but Mateo insisted Nandin continue his education and improve his penmanship. As the Commander of the Yaru, he was responsible for reporting all of the missions and their outcomes, not once, but twice. The first time at camp on scrolls and in point form, more for keeping the details straight for when he wrote his final report in, what Mateo called: The Gathering Compendium. In addition to filling the pages with the events, he had to reference them in an index at the beginning of the book so that it was easier for Mateo to find any particular piece of information. Nandin found this process quite tedious and looked forward to the day he could pass this task onto someone else.

The only perk of this particular chore was being able to do it in the library. Typically Nandin preferred to be outside in the fresh air in the trees, garden or even in the village, but the library was a space that filled him with awe and brought him a different sort of peace of mind. One wall was covered in maps that danced with multi-coloured light from the immense stained-glass windows across from it. Floor-to-ceiling wood shelving lined the walls of both the upper and lower levels. They encased books, scrolls and incredible artifacts; some handmade and some natural art such as rock geodes. Leather club chairs clustered around the hearth of a sizeable stone fireplace, which was flanked by stone draka: a breed of reptilian-like Mystic Fliers that favoured the eastern mountains. Three massive, candled chandeliers lit the whole space in the evening.

The Yaru had begun to frequent the library, as it was a great place to discuss upcoming missions or even to share a drink at the end of the day. The room had a feeling of warmth and luxury especially compared to the stark space of the dining hall, dim and dull with its few tapestries and sconces.

Nandin pushed back his chair and then, gathering up his map scroll, stood and made his way across the room to the map wall. Hundreds of pins with tiny, coloured ribbons attached to them, marked the locations of everything Mateo was tracking. One map consisted of Black ribbons that symbolized where Potentials were from, as well as light blue flags where the roaming Kameil had been found. The second map contained green pins that represented Essence-rich plants. Other Essence sources, such as fumaroles (pockets of Essence gas spewing from the

129

ground), were marked in pink. Beneath the maps was a step stool that was used to reach the upper locations, and a tall, narrow table that held several containers of the ribbon and pins. Nandin placed his scroll on the table and stood back to study the maps.

"It looks like a work of art, doesn't it?" Mateo asked startling Nandin.

Mateo chuckled at Nandin's exasperated expression. After all his training, Nandin thought it would be impossible for someone to sneak up on him, but Mateo still had the remarkable, if not irritating, ability to do so. Nandin resumed scrutinizing the maps.

"I was just thinking," Nandin said, "the connection between the Essence and the Kameil is interesting."

Mateo moved to stand beside Nandin and look at the maps. "It is," he stated.

"It makes sense," Nandin continued. "The Kameil need to be as close to the Essence as possible."

Mateo's crooked grin subtly showed his approval. "And what does that tell us?"

Nandin thought a moment. "Well, I guess you could reason that the Kameil would know where to find Essence."

Mateo squeeze Nandin's shoulder. "Yes, you could."

Mateo turned and strode toward the group of chairs around the fireplace.

"Come, sit with me and tell me a little bit about your reports. Did you get a chance to finish them?"

Nandin nodded. "Yes, all I have left to do is mark our findings on the wall maps."

After briefly summarizing each mission, Mateo asked a few questions that he knew would not be part of the written report, but may prove to be relevant. They had only been in discussion for a short time when Jon came bursting in the room.

"Nandin!" he shouted enthusiastically, "you still in here?"

Nandin stood and walked a few steps towards his friend. "I'm here."

Jon beamed. "She said yes! Can you believe it?" Noticing Mateo for the first time, Jon bowed after giving Nandin an anxious look. "Sorry for my intrusion, I didn't realize — "

Mateo stood and returned Jon's bow. "No apologies necessary. Please, come and join us."

Sensing Jon's hesitation, Nandin wished he had spoken to Mateo about Jon's plans so that he could be sure as to how the conversation was going to turn out. He had been the unofficial voice of the Yaru; if they had an issue, Nandin brought it to Mateo. Also, it was his duty to keep Mateo informed of what went on with the Yaru. He hoped his negligence would be inconsequential.

"What seems to be the cause of your obvious happiness?" Mateo asked.

Preferring the direct approach, Jon replied, "I asked Sarah to marry me and she said yes."

A dark cloud drifted across Mateo's features causing Nandin to doubt his earlier conviction that Mateo would support a Yaru marring a Kameil. After an intense silent moment, the cloud dissipated and a grin lit up Mateo's face.

"That's wonderful!" he said reaching across and grabbing Jon by the forearm, shaking it in congratulations. "Let's set the date for the ceremony to take place in say, two months time? That should give everyone a chance to complete their current assignments and reconvene back here."

Jon nodded, feeling a little taken aback by Mateo's quick change in demeanour and his current enthusiasm.

"Yes," Mateo muttered almost to himself, "that should give us time to get your new accommodations prepared."

"New accommodations?" Jon asked a little puzzled.

"Your quarters are sufficient for you, but it's not sufficient for a couple. Besides, you can hardly raise a family in the one room apartment you are currently residing in, can you?"

Jon had been thinking along the same lines, but hardly thought Mateo would want Jon to start a family. He said, "No, of course not. I was actually thinking we might move into one of the houses down in the valley."

Mateo shook his head. "Don't worry, I will have a suite done up that both you and Sarah will enjoy. Better than any of the houses down there."

"That's okay, sir" Jon persisted, "We don't need anything fancy. Besides, it's quicker for me to get out of the valley to go hunting. The valley makes more sense for us."

"No, I don't think so. I've been meaning to say something for a while Jon. You spend too much time in valley."

As Jon's face flushed, Nandin tensed. It seemed, somehow, the conversation had just taken a turn.

"Too much time? What? Am I a prisoner here? "

"Of course not, I'm just worried about your wellbeing. Trust me Jon, this is the best place for you."

Jon stood, raising his voice. "Haven't I done everything you've asked? Don't you trust me yet? I don't plan on running away."

Mateo stood as well, anger flashing in his eyes. "Don't you trust me yet? You're well being has always been my priority. Curse your Jagare cynicism!" Mateo hollered. "I'm just trying to keep you safe!"

"Safe from what? Are the Kameil not good enough for you? I saw the disgust on your face when I told you I was marrying a Kameil. You're worried that you'll taint your superior race aren't you? You're precious Yaru mixing with your slaves!"

Even Nandin thought Jon had gone too far that time, but instead of shouting back, Mateo dropped back onto his chair and calmly replied. "No Jon, you've got it wrong. If you live in the valley, you will get sick and die."

Ready to retaliate, Jon's mouth opened, but when the words Mateo had spoken registered, Jon also collapsed on the couch.

"What?" he asked quietly.

Mateo sighed. "When The Three first came to this valley, around a hundred and eighty years ago, they didn't realize what they had stumbled upon. Once they began building the outer wall though, it quickly became clear to Kenzo, the Juro, that the quarrying released Essence into the air. This posed a problem. To prevent anyone from being exposed to dangerous levels of Essence, they built the castle on the largest of the floating rocks, surrounding it with the high walls to protect their followers. Since the Essence mostly drifted out instead of up, the castle proved very effective. Unfortunately, before it was completed, many had become ill and some became Addicts. Kenzo's attempt at curing them succeeded in removing all of their natural Essence, making them Kameil. The upside was that the Kameil could live and work in the valley without any side effects; the downside was that they couldn't leave the valley or they would become ill and die, unless they found another source of Essence."

Mateo paused allowing Jon and Nandin a moment to consider what he was saying. Unsurprisingly it was Nandin who spoke first.

"So that means that all the Kameil working in the castle have some form of Essence, like the tablets you make, and that's why all the Kameil in the village don't have to take them?"

Mateo added, "and why those in the village can't stay here for too long or vice versa."

Jon sat up. "Then how can Sarah live here? Wouldn't she die?"

"She could take the capsules, but those are really a short-term solution. I'd rather give her liquid Essence, which would essentially cure her. I would like to do this for all the Kameil, but at this time, liquid Essence is rare. I use it only out of necessity."

"You used it on us," Jon said unsure of what to think.

"Yes Jon, I did. But let me ask you: who is currently out searching for Essence plants? Who is gathering the sick and lost Kameil? Who is putting a stop to the reign of terror that the Addicts are causing? And who is protecting the farmers from raiding beasts or adding much needed game to the Kameil's diet? Do you think the Kameil could do this?"

Jon considered for a moment, really thinking about Mateo's argument.

"Probably not."

Mateo continued, "Even if I cured them, they would not be warriors. Their condition would stabilize, but they are not, nor could they ever be, Jagare."

Jon conceded. "No, you're right, the Kameil could never achieve what the Yaru can."

"As for the Kameil that I have treated with the liquid Essence, the ones that live in the castle, they bravely volunteered to test it — to see what the effects would be. I didn't just use it to create staff for the castle. Now that I know it works, and I have successfully created Yaru, I can spend my energy in finding a way to increase our supply so hopefully, one day, all the Kameil can benefit from it."

Jon sat back completely in awe of Mateo's grand plan of treating all the Kameil. He had been raised to fear and despise Mateo and the Kameil; his reason for coming to the valley was to gather intelligence that he could take to the Sanctuary. Since he came to the valley, even though his opinion of the Kameil had changed, he had still distrusted Mateo. Every action, every word and every mission that Mateo had given, Jon had come up with a devious and selfish reason that had motivated Mateo. Now that Mateo had explained his real purpose, Jon felt ashamed for his prejudice.

"Why would you give Sarah the treatment then? She's just one of many who could use it."

Mateo smiled. "Because Jon, she makes you happy." Jon suddenly lit up at the thought of Sarah being able to travel with him outside the valley, but realized that accepting this gift would be rather selfish. Sensing Jon's hesitation, Mateo continued.

"The Yaru have sacrificed much to become part of our community: your homes, your family. Aside from your sense of wellbeing, your rewards are few. I would be most pleased if I could do this for you and Sarah. And I promise, your children, should they require it, will also be cured."

Jon choked up at Mateo's sentiment. "Really?" he gasped.

"Absolutely. Who knows? Perhaps your children will be Yaru naturally and what an amazing addition to our family that would make."

"See," Nandin said, "Nothing to worry about."

Mateo stood. "Nandin, I think Jon and Sarah would enjoy celebrating their happy news with a friend. I will get Hatooin to finish the map work for you."

"Thank you sir. I'd appreciate that." Nandin stood and bowed, quickly followed by Jon.

"Thank you," Jon said clearing his throat, "thank you for everything."

Mateo just nodded and then watched the two quickly exit the room.

Hatooin, who had discreetly entered the room some time earlier and remained hidden, emerged to stand by Mateo.

"Nice speech," he said.

"Yes," Mateo replied scratching his chin, "I think it went rather well."

"Still, I was surprised that you decided to go along with this marriage."

Mateo cocked his head to one side, "You don't approve?"

Hatooin shrugged. "I don't feel one way or the other. I just thought you were planning on creating female Yaru for their spouses."

"That would be preferable," Mateo admitted, "But you always said Jon was a fence sitter. I'd say we now have him completely committed to our cause. In fact, I'll bet he quickly becomes one of our biggest advocates."

Hatooin grunted. "I think I'd have to agree. Well played sir." Hatooin paused, unsure if he should point out the flaw that he saw in Mateo's plan.

Sensing that Hatooin was not finished expressing his concerns, Mateo nudged him, "Come on, out with it."

"It's just that your explanation of the use of liquid Essence…how will you be able to justify using it to make more Yaru?"

"I'll come up with something. As long as it appeals to his sense of honour and equality he'll accept it—especially after I treat his wife. In fact, he'll have to, otherwise he would be a hypocrite and I know that's something he couldn't accept." Mateo chuckled to himself. "I think I've played this hand rather well."

CHAPTER FIFTEEN

Fowl Play

HANNA WAITED PATIENTLY.

For the last week, Dylan had been coaching the team on hiding and moving through the woods with stealth. He showed them to watch for sticks that would snap if stepped on and when to slide your foot under dried leaves instead of walking right on them. Kazi was proving to have the least amount of patience at moving slowly and diligently. Tasha and Karn, both experienced hunters, were used to moving silently, but neither of them were as skilled as Dylan.

Dylan seemed to glide as he moved, barely disturbing a thing as he ghosted among the trees. It was a skill that he loved to practice even though he had no use for it, until now. As part of the regular training at the Citadel, students all took a course on tracking and hunting. It was unusual for Jivan to become hunters, but they were still given the opportunity to learn the techniques. Dylan's ability with throwing knives and being stealthy had caught Master Jagare's attention.

Karn knew of Dylan as they had attended the Citadel at the same time, though Dylan was a year ahead of Karn. Since finishing his schooling at the Percipio, Dylan had returned to the Citadel to become part of the Huntmasters

Guild as a tracker. It was a rare honour to be part of the Guild as a Jivan. His skills made him an excellent addition to Hanna's team.

As he walked to the back gate towards Hanna, she burst out laughing.

"What are you wearing?" she asked.

Dylan wore the usual leather pants and vest with a beige shirt, however, the shirt was splattered with dirt making the colour hard to discern. In addition to this grubby look, twigs and leaves were affixed to him randomly, even in his dark hair.

"It's my own creation. It will help me blend into the woods" he said proudly, "I thought this was the perfect opportunity to try it out." He looked around. "Where's everyone else?"

"Kazi and Tasha went on ahead, Karn should be in position in the clearing," she replied. "So, what's our plan?"

For the end of the week's lesson, Dylan had requested a challenge for the team to test out their new skills. Karn was stationed in the centre of a small clearing where he was supposed to try to catch the others trying to sneak up on him. They were split into pairs each consisting of one student (Kazi or Hanna) and one graduates (Tasha or Dylan). The group that got the closest to Karn before detection would be the winners. Hanna had the feeling though, that there was more to it than Dylan was letting on. Tasha grumbled about being stuck with Kazi, but Dylan pointed out that Hanna didn't have any more experience being stealthy than Kazi.

"My guess is that Tasha is going to lead Kazi on a fairly direct course. The less he's traipsing through the woods, the better. I thought we would circle around, split up and come at the clearing from two sides."

"Got it coach," she said with a smile, "lead on."

It took them the better part of an hour to quietly make their way to one side of the clearing. Not nearly as talented as Dylan, Hanna was still adept at moving quietly. She attributed this to being small and lightweight, which made it easier to move around without disturbing much.

"I'm going to move into position around the opposite side of the clearing," Dylan explained in hushed tones. "While I'm doing that, I want you to move in closer. There is some brush that will hide you from view, just move slowly until you get to it and then wait for Karn to be distracted before you enter the clearing."

"Distracted? What are you planning on doing?"

"Getting his attention," he replied evasively. "He'll be so focused on me, he won't notice you coming up behind him. Just keep low and move slowly. If your movements are too big, it will draw his attention." He patted her on the shoulder. "You'll do great. It won't take me too long to get into position. I can move faster now that I'm on my own."

Hanna noticed him adjusting the small pouch he carried, again wondering what he was up to. Whatever it was, she was sure it was going to be entertaining.

From Hanna's crouched position, she peeked through the bush. Karn had just resumed his seated position on a stump after walking around the clearing, peering through the trees. She waited with bated breath as he walked past her hiding spot, convinced he would be able to spy her. When she allowed Dylan to put greenery in her hair she scoffed at his efforts. Now she was grateful.

Karn began whittling a stick, seemingly intent on the task, when he paused mid-stroke. A sly smile spread across his face.

"Kazi," he called nonchalantly, "if it wasn't for your behind protruding from that tree, I would have sworn it was a beast making its way to the clearing."

Kazi stepped out onto the path and looked over his shoulder into the woods. Even though he was still too far away to be heard it was clear he was speaking. Without realizing it he had just given away his teammates position.

"Tasha you may as well come out," Karn hollered, "I doubt even Kazi talks to trees."

Tasha's growl of frustration clearly echoed across the open space. Karn set aside his branch, rose to his feet and began making his way towards the two when something smacked into the side of his head. Karn whipped his head around trying to spy the culprit that launched the projectile.

Barely able to contain her laughter, Hanna slowly inched forward as she watched the egg drip down the side of Karn's face. Karn took a few steps toward the trees, squinting to focus. Hanna took her first tentative step into the clearing when Karn turned his head. Before he spied Hanna though, another egg crashed into his stomach, again drawing his attention.

"Dylan!" Karn cried shaking his fist. "I know it's you!"

Another egg flew towards him, but this time Karn was able to jump out of the way. He got the impression that the egg had come from above and he had just started to search the trees when he felt a gentle tapping on his shoulder. He jumped at the unexpected touch and spun in place.

"Hi," Hanna said, a huge grin across her face.

"Where the heck did you come from?"

"I'd say from the woods," Dylan answered as he swung down from the tree, landing nimbly on his feet. He pulled another egg from his pouch, tossing it up and catching it repeatedly.

"Dylan, you fiend! Don't you even think about chucking another one of those at me!" Karn attempted to look menacing, however, with the egg bits clinging to him, it was hard to take him seriously.

"Well, it wouldn't be any fun doing it from here. Perhaps I should give you a head start?" He paused, then added with a sly grin, "It's perfectly safe."

Karn wiped the guck from his face. A tight smile toyed at his lips. "Alright. Point taken. I'm sorry about the target practice."

"Good." Dylan tossed the egg into the trees behind him. Kazi and Tasha, who were observing the scene from the safety of the tree line, entered the clearing to join the group.

"I told you it wasn't a good idea," Tasha said, shaking her head at the mess that was Karn.

"Yes, yes. Valuable lesson: listen to your team. Don't use them as prey. Tell me Dylan, you learned that lesson as well, right?"

Dylan smiled and grabbed Karn by the shoulder as they began heading back towards the Citadel.

"Absolutely, we're even. You got off easy though. One quick wash and it's all history for you. I'm still sporting a nasty bruise that I feel every time I sit down."

"That was hilarious, Dylan" Kazi piped up.

"Yes," Hanna agreed, "talk about egg on your face." The others nodded, yet Hanna had the feeling this was another one of those sayings specific to her home.

They had just made their way through the back gates when a Jivan rushed towards them. Panting, he approached Karn.

"Master Jagare wishes to see you, sir."

"Just me or all of us?" Karn asked.

"He requested you to report on your progress. I'm assuming you would know best who should accompany you."

Karn nodded and the man returned to the castle, this time at a much more casual pace since his message had been delivered.

Karn said to his team, "We'd better go wash up. I'd prefer to meet Master Jagare with a little less...nature all over us."

CHAPTER SIXTEEN

Climatic Seen

HIS JOURNEY WAS RUSHED.

After an enjoyable evening spent with Jon and Sarah celebrating their engagement, Nandin allowed himself one night's stay at the castle before heading to Senda. He traversed the Valley of 1000 Rivers making good time regardless of the zigzagging route the rivers enforced on those wishing to cross from east to west. The weather was in his favour with no more than a spring mist to hinder him. His rendezvous at base camp in Thickwood Forest was enough to replenish his food supplies, drop off Mateo's messages and rest his horse before continuing his journey. Thais, a Kameil that Nandin had met on his first journey to the valley, had elected to travel with him to Senda. In addition to guiding Nandin there, he would also return Nandin's horse back to the camp, as he would be unable to take the horse into the city.

He was glad to have Thais's company. He had spent many days and nights travelling to the valley and back to the forest on his own. Now his meals and campfires were filled with talk and stories, which was much more to his liking. Over the past year, Nandin had grown in respect and authority in the eyes of the Kameil as well as the Yaru and was therefore, privy to information that was originally undisclosed. Now that Thais no longer concealed the details of his past, he was a fountain of information. Nandin was impressed by the man's knowledge of plants, recognizing animal tracks and general awareness of the forest they were travelling.

"There are some sources of Essence in here," he had admitted one night, referring to the woods around them, "but they are few and far between. They're also small and difficult to find. I think that's why no village has risen in the area."

He assured Nandin that he had apprised Captain Sim of the whereabouts of these sources, since Sim's mission was to collect the Essence for Mateo. Mateo would then, depending on the source, create capsules of Essence that the Kameil could use to keep them healthy and allow them to safely travel outside the valley.

Now the two men sat on their horses in the shadow of the woods outside Senda. Nandin marvelled at the size of the place. He had never been to any city before. When he was a youth, his travels only included Kokoroe and the Citadel and even then, he had slept in the woods or small villages rather than staying in any of the cities along the way. As Mateo's commander, his missions kept him mostly traversing back and forth from the woods to Mateo's valley.

As if reading Nandin's thoughts, Thais said, "It sure is impressive."

Nandin eyed his companion. Thais was seated on a slender, light reddish-brown horse that occasionally bobbed it's head as if anxious to continue on. As he watched Thais rubbing the nape of the horse's neck, he got the feeling that Thais was agitated also, as he viewed the city before them.

Definitely no Yaru, Thais was a good head shorter than Nandin and lacked the chiselled physique the Yaru had, but the man had showed his courage and dedication to Mateo on many occasions. He often elected to guard the camp, keeping watch for possible outsiders or even attacks from wolcott, Draka or other beasts that had been known to inhabit the forest. Of course, on the occasion he spotted any of these beasts, his task was to alert the Yaru, who would then hunt the creature down. It was still a brave posting to patrol at night, keeping a watchful eye out for these killers. Nandin wondered what it was about the city that was testing Thais's courage now.

"Are you really going to climb that wall?" Thais asked nervously.

Nandin turned his gaze back to the sight before them. The wall in question completely surrounded the city and stretched further north than they could see. To the south, a road led up to the main gate and they could make out a few travellers coming and going; some with carts or wagons, some on horseback and others on foot. Had the gate been guarded by Jagare alone, he may have risked entry that way. The fact that there was always a Juro who greeted people coming and going prevented the gate as an option though; a Juro would recognize a Yaru. A few sentries could be seen pacing along the top of the wall, undoubtedly keeping a watch for anything out of the ordinary. Since the Kameil were unlikely to show themselves in the bright afternoon sun and very few predators lurked near the city, the sentries seemed to spend more time observing the goings on inside of the walls than outside.

A few of the taller buildings were visible above the wall, but they were still too far away to make out any details. Nandin estimated the wall itself to be four times his height; compared to Mateo's walls, it was not much of a challenge to climb.

He replied, "That's the plan. I don't think it will be too difficult. I'll just have to time it right. I'd hate to reach the top in time to have a conversation with the passing guard." He smiled at Thais to see if his nonchalant answer had calmed him — it hadn't.

"What's the problem Thais? You are as jittery as a Kameil walking into Kokoroe." Since Kokoroe was a school mainly populated with Juro, who had the special ability to recognize the Kameil, Essence tablets or not, the comment clearly communicated Nandin's interpretation of Thais's behaviour.

"You've got that right," Thais agreed. "We may be in the shadows here and those sentries may not be spending much time looking this way, but if they do catch a glimpse of us I wouldn't be surprised if they send a few Jagare our way to see what's what."

"You've a good point, let's move back a bit, I've seen all I need to for now. I'll come back after the sun sets to study the situation further, and I won't bring you or the horses when I do."

Gratefully, Thais led the way back into the trees to an area they had passed where there was some grass for the horses to feed on and a fallen log the men could lean against while eating the cold rations they had brought.

* * *

As the sun began to set and the shadows in the woods grew longer, Nandin prepared himself for the task ahead. He had been wearing a simple cotton tunic and pants with a leather vest and soft leather boots. Now he donned the specialised Yaru clothing. The black outfit covered him from head to toe with openings only for his eyes. Soft, fabric boots with leather soles were tied over his pant bottoms, a wide black sash held the tunic snuggly to his body and also allowed for various tools and weapons to be tucked into. He wore black gloves with the finger tips removed to allow for better grips on the walls as he climbed. Nandin chose not to carry any swords or bow and arrows as they would encumber him, and instead elected to fill a pack of a few necessary supplies including a change of clothes, a dagger, a few throwing knives and the Essence capsules that the Kameil outside the valley use as their source.

"Thais," he said, "thank you for accompanying me, but there really is no point for you to stay longer. Go ahead and make your way back to camp."

Thais bowed. "I will do so as soon as I see that you have safely climbed the wall."

"I appreciate you're concern, but if I have any problems, I don't think there's much you can do to help."

148

Thais nodded several times. "I will be reporting to the Yaru back at camp. They will want to know whether or not you got into the city unobserved."

"Of course," Nandin replied feeling a little foolish that he hadn't recommended that himself. He was relieved to think that if he encountered trouble, help may come. As he thought about it further, he wasn't sure what anyone would be able to do if he was caught. If the Jagare captured him he would likely be taken somewhere, well guarded, and then probably hung before long — a rescue would unlikely be successful. Getting caught was not an option.

Nandin shook Thais's hand.

"I'm going to study the sentries movements and then I'll move out in about an hour's time. There's no need for you to keep an eye on me just yet." He turned to go, then glanced back. "I probably don't need to tell you, but make sure you stay in the cover of the woods while observing me and try not to move around or you may attract attention."

Thais smiled. "Yes, you don't need to tell me. I've spent a lifetime of watching and not being seen."

Nandin nodded and then made his way back to the tree line, crawled the last part of the distance on his belly and hid under the brush to watch. He knew that he was probably being over-cautious, yet decided it was a good habit to get into since, once he was in the city, the risk of being seen was greater.

CHAPTER SEVENTEEN

Over Shadow

NANDIN SLITHERED FORWARD.

After an hour of lying low, it was finally time for him to make the trek across the open field to the city walls. He had observed that there still weren't many sentries; those that were there still watched the city more than the surrounding area. Nandin waited until the guards were at the farthest distance from where he was before he began his approach. He kept low, even though he was sure that he could probably walk without being noticed. His dark clothes would make him practically invisible; nevertheless, someone could still notice the movement drawing their attention to the darker, man-shaped shadow. Even if they couldn't quite tell what it was, they would know something unusual was there. If they looked at him when he was low, they would more readily accept that the shadow was a rock or bush as many were scattered between the tree line and the city wall.

It only took him twenty minutes to ghost his way across the open space before he reached the wall. He had made sure to count the amount of time between the guards crossing this point of the wall and knew that the next one would be arriving soon. Closing his eyes, he waited, focusing on all the sounds around him. As expected, within minutes, he heard the approach of the sentry: the slight scuffing of his feet as he dragged them along, the swishing of his clothes as his arms swung past his body and his thighs rubbing together with each stride. The sentry's occasional snuffling or clearing of his throat was by far the most revealing sound to let Nandin know of the man's whereabouts.

Again, he began to count, timing when the guard would be well past the point where he could see Nandin if he should so happen to look over the wall. When he reached the designated moment; Nandin ran his hands over the rough surface of the wall and smiled. There were plenty of hand and foot holds for him to use and it would be a much easier climb than the walls he had practiced on in the valley. Some of the stones only protruded a knuckles width and for the average person would prove challenging, but after the many months Nandin had spent strengthening his fingers, it would be wide enough. Slowly he began to ascend until he became confident the stone wouldn't crumble under his weight, then he quickened his pace, zigzagging as required by the protrusions he chose.

When he crested the wall he placed one hand, then the other on the smooth ledge and carefully lifted himself up and over. He had continued to count as he climbed and was confident the guard would still be far enough away. Crouching in the shadows of the wall-walk, Nandin studied the city below.

"Incredible!" he mumbled. Even in the grey light of the evening, he could see the vastness of the city, the countless multilevelled buildings, and the hint of architectural marvels. He scanned the buildings, but his eyes were quickly drawn to the aqueduct: the agreed meeting place that Nandin and Nean had arranged a week earlier. Neither of them had been to Senda before so they relied heavily on the information documented in Mateo's library. From what they read, the aqueduct seemed like the easiest, and safest place to rendezvous. First of all, it towered over every other building in the city and therefore, would be easy to spot. Secondly, no one paid much attention to the aqueduct unless there was something wrong with it or it needed cleaning, so it would be a fairly safe place to loiter.

After studying the grid-like pattern of the streets, he made a mental note of how to traverse through them to reach the aqueduct, then he glanced around to determine how to get off the wall. He was pleased to note that just a few paces to his left was a set of stairs; conveniently they were also in the opposite direction that the guard would be facing when he returned this way, making it a quick and easy climb down.

Once at the bottom of the stairs, he walked along the perimeter of the wall to the alleyway he had chosen to follow. Sure that no one was watching he slipped from one shadow to the next until the surrounding buildings safely hid him. Now that he was in the city, being seen would only be dangerous if it was by a Juro, but he wasn't about to take any chances. Silently he made his way down the narrow gap between two three-storey-high stone buildings. When he came to the first main roadway, he checked that it was clear and turned right. Obviously, it was not one of the more common roads used at night as it was only lit by the light of the moon. Although the middle of the road could clearly be seen, the various heights of the buildings provided enough darkness to conceal his passing...or so he thought. He took a few strides along the passageway.

"Commander," a hoarse voice called.

Nandin froze. At first he panicked at the thought that he had been caught, but then it quickly dawned on him that the only people who knew him as Commander were the Kameil and the Yaru. A figure stepped out of a covered doorway.

"Sir, it's me, Lazar."

Instantly he relaxed. Lazar was a Yaru appointed to Nean's team, one of the original Potentials from Nandin's training group. As Lazar came towards him, another disturbing thought occurred to Nandin.

"How did you find me?" he asked.

"Captain Nean had us keep watch for your arrival. He figured you would be showing up soon. We've been taking turns camping out on top of this building for the last two nights, " he said indicating with his thumb the building he had just materialized from.

"Was I that easy to spot?" Nandin asked somewhat disheartened. He had thought he had been the ideal example of stealth.

Lazar shook his head. "When you first appeared I thought I had just imagined it. I wasn't looking right where you came out, but I thought I caught a movement. Then there was nothing there. It wasn't until you were partway down the stairs that I saw you. Once I knew which way you were going I came down hoping to catch you."

Nandin nodded, his pride intact. "But why here? I thought the meeting place was at the aqueduct."

"That was the original plan sir, but the Captain figured it would be easier to intercept you sooner so we could take you straight to headquarters — it will save time."

"Headquarters?"

"I think the Captain would prefer to explain." Lazar looked around nervously, "May I suggest we move on? This isn't the most secure place to be."

"Yes, of course, lead on."

For over an hour, Lazar guided Nandin deeper into the city. The roads may have been straight, but Nandin was completely turned around about twenty minutes in, partly because of the darkness and partly due to his compulsion to look around. He was surprised at the apartment dwellings that housed multiple families, the size of some of the single-family residences and the general opulence of the place. Buildings had carved figures on them and statues lined some of the more prestigious streets. Even though they were angling away from the aqueduct, they were still closer to it than when Nandin entered the city. The towering structure was awe-inspiring with its many arches and multiple levels.

Finally Lazar stopped. He pointed to a single-storey building across the street from where they were standing.

"That's where we have to go," Lazar said quietly, "but it's crucial we're not seen heading towards it. We'll cross the street a little further up and then double back behind it."

Nandin nodded his understanding and followed Lazar once more. Curiously, he noted that there weren't any windows in the surrounding structures, aside from what he thought must be storefronts, but even those were boarded up for the night. He wondered who would possibly see them. It took them another ten minutes to cross the street then loop back around to the place Lazar had pointed out.

Nandin followed Lazar as they made their way between the building and its neighbour. Halfway to the front they came to a recessed door. Nandin would have never noticed it if Lazar hadn't stepped into the alcove. Lazar knocked once, paused, knocked three times more, paused a second time and then quickly tapped twice. They waited patiently for a minute before they heard movement on the other side. Nandin thought it sounded like wood scraping against stone and figured it was most likely a wooden brace being lifted to allow the door to swing in. As the door opened, a soft glow of light flickered somewhere deeper in the building causing shadows to dance and making it difficult for Nandin to make out the features of the individual who had let them in. Shorter than Nandin and slight in form, he thought it likely to be a Jivan.

Lazar entered, but remained silent until the door was closed, at which point he turned to the man.

"Thank you Rodrick. Sorry to disturb you so late."

Rodrick replied, "No apologies required, we hoped you'd return tonight. Besides, the evening's delivery was here less than half an hour ago so I was still up…this is your Commander?"

"Yes. Commander Nandin, this is Rodrick. He owns this house."

As the Jivan began walking further into the building, he glanced over his shoulder and noticed Nandin hesitate.

155

Rodrick said, while gesturing, "Come in, come in. Formal introductions will be better with light and a more hospitable setting."

The two Yaru followed Rodrick through the darkened hallway to a columned passageway that surrounded an open-ceilinged, inner garden. They followed the hallway until they reached the opposite side of the garden where light seeped from under a wooden doorway. Rodrick knocked once then entered the room. Nandin squinted as he set foot in the illuminated space. As his eyes adjusted, he noticed the familiar faces of Yaru, looking up from low, cushioned sofas.

"Ah, you made it!" Nean exclaimed rising to embrace his friend. "I hoped you'd arrive soon." To Rodrick he said, "You are welcome to join us."

Rodrick inclined his head in acceptance of the invitation. "Just for a little while, I'm intrigued to meet this Commander I've heard so much about."

Nandin, Rodrick and Lazar took a seat as Nean poured each of them some wine. Nandin greeted Aaron, the remaining Yaru from Nean's team, who was seated in the room.

"Did you have much trouble finding him Lazar?" Nean asked the Yaru.

Lazar shrugged. "Not too much. Fortunately he entered right where you predicted. If he hadn't, I probably would have missed him."

Nean smiled. "It wasn't much of a prediction. Nandin and I did discuss the best location to climb the wall based on drawings we'd seen, even so, Nandin is very stealthy, spotting him would be a challenge — well done," Nean said raising his glass.

Lazar lifted his glass in response and took a sip while lying back into the cushions. "I just want to say thanks to Nandin for arriving so soon after dark so I could get a decent night's sleep."

Nandin chuckled. "I'm up for that."

"Right," Nean said, "so let's get to it. First of all, Rodrick, this is Commander Nandin and Commander, this is Rodrick our most generous host and owner of this fine house."

Now safely indoors and reunited with his fellow Yaru, Nandin was decidedly interested how they had come to this dwelling of a Jivan and into his confidence no doubt. Nandin opened his mouth to voice a question when Nean cut him off.

"I know you're going to ask about the mission so let me tell you straight off: yes, we found the Kameil." He smiled knowingly. "And Nandin, they're in greater numbers than we could have imagined. When we first arrived, we headed straight to the aqueduct so we could get the best view of the goings on in the city. We made a rough map of the city and after a few hours observation we decided on an old warehouse to make our base camp. The next day we checked out one of the marketplaces. We figured if there were rumours of Kameil in the city, it would be as good a place as any to hear them."

Nandin raised his eyebrows. Even dressed as the city folk, there was incredible risk of being discovered as 'not normal.' All it would take is one look from any Juro to see that their Essence was more than any Jivan or Jagare."

157

Noting Nandin's expression, Nean waved away his concern. "We were careful, not to worry. We kept mostly to the side roads and shadows…no one took any notice of us."

"It was a waste of time though," Lazar mumbled.

"Not entirely," Nean said defensively, "we did discover we could get around the city without being noticed."

Aaron smiled, "Exactly. It was awesome!"

Nean chuckled as he resumed his story. "Anyway, as Lazar so kindly pointed out, we didn't glean any information so eventually went back to the warehouse. My next plan was to go out once it got dark, since that would probably be the only time it would be safe for the Kameil — "

"That was a good plan," Lazar interrupted.

"Yes, thank you Lazar. As soon as I left the warehouse, I spotted movement in one of the alleyways. Typically, they only light a few of the more travelled roads at night and even then most people tend to stay indoors, so someone moving in a darkened, little-used pathway immediately caught my interest. I set off to investigate and left Lazar and Aaron to search for other possible leads."

"I was able to follow, but I had to keep my distance because the guy kept looking over his shoulder like he was afraid of being followed." Nean grinned mischievously. "Of course," he added, "I was only capable of remaining unseen because I've been trained. Any mere Jagare or Jivan wouldn't have been able to keep up unnoticed."

Nandin noticed the amused expression on Rodrick's face and realized Nean had added this last tidbit for Rodrick's sake. Nandin was curious as to why.

"Once I discovered where the Kameil was going — "

"Kameil?" Nandin interrupted.

Nean closed his eyes for a moment, as if admonishing himself.

"Oops," he said, "I didn't mean to let that slip yet." He sighed then continued, "Anyway, I followed and he led me here. At the time I didn't know if it would prove to be important, but my instinct told me it would, so I perched on the roof, got really close to the opening above the garden and waited." Nean looked at his host and shrugged his shoulders in an apologetic gesture.

"Well," Rodrick responded, "I figured you must have done something to that effect, how else would you have been able to waltz in here claiming to know that I was a friend of the Kameil?"

"At least we're on the same side," Nean said. "I didn't hear much though, just that our friend Rodrick here was exchanging goods of some kind with the Kameil. I returned the next morning when his shop was open, and confronted him like he said, but I hardly waltzed."

Rodrick chuckled as he refilled glasses.

"He quickly brought me inside where I was able to convince him that, I too, was on friendly terms with the Kameil and I wasn't about to expose him, and he shared his story with me. Rodrick, tell Nandin what you do here?"

Rodrick swallowed a mouthful of wine and leaned back to get into a more comfortable position.

"About five years ago my younger brother, Gareth, finished his schooling at the Percipio and was heading home to join me in my shop. You probably couldn't see the sign out there in the dark, but I'm a Clothesmaker," he added as an aside. "On his way, he and a couple of his friends encountered a very persuasive individual who convinced them to take a detour with him."

Nandin noticed the Yaru were looking everywhere but Rodrick. He too was feeling slightly uncomfortable as the story sounded familiar.

"He was led back to Mateo's valley, as I understand it, and was experimented on." Nandin crossed his arms and shifted in his seat. "You've probably figured out that the experiment failed, and all his Essence was removed. Once my brother realized what had happened, he tried to convince his friends to leave. One decided to stay in the valley, convinced his village would never take him back. One accompanied Gareth back to Senda, and the last stayed with Mateo. I understand you know him.

"Sim," Nean explained.

Again, Nandin shifted uncomfortably, wondering where this was leading.

Rodrick continued. "When my brother returned to the city, he was very ill. I begged the leaders to help him, but they scoffed at me and banished him, threatening to hang him if he returned. Gareth left the city and waited for me in the woods where I found him close to death. I then smuggled him back. Fortunately, the Kameil that live in Senda had heard about our predicament and took my brother to their home and restored his Essence. When he was well enough he returned here, but he couldn't stay —

too long away from an Essence source and he became ill again."

Nandin glanced at Nean. Rodrick had said that Kameil live in Senda and had a supply of Essence. That was what they were here to find out. Nandin patiently waited to hear the rest of Rodrick's story. At some point, someone would tell him where these Kameil were living.

"So," Rodrick smiled, "we made an arrangement: Gareth would come and get my fabric to make it into clothes and in exchange I'd provide him with food and anything else he needed. It worked out so well that I began making similar arrangements with the other Kameil, they provide a service for me and I get them whatever supplies they need. Until Nean showed up, no one had ever found us out. If they had, it wouldn't just be me out of a home but many Kameil families. That's why all of our dealings have to take place at night; we can't risk anyone discovering that the Kameil are coming here."

Nandin had newfound respect for his host. Rodrick was risking everything by helping the Kameil. As he thought about it though, he couldn't help but wonder why.

"Rodrick, why didn't your brother, or the other Kameil for that matter, just go back to the valley? Mateo would have looked after them."

Rodrick couldn't hide the contempt he was feeling. "Trust someone who shattered our lives? Gareth was just a kid with a great future in front of him and now he has to spend everyday in hiding."

"But he wouldn't be hiding in the valley."

"No? Living in the far eastern quarter isn't hiding? Never being able to see your family again isn't hiding?

Not free to travel throughout Galenia for fear of dying or being hung isn't hiding?"

"But that's just the thing Mateo wants to change," Nandin argued, "this unyielding prejudice that people have towards the Kameil or anyone else who's different."

"Nean said something similar," Rodrick chortled, "but how could we ever trust the man who made my brother a Kameil. If it wasn't for him, none of this would have happened."

Nandin slid forward in his chair. "He has spent his years trying to cure the Kameil, to help them. Unfortunately, it didn't always work. He never intended to harm your brother. He was trying to empower him. He is searching for a way to help the Kameil, which is exactly what Sim is doing and he's doing it in a way no ordinary Jivan or Jagare could." Nandin thought for a moment. "You know, if there were more people like you, he wouldn't need the Yaru to save them."

Rodrick turned to Nean. "You're right, he is pretty convincing." Turning back to Nandin he asked, "You really believe all that? That Mateo is actually trying to help?"

"Absolutely." Nandin swung his bag around that he still carried on his back, reached in and pulled out one of the small pouches he carried. He handed it to Rodrick. "Here, this is for Gareth."

Holding it in the palm of his hand, Rodrick untied the string that was securing the cloth-wrapped bundle. He folded back part of the cloth to reveal tiny pink capsules.

"What are they?" he asked.

Nandin smiled. "Your brother's freedom." When Rodrick raised one eyebrow in question Nandin explained, "They're Essence pills. If Gareth takes two pills a day he won't need any other source of Essence...he can go anywhere he likes." Nandin watched Rodrick's eyes widen as the full impact of what he had said registered. "It gets better, once he's been on them for a few days he'll look as healthy as any Jivan and no one other than a Juro will be able to tell the difference. Like I said, in his own way, he will be free."

Rodrick looked at the men around the room checking for any deception, but when he saw only determined faces, his eyes began to tear up.

"How's this possible?" he choked.

"This is one of the things Mateo's been working on. He's on the verge of a complete cure. These are just to help until then."

Rodrick fingered the little pills. He held in his hand just over a month's supply of Essence. "What will he do when we run out?"

"If Gareth chooses to remain in Senda, I'm sure we can make some sort of arrangement. We'd like to establish a connection with the Kameil here. We need a way to send messages and, if they request it, assistance in smuggling out the Kameil."

"And if Gareth agrees, Mateo will keep supplying him with these pills?"

"Yes. And a cure once it's readily available."

"This...this will change his life. How can I thank you?"

Nean spoke up, "You don't need to, just do us one last favour."

Rodrick nodded. "What?"

Since they had arrived, Nean had been trying to get a meeting with the leader of the Senda Kameil. Unfortunately, the request had been denied — repeatedly. The leader, Demetrius, never left their hideout and non-Kameil were not allowed in. They had been at a stalemate for days. He wondered if Rodrick was now motivated to find a way to make it happen.

Nean leaned forward "Get us that meeting with the leader of the Kameil."

Rodrick grimaced. Even he hadn't met Demetrius. It would take some convincing, he may even have to sacrifice some of the capsules he had just been given. He gazed down at the precious supply he held, he was reluctant to part with them. Sensing some sort of internal struggle, Nandin reached into his bag and pulled out another pouch.

"Here, maybe this will help. Our gift to the Kameil leader."

Rodrick brightened. "Yes, this will help. I will speak with my brother tomorrow."

CHAPTER EIGHTEEN

Underground Trade

SHADOWS DANCED ON THE WALL.

In the candlelight, Nean's eyes gleaned with irrepressible mischief; he enjoyed watching Nandin struggling to comprehend what he had told him.

"The sewers? Really?" Nandin asked for the third time.

Nean shook his head. "Why is this such a difficult concept for you to get?"

"I just can't image it…sixty-some families living in the sewers. It's just…wrong."

Nean spread out his hands. "Of course it's wrong. That's why we're here. We can offer these people a better life."

Nandin leaned against the wall and stretched out his legs on his mat. When Rodrick retired for the night ten minutes earlier, the Yaru also made a show of going to bed. Since the Yaru already occupied the three guest rooms in the back of the house, Nean offered to share his with Nandin. Rodrick had supplied him with a thick floor mat, yet promised that he would find a bed for him the next day. Aaron and Lazar had joined them in Nean's room to continue their discussion without their host.

"It's quite clever actually." Aaron sat on the floor across from Nandin. He had never been one to talk much. When he did, Nandin knew he was worth listening to.

Nandin asked, "Why's that?"

"It's pretty safe. Who's going to go down there?" Aaron replied.

Nandin asked, "What about the people who clean the sewers? Surely someone has to go down there once in awhile."

Aaron nodded. "Again, that's why it's clever. Years ago some Kameil were hired to clean and maintain the sewers. Of course, the Jivan that hired them had no idea they were Kameil — guess they were still healthy looking at the time. Now the Kameil are the only ones who go down there and they still get paid to keep it up."

"Really?" Nandin asked. "No one's noticed they're Kameil?"

Nean interjected, "Think about it, Nandin. Sewage workers dress from head to toe in cloaks and are foul smelling—no one gives them much notice. They just pay them and go. In fact, they told us they even chance going to a few shops to buy supplies. People just serve them as fast as possible and send them on their way."

"Of course," Aaron added, "the fact that the sewers run right under all the cities crystal pockets never seemed to dawn on anyone. The Kameil just build their homes right underneath and have all the Essence they need to survive."

"Huh." Nandin said. "Well then, why would they want to leave?"

Nean rolled his eyes. "They're living in the sewers! *Geez*, Nandin."

Nandin threw his hands in the air. "Well you guys were making it sound like they had it pretty good."

Aaron replied, "They're just finding a way to survive."

"And I just love that they're doing it right under the smug Juro's noses," Lazar stated vehemently.

Nean laughed. "Literally."

Nandin crossed his arms. Personally, he didn't really have a grudge against the Juro, just how the system itself was being run. He tended to feel a little uneasy at his companions dislike, and for that matter, disrespect for the Juro. One day, under Mateo's leadership, he was sure that the misunderstandings of the Kameil would be cleared up, and there would be a change in the way things worked. The missions were about bringing people together, not encouraging disdain.

"Have you gone into the sewers yet?" Nandin asked.

Nean shook his head. "Nope. That's why I asked Rodrick to get us a meeting with the leader. So far we've only met Gareth and a few other Kameil that work for Rodrick, but they don't have the authority to take us. Of course, we could just let ourselves in, but I'd rather have an invitation."

"Agreed," Nandin replied. "Which reminds me: why didn't you offer the Essence tablets earlier? Obviously it won Rodrick over pretty effectively."

Nean grimaced. "I forgot to restock my supply before we came. As it worked out, it was a quick way for you to gain trust."

"That's good, we need their trust. If they won't take us to the sewers, do you think Rodrick can convince the leader to meet us here?"

Nean shook his head. "Gareth said Demetrius, the Kameil leader, hasn't left the sewers in years. By the sounds of it I'd say he's a little bit paranoid."

"With good reason," Aaron interjected. "If he was caught I'm sure he'd be hung. As a rule, Kameil are banished, but I wouldn't put it past them to make an example out of him."

Nandin nodded. The city of Senda made every attempt to prevent Kameil from entering and purged itself of outcasts. Those that were discovered risked the gallows. The walls, sentries and Juro at the gates were an attempt to ensure the city stayed free of them — finding Kameil inside would cast doubt on their security leading to a search for more Kameil that may be around. Fear of hanging was just one more attempt at control should all else fail.

"So Gareth needs permission to takes us to meet Demetrius."

"Right," Nean replied.

"And then we get a tour and go about our usual routine of inviting them back to the valley."

"Yes," Nean said, "but it'll be a bit trickier than usual. I'm not sure what our chances are that they'll show us their Essence sources, let alone convince them to leave."

"I don't think we need to," Nandin said. Seeing the confusion in his comrade's expressions he explained. "Convince them to leave I mean. Those who wish to go to

168

the valley are more than welcome, of course, but Mateo wants to establish a connection with this group. He said that if we found Kameil here we were to try to make an arrangement."

Lazar leaned forward. "What kind of arrangement?"

"He's offering to make a trade. He'll give them food, pills or whatever they need."

"In exchange for what?" Lazar asked as he tapped his legs, unable to sit still.

"Well, information for starters. He wants to know how they get around and survive without being noticed."

"Yes, but we already know that," Lazar said impatiently.

Nandin sat back. "We know it in theory, but we need to know more. We need to learn how to get in and out of the sewers and move about the city unseen. And, of course, Mateo will be wanting some of those crystals."

Lazar whistled. "That's a tall order. Why would they ever let us take the crystals? I mean, if they're not leaving, they'll need them, right?" He looked around the room at the Yaru trying to ensure he didn't miss something.

Nean answered, "True, but crystals are the best source of Essence. I guarantee Mateo will want whatever we can get. Besides, if any of them decided to leave, crystals will be a fair payment for their secure passage, and they can use them to safely travel to the valley."

"That's right," Nandin added, "they won't even need the Essence tablets. They can just carry the crystals until they get there."

Lazar still looked apprehensive. "That's if any of them decide to leave."

Nandin shrugged. "Why wouldn't they?"

Lazar replied, "Well, they don't trust Mateo, and they have Essence and homes here."

"Yes, but they're living in the sewers."

Nandin and Nean looked at each other and said together, "*Geez,* Lazar."

* * *

"Good morning gentlemen," Rodrick said as he entered the dining area with a fresh pot of tea. "I trust you all slept well?"

The Yaru greeted Rodrick and were grateful for the refills, as the spring mornings were still somewhat cool, especially since there was no fireplace to heat the space.

"Again, thanks for your hospitality Rodrick," Nandin said.

Rodrick bowed. Now in the bright light of day Nandin could see the man more clearly. His hair was cropped short and he had a friendly, if not tired, smile. His clothes were well made with fantastic details. A white tufted shirt was topped with a close fitting, dark green, velvet jacket with detachable sleeves. Several lustrous gold button closures adorned the jacket. His simple black cotton pants were tucked into soft leather boots. Nandin's simple white tunic and beige trousers paled in comparison.

Rodrick said, "Please make yourselves at home. My wife, Fay, and I will be in the shop as usual so if you need to get in touch with me just ask Eva."

Nean leaned over and whispered to Nandin's, "That's the cook."

170

Rodrick smiled, "And my sister-in-law. She is aware of who you are and our arrangement. Most importantly, she can be trusted." Turning to Nandin, he asked, "Perhaps you'd like to come with me? I'll show you around and then you can stop in the kitchen to get the mornings meal. Eva should be almost done preparing it."

Nandin had to admit he was curious as to what the rest of the place looked like. So far all he had seen of Senda had been in shadows and this was probably one of the few places he would ever really be able to see. Nandin glanced at Nean.

"Go ahead, we've seen it." Nean waved him on.

Rodrick led the way along the covered passage that was lined with white marble columns. The garden in the middle included benches and a small fountain. The next room over from the lounge had two-tiered stone benches in a semi circle and were topped with many cushions.

"This is where my formal meetings are held."

"Do you typically have large groups at your place?"

Rodrick shrugged. "It is expected that shopkeepers meet monthly to discuss business, and even though I may have unconventional employees, I am still running a business."

They continued on, passing the last room on the back wall. Nandin was surprised to discover the room had no ceiling, in order to expose the fruit and vegetable garden within to the sun and rain.

Rounding the corner, Nandin realized they were in identical hallway to where his room had been. The layout was a simple square pattern with a garden in the middle and rooms all around.

171

Rodrick gestured to the closed doors as they walked by. "Another guest bedroom and the lavatory. This hallway ends with the door you came in last night. It is the back entrance and the only one the Kameil use because it hidden from the road."

At the front of the courtyard, Nandin could see a central door flanked by two more hallways.

"My study lets out into this garden and is a walk-through to the main house, but I'd prefer you use the hallways on either side to enter the front area."

Walking down the darkened hallway, Nandin ran his hand along the cold, stonewalls. The hint of light ahead steadied him as he fought the urge to run. It was rather early in his association with Rodrick to trust him completely and this rather confined, dark space left Nandin feeling quite vulnerable.

As they emerged, Nandin sighed with relief. Mistaking Nandin's thoughts, Rodrick said, "Yes, it is quiet beautiful, isn't it?"

The front of the house had a similar layout to the back: rooms lined the exterior walls and the centre courtyard was surrounded by a square tiled walkway all around. The main difference in the front was that instead of a garden, there was a reservoir where rainwater collected from the open slanted roof above. What made the room stunning was the brightly coloured, complex mosaic tile on the floor and the hanging brass lanterns that shimmered as they lit the walls with their fresco paintings of scenes of nature.

"Just a few more bedrooms, kitchen and the formal dining room make up most of this part of the house. That narrow hallway at the front opens onto the street as well as to my shops. You might enjoy seeing those, but now is not a good time as they are currently open for business...I think we both would like to keep your presence here a secret."

Nandin nodded. "Absolutely. But I am curious, what are in your shops?"

Rodrick smiled, obviously enthusiastic to speak about his trade.

"The shop on the right is where I keep fabrics, threads, buttons and other such items that I have purchased from all over Galenia. I do sell some of those materials, but mostly it's for display and storage items for the clothes I make. Many customers like to choose the fabrics themselves and then I can custom make their orders. The shop on the left is my collection of clothes — all my own designs. My brother and his friends help with the basic stitching and I add the details.

"Are all the houses like this in Senda?"

Rodrick shook his head. "No, no. The successful shop owners have places like this, but there are multilevelled apartment buildings for those that work outside of their homes. Also, I often have guests stay over because I hire others to bring me my fabric so I don't have to leave my store. That's why I have so many guest rooms." He added wistfully, "My brother would have lived here as well with his family and run one of the stores."

Sensing Rodrick's cheerful mood slipping Nandin said, "You have a lovely home Rodrick, thank you again for your hospitality."

Rodrick smiled. "You're welcome. I'm sorry you and your friends won't have much to keep you entertained while you're here. I won't be able to get word to Gareth until tonight. Hopefully he can arrange a meeting with Demetrius."

Nandin looked around at the extravagant surroundings, "Oh, I think we'll manage."

Rodrick nodded. "Alright, let's see if Eva has your meal ready."

CHAPTER NINETEEN

Outsiders Track

TIME DRAGGED.

For what seemed a long stretch, Nandin and his fellow Yaru had been blindfolded and led through the sewers by their Kameil guides. It had taken an additional two days at Rodrick's place before a meeting was arranged. The Yaru, becoming restless, had begun scouting the city. Nandin thought it was this more than anything that convinced Demetrius to see them — he probably wanted them out of the city before they inadvertently exposed the Kameil. The Yaru agreed to accept the terms that allowed the whereabouts of, and the entrance to, the Kameil's home a secret.

It was a slow decent at first, as the Kameil insisted they take them from the street side one-by-one into the underground. Nandin paid attention to the change from the hard cobbled-stone street to the slightly sinking grass as the ground steadily sloped downwards.

Even with the blindfold securely in place, it had been obvious to him when they entered the sewers. Aside from the slight drop in temperature, the deadening of noise from the creatures of the night, and the sound of water rushing past, it was the odour of the place that was the telltale sign. It reeked like rotten eggs and made his stomach turn. He hoped the Kameil would allow them their sight back once they were in, but their guides made no move to do so. Finally, his guide removed Nandin's hand from his shoulder and placed it on the cool, moist wall of the sewer passage allowing Nandin a chance to steady himself.

"You may remove your blindfolds now," one of the guides said.

Nandin didn't really know what to expect once he could see. The eerie green glow that was diffused throughout the tunnel had never entered his imagination.

"What is it?" he asked more to himself than anyone in particular.

Gareth smiled and pointed up. The expression was almost lost to those around him as the light was barely enough to make out shapes let alone faces. The Yaru looked up and gawked at what they saw. Thousands of silken worms dangled from the ceiling emitted the green glow.

"How — " Nandin began to ask.

"We breed them and use them to light the passages," responded Gareth. "They require hardly any Essence and their glow provides a relief from the utter darkness. Candles or fuel for our lanterns are a most precious commodity and cannot be wasted for navigating the underground. Come on," he said as he picked up the pace, "we have a ways to go. Keep close, there are many twists and turns. Even after six years, I can still get lost down here."

The four Yaru followed Gareth and the other three Kameil who had led them safely so far. Lazar and Aaron were content to let Nandin do all the talking; they trusted his leadership and knew he would ask the questions that were on their minds. As for Nean, he had been busy counting the turns ever since they entered the sewers. Without the opportunity to draw a map as he went though, keeping track of the entire route was unlikely even with his restored ability to see.

* * *

Sitting cross-legged on the ground, Nandin casually returned the piercing gaze that Demetrius had fixed on him. The room chosen for the meeting was carved out of the ground. It had dirt walls instead of the stone that was in the sewer passageways. The ceiling was low causing Nandin to stoop when he entered. He sat awkwardly on a small cushion placed on a mat covering the dirt floor. The room was small with barely enough room for two people to sit and he found Demetrius's proximity a little too close for comfort. Nandin was of the opinion that making him uncomfortable was done purposefully.

Finally breaking the silence, Demetrius spoke. "What do you want?"

Nandin was surprised by the husky voice that the frail looking man produced. From the single lantern that lit the space, he was able to discern the dark circles under Demetrius eyes on his wrinkled, paper-thin skin. The smoky colour of his shaggy hair and mangy beard contributed to his frail, elderly appearance. Yet the authority behind the man's voice left little doubt of the strength he still possessed.

"We've come to offer our help," Nandin replied.

Demetrius sniggered. "Right. What makes you think we need your help?"

Nandin paused trying to choose his words carefully. "Mateo wishes to invite the Kameil to come to the valley."

"Why would we want to do that?"

"So you don't have to live in the sewers anymore. To give you a choice how you live."

"A choice? You mean he wants to make us slaves."

"Mateo doesn't enslave people."

"No? That quarry of his…he'd have us breaking our backs hauling stones."

"The Kameil who work the quarry aren't slaves."

Demetrius leaned forward closing the already narrow gap between them. "Are you sure about that?"

"Of course," Nandin said, unshaken by the man's attempts to intimidate him. "The whole point of the valley is to allow people to have choice."

"Hmm. You mean, to choose whether or not to be experimented on?"

"That is one of the choices, but — "

"Right." Demetrius interrupted. "Cause who wouldn't chose to be a Kameil?"

He leaned back again and smirked, as if he had just scored a point. Nandin remained steadfast.

"Mateo only treats volunteers and it is never his intention to make Kameil."

"And what lies did he tell them to get them to volunteer? Promises of power and glory?"

"Those weren't lies and I'm living proof. I have abilities beyond any Jivan's dreams. He freed me from a life without choice. A life dictated by the Juro. I was nothing more than a servant, spending my life doing what I was told. Now I am so much more."

"Are you sure you didn't trade one servitude for another?"

"Absolutely! I have a say in what I'm doing and how I'm doing it. I'm saving lives. We've rescued so many Kameil who were barely able to survive and gave them lives worth living."

"Oh really? And how exactly are you saving lives? From my perspective, turning Jivan or Jagare into Kameil is not saving anyone."

Nandin pressed on. "That was an unfortunate accident. And now he's able to treat them. He created those Essence capsules that I sent to you. They're not a permanent fix, but they will restore a Kameil's health to the point that they can pass for Jivan."

"So then why not just get the Kameil to rescue Kameil? Why create Yaru?" he asked looking down his nose at Nandin, still determined to find the flaw in Mateo's actions.

"Tell me Demetrius, could you or any of your people travel across Galenia in search for Kameil? Do you have the strength? And how would you survive without constant contact with the Essence?"

Demetrius crossed his arms. "With these wonderful pills you've been telling me about. Didn't you say they'd restore our health? What would we need Yaru for?"

Nandin shook his head. "Where do you think he got the Essence to make the pills in the first place? He created Yaru to go and collect it, which is not an easy job mind you, Essence isn't just laying around waiting for someone to just snatch it up."

Demetrius pressed on. "To what end is this all for? Having us rely on these pills sounds like a trap to control us."

"The point isn't to create pills. It's to find a cure...and he has."

Demetrius opened his mouth ready for another witty retort, but was momentarily dumbstruck.

Nandin spirits lifted as he watched the Kameil leader's eyebrows rise in disbelief. "The tablets are just a temporary fix so that you're not tied to an Essence source. The Kameil have the ability to go where they want. We even have Kameil working on farms and hunting, by their own choice of course."

"You mentioned a cure?"

Nandin refrained from the urge to roll his eyes. "He has created a cure, but he needs a more pure form of Essence to make it. The pills are just to make due until that time."

"What do you mean 'a pure form of Essence'?"

"He can make the pills from any form of Essence, plants or gas for example, but he needs crystals for the cure."

Demetrius nodded. "That's it then, he wants our crystals."

Nandin shrugged. "Only to help you. Mateo doesn't need crystals for his survival, he has all the Essence he needs."

He reached into his pocket and pulled out the last pouch loaded with pills that he had brought and handed them over.

"A gift from Mateo, regardless of your decision."

* * *

Nandin and his fellow Yaru waited in the sewers alongside the caves that made up the Kameil's' living area. While Nandin had been in discussion with Demetrius, the others were shown to a larger, but completely empty, carved-out room. Once Nandin emerged, they had been asked to wait back in the sewer while the Kameil decided what to do.

Aaron paced along the dimly lit, narrow edge. "What could be taking them so long? Didn't you just offer them a choice to come back to the valley?"

"It was a bit more complicated than that. Demetrius doesn't seem to trust our motives."

Aaron frowned. Clearly he wasn't empathizing with the Kameil.

"Think about it, Aaron, some of these people were given the treatment and they became Kameil, not Yaru...how would you feel?"

Aaron paused in his pacing and looked up at Nandin. Then he threw his hands in the air and resumed walking. "Yes, but we're here to make up for that, right? I mean what do they have to lose? It's not like they'd be giving up a life of luxury to come live in the valley."

"No," Lazar interjected, "just their source of Essence, which is currently their only means of survival."

Aaron turned to Nandin and asked, "Did you ask for their crystals?"

"Well, not in so many words — "

Aaron clasped the sides of his head. "You asked for the crystals already? I thought you were just going to start with offering them an invite to the valley and asking for a tour of the sewers."

Nandin sighed. "Yes, that was my plan, but their leader wasn't satisfied with a simple *we're your friends, let us help you for no apparent reason*. It's going to take some time to build their trust."

Nean grasped Nandin's shoulder. "At least we got this far."

At that moment a Kameil emerged into the tunnel.

"Gentlemen, if you would come with me."

They were led into another dugout room. Leader Demetrius was accompanied by a handful of other Kameil. The only one they recognized was Gareth.

Nandin was relieved this space actually had low stools to sit on in addition to pillows, his legs were still feeling cramped from sitting on the floor earlier.

"Please, sit down," Demetrius said in a more gentle voice than Nandin had heard him use. Without preamble he asked, "If anyone chooses to go to the valley with you, you would provide them with Essence pills?"

"Yes," Nandin replied.

"For how long? All their lives?"

"If they decide to live in the valley they won't need them."

Demetrius rubbed his chin. "Why not?"

"That's the point of the quarry. Digging out the rock releases enough Essence for those in the valley to survive. It's just the Kameil who wish to work outside the valley who need the pills."

"Mateo would give us these?"

Nandin nodded, "If you were contributing to the community in some way...farming or helping us find Kameil, for example."

"And if the Kameil chose to return to Senda, he wouldn't stop them?"

"We would escort them. In, fact it is our wish to establish an on-going communication between yourself and Mateo."

"What if we decide never to leave? Would Mateo still consider giving us the pills?"

"I think he would, if you were willing to trade."

"The crystals?" Demetrius asked shrewdly.

"Yes," Nandin simply answered.

Demetrius studied the Yaru as he considered Nandin's answers. Finally, he came to a decision.

"I am not prepared to hand over our supply of Essence solely on a promise from a Yaru and a few pills to get us by. If it were solely up to me, I'd have you escorted from the city and hope to never see you again," he paused as he gazed around at the gathered Kameil. "However, it is not only my decision. There are those who wish to leave with you. In exchange for their safe passage, along with a supply of those Essence pills, we will give you a few crystals as payment."

Nean bowed. "Thank you for entrusting us with their lives. We will not disappoint you."

"Yes," Nandin agreed, "the biggest challenge will be to get your men in and out of the city. Climbing the wall requires a certain...skill."

"I'm sure that it does, but it is not necessary. There are much easier ways in and out of the city."

Nean and Nandin quickly glanced at each other, both holding their breath. They had suspected as much, but had refrained from broaching the subject.

Aaron, who seemed oblivious of the delicacy of the moment blurted out, "And where would those be?"

To Nandin's and Nean's great relief Demetrius replied.

"Through the sewers, of course."

CHAPTER TWENTY

Identity Theft

HANNA'S CURIOSITY WAS PIQUED.

Her team had been summoned to an unscheduled meeting with no explanation as to why. They had been called away from their morning's training and brought to the main meeting hall.

"I think we've found your cover story, Hanna" Master Jagare said without preamble.

The team sat around the large meeting table, accompanied by Master Jagare, Leader Puto and another Jagare Hanna had yet to meet.

"Jarek," Master Jagare said turning to the unknown man, "would you please recount your story for us."

Jarek looked uncomfortable sitting at the table. His bulky frame made the large chairs seem cramped. As he adjusted himself, attempting to get comfortable, Hanna had the feeling this weathered-looking individual, with dirt stained hands and twigs in his hair, would be much more at ease if the discussion was held out in the woods.

Jarek cleared his throat. "My hunting party was out chasing a wolcott. It attacked a Kameil family before we caught up to it. The family had been living in a cave, half of a day's hike north of here. They had obviously been there for some time."

"What happened to the Kameil?" Hanna asked, remembering all too vividly her encounter with a wolcott the previous year.

"They were killed." Jarek looked down at his hands, not wishing to elaborate. Everyone in the room knew what the beast was capable of, the gory details of the attack did not need to be divulged.

Master Jagare spoke up, "The point is this accident provides Hanna with an identity."

"How?" Kazi asked, too impatient to wait for an explanation.

Karn scowled at him showing his irritation, yet Kazi was oblivious to the silent reprimand.

"The family consisted of a mother, father, and two children," Master Jagare continued. "Their daughter looked to be around your age, Hanna."

Silently, Hanna tried to figure out where this was going. Karn was quick to puzzle it out.

"So, she can claim to be this girl, tell the Kameil she meets that her family was killed by the wolcott and now she's all alone."

"You've got it exactly, Karn," Master Jagare said. "And since it appears the family has been there for some time, there's little chance anyone would have met this girl before. I've asked Jarek to take you and Hanna to the cave. I need you to find out everything you can about these people so, on the off chance someone has heard of them, you'll still be believable. Leader Puto will be accompanying you to search for their Essence source. We need to know how they survived for so long, unharmed or undiscovered."

"What about the rest of us?" Kazi asked, "can we go too?"

"Not this time Kazi. There will be enough people there with Jarek's hunting party and I understand the area isn't that large, we don't need you all huddled into the cave. Besides, you still have your other studies to attend to." Master Jagare's stone expression was enough to convince even Kazi not to push the matter further.

"When do we leave?" Karn asked.

"Now. If you hurry you can be back before nightfall."

Using her imagination to picture the scene of the attack, Hanna didn't have much desire to go during the day, but being caught out there in the dark was positively bone chilling.

* * *

Hanna swallowed, trying to keep the contents of her stomach from making an appearance. The Jagare who had found the Kameil had covered the bodies, but the blood still stained the ground and small bits of flesh and entrails' still clung to the bushes where they had landed. She noticed the Jagare were wearing cloth masks that covered the lower half of their faces — she imagined it was to block out the smell of death that surrounded the area.

"We're assuming the mother and the children were picking berries off these bushes when they were attacked. It's fairly clear the father attempted to come to their rescue, but he was too late. His body is further away." Jarek explained, his voice muffled by the cloth he wore.

"I don't understand." Hanna croaked. "Why did it attack? From what I've read, the wolcott are territorial and usually just attack intruders in their area. If these people have been here for a while, I can't imagine it lived around here. Where did it come from?"

"The beast was young and probably looking for its own territory after leaving its mother. We keep the woods surrounding the castle free of wolcott so it was new to the area. We discovered it making a den and chased it out. An older wolcott would have turned and attacked us, but this one fled. We got close a few times, but only managed to scare it. When it saw the Kameil, it ripped right through them to get away from us."

"Hanna, Karn, come with me," Leader Puto said.

He approached the three blood-soaked blankets that covered the bodies and knelt down next to one. Karn watched, but remained at a distance.

"Have you ever been in the presence of someone who has died since you've been on Galenia?"

"No," Hanna whispered.

"Sit with me. We must learn what we can while there is still time." Carefully he pulled back the shroud revealing the mauled body of a middle-aged women. Hanna wanted to look away, but something compelled her to watch.

"Their Essence has not left them yet, not completely that is. As the body begins to decompose, the Essence is released. If we get to it soon enough we can pull it out and let it pass through ourselves."

"Why would we want to do that?"

"To catch a glimpse of the person that was. The Essence will hold a thread of a person before it dissipates.

188

Sometimes loved ones wish to hold onto those that have passed. In subtle ways it will allow them to see the world through their eyes. Today we do it to gain knowledge of these forgotten souls. Watch."

Leader Puto touched the lady's brow and then quickly touched his own. He repeated the action over and over. As Hanna watched, she saw the Essence following the movement as it left the dead body and entered Puto's mind. When no more Essence remained, the leader closed his eyes and sat back on his heels. She noticed the growing repugnance on Karn's face and wondered if it was just from the dislike of seeing the corpses or something more. Surely he had seen this death ritual before.

Leader Puto breathed in slowly. "It is very faint. The Essence just didn't connect with her mind like it normally does. Quickly Hanna. You must do the same with the girl."

Hanna crawled around until she sat in front of the still form of the girl as Puto pulled back the shroud. There was a gash across her face and her nose was bent so much that a bit of bone poked through the skin. Again Hanna swallowed. The smell of blood was strong; she could taste it. Once she touched the girls cold temple, she closed her eyes — not only to help her concentrate, but to help shut out the carnage before her.

She repeated the process Leader Puto used and concentrated on pulling the Essence towards her. As it entered her mind, a warm tingling sensation filled her. When she could no longer feel the drag of the Essence, she sat back and attempted to comprehend the memories that were not her own. She concentrated, but the greater the effort, the more elusive the thoughts became. It was like

189

attempting to remember a dream upon waking. The harder you tried, the quicker it would fade.

A hand gently squeezed her shoulder.

"All in good time, Hanna," Puto said apparently aware of her struggle and frustration. "She will reveal herself to you soon enough. Let us examine their home now."

"What about the boy?" she asked.

Puto shook his head. "I'm afraid his damage is too extensive, I looked while you were busy."

Karn pulled Hanna to her feet and held her steady. Unsure whether it was the nausea that made her lightheaded or from acquiring the Essence, either way she was grateful for his assistance.

* * *

Hanna kept her eyes on her feet as she walked in an attempt to block out anything else unfavourable. Karn followed in silence but stopped at the entrance to the cave. The cave was a very different scene. The walls were covered with brightly painted scenes. Maps of the woods, pictures of flora and fauna all told of the life the family had lived. Roughly woven mats topped with tattered blankets made up four beds. Chairs were created from small branches entwined. Shelves and cabinets kept food stores and clothes dry and out of reach of creatures. It was all very primitive looking, yet it hinted at knowledge outside the wilderness that surrounded it.

Leader Puto held up a plain beige tunic and trousers. They looked to be relatively Hanna's size and in fairly good condition.

"What do you make of these?" he asked.

"They're...ok?" she replied, unsure of what he was looking for.

"But where did they come from? I don't see any spinning wheels, do you? And they are relatively new. Either they got these awhile ago and only started wearing them or they are recently acquired." He folded them back up and slipped them into a bag he had placed on the floor. "Look around for anything you think would be useful. Karn, are you going to help out or just watch us?"

Karn hesitated, then finally joined Leader Puto examining the items on the shelves, Hanna walked deeper into the cave. At the back, she discovered several honeycomb like holes that had been dug into the wall; they were similar to those she had seen in the Citadel's library. The first one she investigated held a display of miniature woodcarvings. They were simple, perhaps done by a child and reminded Hanna of the figurines that Hamlin made her, although they were not nearly as well crafted. In the next hole she found two scrolls. The papyrus was worn and delicate. Carefully, she carried the scrolls to the bed closest to the cave opening to sit with enough light that would allow her to see more clearly.

"What have you there, Hanna?" Leader Puto asked.

"I'm not sure."

Puto and Karn made their way over to watch as she unrolled the first scroll. On it was a maze-like drawing.

"Senda," Karn said.

"What's Senda?"

"It's one of our major cities, three days south of here."

"Oh." She looked back at the drawing. "You can tell it's that city by just looking at this jumble of lines?"

Karn shook his head. "No. I can tell that by looking at this symbol." He knelt down and pointed to an image at the top of the scroll. "This is Senda's sign. The broken circle indicates the cities walls. The gaps represent the two gates leading into the city and the three arches in the centre are for the aqueducts that supply it with water. The aqueducts tower over the city, bringing water all the way from the mountains into the area."

"Yes," Leader Puto said leaning in closer, "but this is unlike any map of Senda I've ever seen. What do you make of it?"

Karn tapped on the paper. "This area looks to be the woods outside the walls, so this must be the city itself. It's some sort of cryptic map."

"Interesting. Hanna, let's have a look at the other one."

Again, being careful not to tear the paper, Hanna unrolled the other scroll. This one was more detailed and more easily understood.

"I'd say this is the cave here, the Citadel, the river...looks like a map leading down to the main road," Karn mused.

Leader Puto nodded. "Two maps. One leading to the road to Senda, one a representation of Senda."

"Why would a Kameil have a map of a city? Are they allowed in Senda?" Hanna asked.

Puto stood up. "No, they are not welcome there. Where did you find these?"

"In a hole in the wall," she said.

Puto indicated that she should show them. She placed the maps on the bed and lead the way to the back. There was nothing else in the hole. In the next one over they discovered a bag. Hanna carried it over to the bed, knelt down and began removing its contents. She recognized a pico wrap as she pulled it out along with a water skin, dried rations and socks.

"It's like a camping kit. Do you think they were about to go somewhere?"

Puto looked around the room. Noticing that the shelves were fully stocked with food stores, and a pile of dry wood took up part of one wall, he shook his head. "No, I think perhaps this was some sort of emergency kit. It's all stocked and ready to use. They probably switched out the food and water on a regular basis. That way they could just grab it in case they needed to leave in a hurry. And the maps indicate that Senda would be the destination. The question is: why?"

"Look," Karn said coming over with another bag. "I found a few more holes, each with a bag including the same contents. One each," Karn pointed out.

"Makes sense. Let's keeping looking, see if we find anything else." Puto suggested.

After another ten minutes of lifting up the beds, going through the jars and combing the walls for more treasures, Leader Puto stood back. Tapping the side of his face, he gazed around the room as if searching for further mysteries. The space wasn't that big and it seemed they had covered the area.

"Leader Puto," Hanna asked, "I've been wondering, if they're Kameil, how have they been surviving out here? I mean, they'd need Essence wouldn't they?"

Puto smacked his forehead with the palm of his hand. "Of course, they would! I knew I was forgetting something."

He sat down on the floor, hands resting face up on his knees, eyes closed. After a moment he turned to the others.

"Would you two mind leaving the cave for a moment? It is hard to discern your Essence from any other."

Hanna's hand went straight to her crystal. She nodded her head and then left the cave, following Karn.

They waited some distance outside the cave entrance. Hanna was relieved to note the Jagare who remained on guard of the area. The smell of blood, strong in the air, was likely to attract any number of animals, most of which Hanna was sure she didn't want to meet. She watched them as they used sticks to drag the father's body toward the others.

"Why don't they just pick it up?" she asked Karn quietly.

"They...don't want to risk touching it."

"Why?"

"They're afraid of catching the disease."

Hanna sat upright, suddenly concerned. "What disease??"

"The one that makes you Kameil."

"There's a disease that makes you Kameil?" she asked skeptically.

"No," Puto replied as he joined them. "It is a myth, even though many people believe it."

Hanna looked Karn over. "Do you? Is that why you didn't want to go into the cave?"

Karn sighed. "It is why I didn't want to go into the cave, but I don't believe in the myth anymore. I grew up believing it. Since I finished school and began working more closely with the Tahtays and Masters, they have assured me there is no disease. I just — "

"Knowing the truth and battling a lifetime of fear is no easy feat. You are doing fine." Puto placed his hand on Karn who nodded, excepting the Tahtay's encouragement.

They followed him back to the cave where he had left a lit torch. He retrieved it from the wall and held it out to Karn.

"If you would be so kind to raise this, your reach is considerably higher than mine," Karn lifted the torch, lighting the cave. Puto pointed to the ceiling.

Small specs glittered as the light hit it.

"Crystals!" Hanna exclaimed. Tiny crystals were dispersed in the rocky ceiling of the room.

"It is not much, but there is enough to have kept the family in good health. Karn, do you think you could carefully remove a few?"

Karn looked around for a tool and found an axe made of sharp rock and a wooden handle. Carefully he began chipping away at a small section. When a chunk of rock the size of his hand came free, he gave it to Puto who then placed it in one of the Kameil's bags.

"We'll take these with us." He passed three of the bags to Hanna and Karn then placed the scrolls in the last bag and swung it over his own shoulder. "I think that's all we need. Let us go home."

* * *

A few days after returning from the cave, it was determined that Hanna would head towards Senda. The maps they had found were reason enough to believe there was some connection. Reading the mother's Essence convinced Tahtay Puto that was their plan if something went wrong, but that was all he was able to glean. Master Jagare's scouts had discovered a Kameil and Yaru camp in Thickwood Forest between the Citadel and Senda so the hope was if Hanna made her way towards the city someone would intervene before she got there.

The team went over the details of the plan, the most important of which was the escape route. If the Kameil found her and brought her to their camp, it was imperative that they find a way to observe her and be able to cover her retreat if needed.

Another troubling detail Hanna had to face was minimizing her Essence. There was no way she could safely take the crystal she currently wore into the camp. If they seized it, she'd never get it back. She would have to make do with a less valuable and more realistic option. The one small comfort she had in this was that Master Juro had been preparing her for this moment and had taught her how to manipulate the Essence. If she was desperate, she could pull Essence from the life around her: even the trees contained Essence. It wasn't an easy trick nor would it be much, but it would keep her alive.

As she lay in her beautiful canopy bed for one last night, she pondered her situation. It seemed disconcerting to her to have all this newfound strength and unique abilities, yet to get close to the Kameil she had to give them all up. She just hoped that in the long run, it would all be worth the risk.

CHAPTER TWENTY-ONE

Mission Possible

NANDIN BEAMED.

His first mission had been a success. Scaling the walls of Senda unseen, seeking out the hidden Kameil that resided there and establishing a connection with them was definitely a noteworthy mission. True, he hardly did all of this on his own, but his negotiations with Demetrius required a skillful round of diplomacy. Even Nean praised him for a job well done.

He knew Mateo would be pleased. Not only was he going to bring a handful of the Senda Kameil back to the valley, he had been given access to a secret entrance into Senda and they each carried a pouch full of the minuscule Essence crystals that they had brought instead of relying on the pills to get them to the valley. Of course, Nandin was yet unaware of the exact location of the secret entrance, Demetrius hadn't trusted them enough for that yet, but the Kameil that left Senda with Nandin knew the way and agreed either to go in their stead or blindfold and lead the Yaru back in if they desired.

Back at base camp, he filled out the necessary paperwork that Mateo would request. He was anxious to return to the valley. Aside from the desire to share his success, there was a wedding to get to. That was one of the reasons he had to remain at the camp just a little longer. So far, only Nean's team and the Yaru guarding the camp were aware of the upcoming nuptials. He could have pressed on ahead, leaving those in charge of the camp to recall the others to the valley, but Nandin wished to be the one to share the good news. Besides, with the extra Kameil in the camp, he preferred if they all returned to the valley together. It would provide them with extra security and assistance while travelling.

Another matter that gave Nandin pause was that he had yet to hear about the mysterious girl Blades had encountered. None of the Kameil or Rodrick had heard anything about a Jivan with the Juro sight. He thought perhaps news of this anomaly had yet to leave the Citadel. If that was the case, it created another, rather dangerous, challenge for him. The Citadel was a fortress. The castle guard knew the comings and goings of everyone so there would be no way he could enter through the front gate without being detained and questioned. The safest thing to do would be to get in unnoticed. Sneaking in the stone structure would require scaling the walls, entering through a window and taking the chance that the room he entered was unoccupied. Succeeding that, he would then need to begin the search for this Seer, but where would he start? He had a few ideas, but he preferred to have more information before risking such a dangerous campaign.

He pushed the thoughts aside as he continued drawing a map of Senda. It was important that he kept focused so he wouldn't miss any crucial detail. Later he could discuss the problem concerning the girl with Nean; for now, it would just have to wait.

CHAPTER TWENTY-TWO

Lofty Liberation

DARRA WAS COLD.

And hungry. Cold, hungry and lonely. It was well into the spring season. The night air was crisp and she didn't have the luxury of a fire to keep her warm. Resentfully she eyed the soft glow produced by the campfire a short distance away. More than anything, she wanted to join the small party that circled it, but she knew she couldn't risk it. She was a thief, an outcast, a Kameil. Definitely not someone who would be welcome to join the Jivan and Jagare that happily sang songs while eating their stew and drinking hot tea. The aroma that wafted through the air taunted her; she couldn't help but begrudge them their pleasures.

In her opinion, it was ludicrous. Just because she was born without Essence, why should she be ostracized? She hadn't hurt anyone and the only reason she was a thief was to survive. Her most recent procurements included a knife she wore on her belt and some dried rations that she carried in her bag. The only other things she called her own were the clothes on her back, her water skin and a pico wrap. She was most grateful for the wrap as it allowed her to sleep in the safety of the trees, sleeping in the woods alone at night was bad enough without the additional worries of being attacked by some wild beast.

She had been following the group of travellers she currently watched for the past three days. It was from this lot that she had taken her food supplies. They were rather careless about guarding their wagon at night and she was able to grab some essentials without being discovered. The group chose to sleep on the ground close to the fire. Every night she waited until they tucked in and then she'd sneak into their campsite and find some food.

It would be few more hours before they'd call it a night so she chose to find an appropriate location to set up her wrap. She wanted to be close enough to their camp so she didn't have to travel too far in the dark, but needed to be far enough away that they wouldn't chance upon her. She wandered a little further into the woods and picked a tree that suited her. Confident her choice would keep her hidden, she began making preparations to climb.

The party camped close to a well-travelled road, just at the edge of Thickwood Forest. From what Darra could tell, most people tended to stay out of the forest, partially due to the reason it got its name: the thick trees grew close together and the underbrush was dense, making it difficult to navigate. Another reason, she assumed, had to do with the fact that it didn't lead anywhere. There were no cities, villages or schools and no crystal pockets. The only thing to be found by heading east into Thickwood Forest was Mateo, or so the stories told.

She was on her way to Senda in search of other Kameil. For the time being, the group she stalked were heading in that direction so it suited her purpose to follow in their tracks until she could find the Kameil.

Once securely set in her tree, she settled in to have a nap. There was no point sitting around doing nothing for hours waiting for the others to fall asleep.

* * *

A bird's hoots wakened Darra as the noises of the forest seemed amplified at night. She thought it might have more to do with her inability to see and the nagging fear that tugged at her than the sounds actually being louder. She waited a moment, considering skipping the nights excursion. The rumbling of her stomach convinced her otherwise. Carefully, she steadied herself as she undid the fastening of her pico wrap and eased herself onto the branch of the tree. She had slept with a safety rope around her waist to make her descent easier as it had proven difficult to try and fuss with it in the darkness.

Grabbing the climbing rope, she attached her safety line and lowered herself, breathing a sigh of relief as she felt the firmness of the ground beneath her feet. Now the fear of falling was dealt with, she just had to face her terror of encountering a flesh-mutilating creature. Trying to calm herself, she concentrated on being stealthy as she made her way toward the campsite. She paused when she reached the edge of the clearing to study the area. As usual, the three sleeping mats were arranged around a lit fire and the occupants were sound asleep.

As Darra began to edge her way over to the wagon, she spied a pot on the edge of the fire — and it still contained some stew. Her mouth watered as she tiptoed closer to the fire. Ensuring that everyone was sleeping, she gingerly reached down and grabbed the pot, wooden spoon and all. She was tempted to sit down in front of the fire, but she knew that would really be pushing things too far. The fire would ward off any beasts, but any experienced party would have still kept a watch out. Still it was best not to risk giving them a reason to change their negligence. Instead of getting cozy by the fire, she contented herself to sitting in the back of the wagon and leaning against the various bundles that resided in it. If anyone woke she could easily hide from view; the chances of them checking out the wagon would be remote.

She finished the stew leaving some gravy and refraining from licking the spoon — that would have been a bit too obvious. Searching one bundle she found an apple and then, after carefully returning the pot to the fireside, she crept back to the woods and up her tree to spend the rest of the night.

The next morning she lay in her bed listening to the sounds of the campers making breakfast, packing up and eventually setting off down the road once more. Darra crawled out of bed and dismantled her pico wrap, stuffing it in her bag, which she then swung over her shoulder before descending from the tree. Tentatively, she entered the campsite. It had been her routine to check over the site after it had been abandoned in case anything useful had been forgotten. So far she had added the knife to her collection of supplies and the odd scrap of leftover food.

Today as she combed the eating area, she found a piece of bacon and a half eaten piece of toast. Eagerly, she settled down to eat.

"Sloppy, aren't they?"

Darra jumped. She swung around in a crouch grabbing her knife from her belt.

"Easy, it's okay. I'm not going to hurt you."

Standing only a few paces away from Darra was a pale lady, with long honey-coloured hair.

"I'm Cassey," she said. "I have food if you're hungry."

Darra eyed her warily.

Cassey approached her and sat on a stump across the ash pit that was what remained of the fire.

"What's your name?"

"Darra," she replied hesitantly.

"Well Darra, I think you can tell I'm a Kameil. Can't you?"

Darra looked at Cassey's delicate figure, her sunken eyes and tattered clothes. Yes, it was easy to tell she was Kameil. There was something else too, but Darra kept that to herself and instead just nodded.

"Good." Cassey smiled. "And I think I would be correct to guess that you are Kameil as well? Although, you do look rather healthy, for a Kameil. You must have a good supply of Essence."

Seeing Darra's panicked expression, Cassey shook her head and spoke softly. "Don't worry, Darra. I have my own source of Essence. But now that you know we are on the same side, will you let me help you?"

This is exactly what Darra had wanted — to find the Kameil and get their help, but she just couldn't suppress her anxiety. Cassey seemed to understand this and became protective of the girl.

"I promise, Darra, I won't let anyone harm you." Darra returned her smile even though she was still apprehensive. Cassey said, "I have a daughter myself. Perhaps you'd like to meet her?"

"How old is she?" Darra asked forgetting herself for a moment. Cassey approached, helped her up and, placing a hand at her elbow, she led Darra into the woods.

"She's only five, and as cute as can be. She's just so full of life, even if she is rather frail."

"Do you live around here?" Darra asked wondering what a mother and a young daughter would be doing out in the woods and so close to the road.

Cassey laughed. "No, no of course not. We are in the process of moving. You probably wouldn't believe me if I told you where I did live."

"Why? Where was that?"

"We just came from Senda, but we're going to find a new home now."

Darra smiled. "I was just heading to Senda."

Cassey turned to her in surprise. "Whatever for?"

"Hopefully to find more Kameil. It's where my father told me to go...I didn't want to be alone anymore."

"Yes, I can understand that. But why are you out here all alone?"

Darra swallowed. This had been the moment she had been dreading. She didn't know if her story would be believable. "My...my family was killed by a wolcott."

Cassey stopped and wrapped her arms around Darra.

"Oh, you poor soul!" In Cassey's embrace Darra couldn't help but well up. She had lost her family and she had been alone in the woods. Now that she was here, she wondered what she got herself into. She was scared and hungry and suddenly it was all just a bit too much.

When Cassey released her and saw the tears rolling down Darra's face, she looped her arm through Darra's and confidently marched her deeper into the trees.

"We're your family now, Darra. We'll take good care of you."

Cassey waved to someone further ahead who was leaning, unassumingly against a tree. Darra would have again felt fear at meeting another Kameil, but the broad grin and easy manner of the man was reassuring, yet there was more to him than met the eye. Right away she realized this was no Kameil. She tried to react appropriately, but she just wasn't sure at the moment what that meant.

"Cassey, I see you've made a new friend."

"Nean this is Darra. Darra this is Nean. Nean and his friends found my family and me just a few days ago and they're taking us to our new home. Isn't that right, Nean?"

"Yes ma'am. Care for some oatmeal Darra? I just had a fresh batch cooked up."

"That sounds wonderful," she said apprehensively. "Do you have any brown sugar?"

"*Brown sugar?*"

Uh-oh, did I already mess things up? Not knowing what to say, Darra just raised her eyebrows, her lips quivering.

Nean nodded. "Well I suppose we do, but we just call it sugar. I mean, is there any other kind?"

"Honey." Darra said, desperately trying to improvise, she'd momentarily forgotten there was no white, refined sugar on Galenia.

Nean laughed. "I guess there is that. Now that you mention it, honey in oatmeal would be pretty tasty."

Darra decided she'd better stick to saying as little as possible. Although this Nean fellow was welcoming and seemed rather carefree, there was something about him that convinced her to be on guard.

As they pushed through a rather thick portion of shrubs, the sight before her made silence achievable as the shock took her breath away. She didn't really know what to expect, but the clearing she walked into housed at least thirty tents of various sizes, the largest one was opposite from where she just entered and was four times the size of any of the others. Unlike the plain beige tents that covered most the clearing, the large one was topped with wide black stripes and a triangular trim.

Men, women and children sat around multiple fire pits eating the morning's meal or washing up dishes. As Darra watched them, she realized there were fewer people than tents. Several horses grazed by the large tent. She wondered who they belonged to. Out of the corner of her eye, she noticed Nean watching her and she nervously looked away.

"It's okay Darra, we're all outcasts here. Let's get you that food, then you can tell us your story."

Darra just nodded and allowed herself to be taken further into, what she had come to think of as, enemy territory.

* * *

Karn listened to Tasha's account. Apparently, the Kameil had taken the bait and invited Hanna into their camp. As instructed, Dylan and Tasha had Hanna under surveillance as she followed Karn, Kazi and another Jagare who was the Wagoneer. When the Kameil had led Hanna away, Dylan followed, keeping a safe distance away and leaving Tasha behind to alert Karn. Dylan made sure to leave markers for Tasha to find so she could meet up with him later.

When Tasha left Dylan, she ran to get into shooting distance of the wagon as it made its' way along the road. She shot an arrow into a target covered by a sack that was in the back of the wagon. The shot, which flew over 160 feet, hit the target dead centre. Kazi jumped up and attempted to cover his response by pointing at a non-existent animal in the brush while Karn, who was in the back of the open wagon, removed the arrow. In case anyone had been observing them, it would be unlikely they had noticed the shot, but an arrow protruding from the back of the wagon would draw attention sooner or later. Karn laid down, obscuring himself from view, lowered a door in the side of the wagon, slid out and slinked into the ditch.

After Tasha had loosed her arrow, she resumed tracking Dylan. His markers were subtle; it took a skilled tracker to notice them and even then they wouldn't understand what they meant. The last marker informed her that Hanna was in place, but not to come any closer. Tasha then added a stone to the marker to let Dylan know she had received the message if he came back to check. Tasha waited for Karn at the campsite he had left that morning as per their arrangement.

"Did you get a look at the Kameil's camp?" Karn asked.

"No, I didn't get close enough. I don't even know how far away it is from Dylan's last marker. As far as I could tell it was just brush, brush and more brush." Tasha replied.

"Ok, well we better get back to the marker and see if Dylan has anything else for us."

When they arrived, Dylan was waiting. In hushed tones he explained that the Kameil's camp wasn't much further ahead and there were four sentries surrounding the area.

"They're all on the ground and they don't move from their posts so I can take us to a spot between their defences. We can get into the trees and have a fairly clear view of the site."

"They won't be able to see us?" Karn asked.

Dylan shook his head. "No. I will place you a bit further back. From my vantage point I will be able to see everything that goes on. Your spot will be a bit more obscured. If something goes wrong, I will use the bird call we discussed."

Karn had hoped all three of them would be able to see into the Kameil's campsite; however, they had prepared for the current scenario as well. Certain bird whistles would signal if there were problems. The general plan for Hanna was to walk or run out of the camp the moment she had gathered enough relevant information or if she was in trouble. Dylan would signal which way she was exiting so the others could be ready. The plan hinged on Hanna being able to escape — if she couldn't, then Plan B required a rescue mission. And it required Kazi's assistance.

Kazi was to wait ten minutes after Karn left the wagon before he too snuck away. His job was to follow the road back the way they had come. An hour behind them a group of Vaktare were slowly heading to Senda. They stayed in the woods opposite of Thickwood Forest. Kazi was to inform them that the signal had been given at which point they would hold their position until further notice. Kazi would then return to the camp they had just left that morning and wait for word from Karn. All the extra comings and goings would be risky; especially when it required Kazi to be stealthy. Karn felt that it was a necessary risk though because he needed the Vaktare close if Hanna had a difficult time leaving the Kameil camp. His team could only buy Hanna time, if there were Yaru in the camp they would need the Vaktare's skill. Karn just hoped it wouldn't turn out that way.

"Okay," Karn said, "let's go."

CHAPTER TWENTY-THREE

Dubious Empathy

THE CAMPSITE WAS BUSTLING.

Once Darra had been settled in with the other Kameil, Nean made his way into the command tent to report. Nandin was diligently making notes on their recent mission to Senda. Nean didn't envy the Commander's task and was rather pleased that he had encouraged Mateo to appoint Nandin to the role. Of course, he was also glad Nandin was still able to partake in the missions; Nean rather enjoyed his company. Nandin looked up as he entered.

"Any news on that group you've been following?" Nandin asked.

"I confirmed they are a Minstrel's party. They're still continuing in the direction of Senda."

"Any potentials among them?" They both knew potentials that could become Yaru had markings such as freckles and moles. One of the missions they were given was to seek out these individuals and win them to Mateo's cause.

"There was one, but in any event, it doesn't matter. We wouldn't be able to recruit them."

"Why not? I thought you said they were a young group. Those are the easiest to win over."

"True, but we never involve ourselves with Minstrels. Their movements are tracked by their guild—if they didn't show up to their next gig, people would notice right away and have a pretty good idea where to start looking for them. We don't want that kind of attention, especially this close to base camp."

"Too bad. It would have been nice to have a musical recruit. What about that girl that was following them?"

"We brought her here."

"What's her story?"

"She's been orphaned and was hoping to come across the Kameil."

"Do you believe her?"

Nean shrugged. "She hardly looks like a Kameil. She could actually be a Jivan, yet it is rather unlikely she would be thieving and scrounging off of strangers if she were. I didn't get a full account of her situation—I thought you'd prefer to speak with her."

"What if it's the Seer Blades told us about?"

"Why would you think that?"

"You said she could be a Jivan. That's what Blades said."

"Out of the hundreds of Jivan's that come and go from the Citadel, we'd just happen upon the same one Blades did? That's kind of a leap isn't it? "

"I guess it is. She's been on my mind lately. We haven't heard anything about her and I was hoping to bring back some intelligence to Mateo."

"Careful you don't resort to jumping to conclusions. Mateo would rather have a lack of information than false accounts."

"And if she was a Jivan she'd never walk willingly into a camp of Kameil, she'd be running the other direction. Of course, there is a fail-safe way of discovering if she is Kameil. What is she using for Essence?"

"She didn't say, I didn't ask. She was just as skittish as any of the other Kameil we've met."

"Well, that's something. Invite her in. I'll see what I can make of her."

"And if your still unsure she is what she claims to be?"

Nandin chortled. "She's in a camp about to be occupied by Yaru who will then escort her to Mateo. She doesn't pose a risk to us. Besides, I'm sure Mateo would be more than pleased to meet her either way."

* * *

Darra had finished eating and was speaking with some of the Kameil in the camp when Nean returned. He requested her to follow him and he led her through the camp, weaving among the tents. Finally, they faced the large, striped tent at the far side of the encampment.

"We refer to this as the command tent. It's where we hand out Essence and make our travel plans."

Darra paused, foot in midair. "You hand out Essence?"

Nean's crooked grin gave the impression that he enjoyed being nonchalant about something so extraordinary.

"We do indeed, but I'll save that for the Commander to explain."

Darra hurriedly skipped to catch up to Nean who had continued to the tents entrance.

"Who is the Commander?"

"Not to worry, Darra, all your questions will be answered soon."

His statement did little to ease her mind. A Commander sounded like just the person she needed to speak with in order to discover what Mateo was up to, but that didn't mean she wasn't terrified to meet him. And what if the Commander turned out to be Mateo himself? Then she'd be in real trouble. Surely, he would discover she was an impostor.

Nean pulled back the tent flap to let Darra inside and then followed her in. Several raised beds sitting on top of small carpets lined the sides of the tent with curtains in-between them to allow for privacy. Wooden trunks sat at the foot of each bed with one extra trunk at the back of the space, a heavy lock securing its contents. Long boards attached to wooden legs made up the table that stood centered in the tent on top of the crushed grass floor.

A young man with ash-blond hair sat on a wooden chair behind the table, concentrating on a piece of parchment. So intent was he that he still hadn't acknowledged the new arrivals.

"Commander Nandin, I'd like to introduce you to Darra."

With haste, the Commander stood up and made his way to greet his guest. Without realizing it, Darra had been holding her breath when she entered. Upon hearing that the Commander was named Nandin and not Mateo she exhaled. As he made his way over to her, her breath caught again.

She tried really hard to react like the traumatized Kameil she pretended to be, but was awed and a bit intimidated by this attractive, ninja-like figure coming towards her. As Nandin approached, she was amazed how the Essence flowed through him. Like Nean, she was sure this was another of the Yaru she had heard so much about, although Nandin's Essence was brighter and seemed to course through his veins like an electric current. She found she had to make an effort to keep blinking to prevent staring.

"It's a pleasure, Darra," Commander Nandin said extending his hand to shake hers.

Again, Darra was caught off guard — this was the first person on Galenia she had ever met who offered her a handshake. The preferred greeting that she had witnessed had been bowing.

"I like to shake hands," he explained, "I find it more of a personal way to greet people."

He smiled warmly at her. Tentatively she offered her hand. "Quiet a grip you have there. Pull up a chair; I'd love to hear your story. Not too many young Kameil girls are found wandering through the woods alone. Would you care for something to drink?"

"No thank you, Commander Nandin, I just had some water."

"Call me Nandin, we can save the Commander stuff for the Yaru. Nean, will you be joining us?"

Hanna flinched. *The Yaru, I was right!*

Nean cocked his head. "If it's alright with you *Commander*, I have some errands to attend to."

Nandin chuckled. "By all means," he replied and motioned to the door.

He pulled out a chair for Darra to sit on as Nean left the tent.

"So, what brings you here and why were you following the Minstrel's party?"

* * *

It took the better part of an hour to explain how her family was killed, her trek down the mountains and her need to find the Kameil. Nandin accepted her reasoning for following the wagon and commended her on acquiring her knife and food. She explained the pico wrap was part of her emergency pack that her parents had made, but left out the map that was also stashed away in her bag that was currently tucked under her chair. Darra tried very hard to stick to the story that had been conjured. With Nandin quietly listening, and asking only a few questions, interrupting here and there, she was afraid it might have sounded too rehearsed. When she finished, Nandin leaned forward and took her hand.

"You've been through a lot Darra. I'm sorry for your loss and the heartache you must be enduring. I do have a few more questions I'd like to ask. Would you mind indulging me?"

As the warmth flowed through his hand into hers she felt less stressed and a bit of a buzz.

"Go ahead," she said.

"Why Senda? You said specifically you were heading to Senda to search out other Kameil?"

She nodded. "Yes. My father told me if anything ever went wrong to head to Senda. I hoped to find other Kameil there."

"He knew of the Kameil there?"

Darra wasn't sure what to answer. If she said yes, he may want more details, which she didn't have. If she said no, then how could she explain why she was going there without showing him the maps?

"I don't know what my father knew. He didn't speak of the others. I guess he thought if I just went there, they would find me…and they did."

"That was a rather risky gamble."

"What choice did I have? Both of my parents were just killed and I was getting low on food. I couldn't survive on berries alone. And what if the wolcott returned? Where else could I go?"

She had not gleaned much when she had taken in dead girl's Essence — just her name, Darra, and the feelings of terror that plagued her. Sometimes, her dreams consisted of images she was sure belonged to Darra, but they did not provide her with useful information. Puto had explained that absorbing someone's Essence was an art form that took time to master. She would prefer if she didn't have to do it again.

Nandin considered her story and agreed her points were valid, but there was another issue he needed clarification of before he could trust her.

"I'm glad we found you and in such good health. Obviously you must have a very good source of Essence."

Darra sat back, releasing his hand. She had been dreading this moment the most. She wasn't keen about revealing her lifeline, yet she was unsure how long she could hide it. Seeing her hesitate, he inched forward and spoke softly.

"I am no Kameil. I have no need for Essence. I will not take whatever it is that you possess that is keeping you alive. In fact, it is my job to ensure that the Kameil in this camp stay alive. I can only do this if I know they have a reliable source of Essence. I promise, you are under my protection."

Full of trepidation, she grabbed the leather string that was around her neck, and pulled it out from under her shirt. Attached to the necklace was a small pouch. Again, Nandin smiled reassuringly at her. Carefully she opened it and shook some of the contents onto her palm. Small chunks of rock with flecks of pink crystals tumbled onto her open hand.

"Those are very precious, Darra. Thank you for your trust." He indicated for her to replace the stones. Once the stones were securely replaced in her pouch, she tucked it back under her shirt. Nandin relaxed. Only a Kameil could wear Essence next to their skin for any length of time. Any other race would become ill from the excessive exposure.

"Where did you get those?" he asked kindly.

"The cave that we lived in had a few scattered on the ceiling. I knew I would need them if I left, so I chipped these ones out."

"Good thinking. I guess you won't be needing any capsules at the moment."

"What do you mean?"

"Oh, has no one told you?" When she shook her head he explained, "Well most Kameil are not fortunate enough to have crystals of any kind. Normally we find them surviving off of fumaroles or plants with high Essence content."

"What are fumaroles?" she asked.

"They're pockets in the ground that hot Essence gas seeps from. The point being, these people depend on these sources and typically can't just leave. Fortunately for them, Mateo has created these Essence pills."

He reached across his desk for a small box and took something out of it. Darra's eyes widened both at the mention of Mateo's name and the little glowing pill that Nandin now held. She wondered if the pills shone for those who couldn't see the Essence.

"Rather amazing, aren't they?"

She hesitated, not sure whether to feign ignorance of Mateo or to ask about the pills. She decided, for the time being, to go with the latter. "How are they made?"

Nandin slipped the pill into the box he had taken it from and placed it back on the table.

"Not really sure. It has something to do with crushing Essence-rich rocks to make a powder and removing the extra, non-Essence bits."

Darra knew Master Juro would want to take a closer look at one of those pills. She made a mental note to watch for an opportunity to get one; at this point she wasn't about to trade her pouch for them. As she thought about this, the significance of the capsules dawned on her.

"So he's curing the Kameil — Mateo that is."

Nandin shot Darra a puzzled look. Inadvertently, Darra realized she had slipped into Hanna mode and referred to the Kameil as if she wasn't one.

"I mean us," she sputtered, "alone with my family in the mountains for so long, I just thought of myself as Darra, not as Kameil."

He accepted her blunder, ignoring his momentary suspicion as he explained. "The pills are more of a medicine than a cure. But that's coming."

"Really?" both the Darra and Hanna personas were intrigued by this new piece of information.

He seemed excited to brag about Mateo's accomplishments. "Oh, yes. He's tested it out on a few Kameil with great success."

"Why hasn't he treated more?"

Nandin paused to consider her question. He liked Darra and now that they had spoken and she had proved she was Kameil, he felt at ease speaking with her. To win people over he had to be open and honest, but it would be foolish to be too trusting. She appeared to be just a young, harmless Kameil, but even so, some questions should not be answered.

"These things take time," he replied.

Darra sensed he was being vague. She wondered how she would get more information out of him.

"Excuse me, Commander," Nean barged into the room, "but I've been alerted that there's a Draka in the woods."

Nandin jumped to his feet.

"Sorry Darra, we'll have to finish our conversation later."

They all rushed out of the tent. As the two Yaru made their way to the horses, Hanna returned to her new Kameil acquaintances.

* * *

Darra was torn as she looked at the Kameil families that occupied the camp: the children playing, the others doing camp chores. She could only feel compassion for them. All the time she had spent with the other races, she was treated with such kindness and charity; how could those same people abandon an entire race? She just couldn't get her head around it. There had to be something more that she just wasn't seeing. The challenge was, how to find out what. How could she gain information about a people that she was suppose to belong to? How could she claim ignorance?

Finally, she approached Cassey, her stomach in knots.

"Darra, there you are! I was wondering where you wandered off to."

"Nean introduce me to Commander Nandin," she replied.

"Ah, yes. He's a handsome, smooth talker isn't he?" she said, winking at Darra.

"I…I guess so," Darra stammered. "He had to run off though. Nean mentioned something about a Draka?"

Cassey nodded. "Thank goodness the Yaru are here. I doubt there's anyone else here who could kill it."

"Yaru?" she questioned. She figured 'Darra' would be unfamiliar with the term and this may be an opportunity to do some digging.

"That's right. From what I understand, Mateo gave them an extra shot of Essence. It makes them very skilled. They're like a Jagare and Jivan all wrapped up in one."

Cassey led Darra to a bucket of water, scooped out a cup and handed it to her. Darra swallowed a few mouthfuls. She hadn't realized she was thirsty. Cassey's intuition surprised her; she figured it must have something to do with being a mother.

"So Darra, you mentioned earlier that you were heading to Senda?"

"That was the plan."

Cassey chose a soft patch of sunny ground to sit on. Darra swung her ever-present bag to the ground and joined her, keeping her back to the sun. She didn't want the bright glare in her eyes, and the heat felt nice on her back.

"What I wondered was, what did you plan to do once you got there? You know you couldn't just walk into the city. They would never let you in."

"Yes, I know. I was hoping this would help." Darra reached into her pack, pulled out a tattered scroll and passed it to Cassey.

Gingerly, Cassey unrolled the parchment. As she studied it her eyes grew wide.

"Darra," she whispered, "Where did you get this?"

"It was my father's," she replied softly.

Cassey rolled up the item and quickly tucked it back into the bag. "Have you shown it to anyone else?"

"No," she lied, noticing Cassey's concern. How worried would Cassey be if she knew that Master Jagare had seen and even copied the map before Hanna had left the Citadel? The map was most likely now in the hands of the very people Cassey feared.

"Good," seeing the question in Darra's eyes Cassey continued. "Let me explain. It's safe to assume your parents decided to make it on their own outside of Senda. Did they ever tell you whether they were born Kameil or if Mateo made them?"

Darra improvised, hoping her back-story would hold up. "They didn't talk about the past. We were more concerned about surviving."

"Of course, something's are better to forget. Do you know what this map is?"

Darra shrugged. "It's confusing. I'm guessing the mark outside, what I assume is the city wall, is an entrance of some kind. There aren't any buildings or names on the roads. I thought maybe when I got there it would make more sense."

"Indeed. The reason you don't see any landmarks is because this map is for under the city — it's for the sewers."

"The sewers?"

"Yes, that's where I grew up. There is an entire community living under there. A few places covered in specks of Essence keep us alive. It's fairly safe. Very few people, other than the Kameil know about it. We haven't even let the Yaru know where the entrances are or how to navigate the tunnels. We guard the secret most adamantly."

Darra took another sip of her water, feeling guilty about lying and suddenly fearful for the Kameil who were in danger of being exposed. It was all she could do to remain calm.

"Why did you leave?" she asked, hoping to steer the conversation away from her guilt.

A look of sadness came over Cassey's face. "Many of my friends and family chose to stay, but when the Yaru came and offered us the chance of a home outside the sewers, I jumped at it. Look."

She pointed to a few children who played in a grassed area. They were spinning and spinning until they fell down, then they got up to do it again, giggling all the while.

"My daughter has never been outside before. How could I deny her this?"

"Never?" Darra gasped.

"It's too dangerous. When she got a little older I would have risked taking her out of the sewers into the forest, right now she is too vulnerable. When she was old enough, I would have let her make the choice herself. Being discovered is not the only danger. What would we have done if a Draka or another beast had come and we were on our own?"

Darra sighed. "I just don't get it. How could they let this go on? Forcing people to hide in sewers? What could the Kameil ever have done to deserve such a life?"

Cassey nodded, oblivious of Darra's slip of referring to the Kameil in third-person. "I know, I've asked that so many times, but the Addicts would have probably scared me to the same extreme."

"Addicts?"

"No offence Darra, but your parents should have told you at least a bit of our history. They didn't expect you to stay in that cave with them your whole life did they?" Mistaking Darra's expression for one of pain and loss instead of fear of discovery, Cassey patted her leg and explained. "The Addicts are Kameil only to the extent that they have no Essence of their own. Their dependency for Essence has become truly disturbing. They just can't get enough. They will suck dry any source they can find and I do mean it literally. Plants, animals, hatchlings, I think they'd suck it right out of a person if they got the chance. They've killed Jagare trying to get into the Crystal Pockets."

Appalled, Darra pressed forward with her questions. "How could they suck the Essence out of crystals? Is that even possible?"

"No, not at all. Instead they crush them and ingest the powder. And Darra, the way they look, like some sort of nightmare. Their eyes bulge out of their grey sunken faces, which are stained with blood from constant nosebleeds." Cassey seemed to go into a trance as she explained. "What hair they have left is long and stringy. Their ragged, gasping breath is foul from rotten teeth. Completely neglectful, their nails are long and yellowed, their clothing nothing more than tattered rags."

"How do you know?"

"I was attacked," Cassey answered. "I was just a child at the time and my father took me for a walk in the woods. The Addict just jumped out of nowhere and grabbed me. He was hovering over me when my dad cracked him over the head with a club — thank goodness." She shook her head as if to clear it. "Anyway, there's this myth going around that all Kameil become those monsters so that's why we are banished."

"Banished." Darra repeated. "What if you come back? I mean what would happen if they found the Kameil in the sewers? Would they just kick them out?"

Cassey sighed. "That would probably be the best case scenario, but I think fear would lead to a more drastic approach, although, I can't really imagine them hanging all the women and children — people are scared, but they're not cruel."

Darra swallowed. "Hanging?"

"Yes, that's the punishment for any Kameil who return. Banishment is the first time you get caught and the gallows is the second time. Needless to say, getting caught twice is not an option."

"But why don't they just arrest them and when they're locked up they could wait and see if they become Addicts."

"More fear of course. Some people think we're contagious and the whole city could become infected. I guess they figured it's just safer for us to go away. Galenia is big enough to cast us off and forget about us."

"Something has to be done. It can't keep going on like this."

"That's Mateo's opinion exactly," Nandin said from behind Darra. She hadn't noticed him approaching, sitting with her back to the camp. She craned her neck to see him.

Cassey asked, "Did you get the Draka already?"

"Not even close," Nandin replied. "We chanced on some Yaru returning to the site so they went on in my place. It's always a good idea to keep at least one Yaru in the camp in case something else comes up."

Nandin knelt down so he wasn't hovering over them as he talked. "Sorry to interrupt your conversation. I just stopped by to invite Darra back to the command tent at the next mealtime. We could finish our chat." He gave Darra a wink, and she smiled feeling the colour rise in her cheeks.

"Thanks, I look forward to it."

Eyeing Darra's bag he added, "Cassey, would you mind finding Darra a tent for her to sleep and store her things in?"

Cassey agreed as Nandin stood.

"Good. Well then, carry on ladies," he said with a bow.

Darra saw Cassey's grin broadening.

"What?" Darra asked.

"I think he's sweet on you," she replied.

"What?" Darra repeated in a startled voice.

"I'm just saying."

Darra sipped her water. "Maybe he likes you," Darra countered.

Cassey laughed. "That's doubtful. I think that was the first time he spoke directly to me. In fact, I'm surprised he knew my name. Aside from the fact that he's way too young for me, I doubt he'd make a play for me with my husband halfway across the field."

"Oh, right." Darra recalled Cassey introducing her to her husband when she first arrived at the campsite earlier.

"Of course, if I wasn't married, he'd be the first to know. Fortunately, you have no such commitments."

"Well yeah, but I'm only fourteen." She was momentarily surprised she had blurted out how old Darra was — Hanna was actually fifteen. There had been no indications of her age at the cave. It must have been another one of those Essence-linked memories she had.

Cassey snickered some more. "I didn't say he was planning on proposing, but there's no reason you can't put your name in for later consideration."

Lifting her glass again, Darra realized it was empty. She wasn't really thirsty; she was just trying to gather her thoughts. She had been talking about Mateo, and then things got all...sidetracked.

"Come on Darra," Cassey said as she stood up and offered her hand to help Darra to her feet. "Let's find you a tent, then you can get ready for your hot date."

CHAPTER TWENTY-FOUR

In-tents Disclosure

DARRA RETURNED.

"Where were we?" Nandin asked, leaning back in his chair and popping cherry-like fruit into his mouth.

She knew exactly where they had left off, but didn't want to seem too eager. "I think we were talking about Essence. How Mateo was curing people?" she said pulling up a chair.

"Oh, right. I was explaining that he's trying to make a cure."

"And how is he doing that?"

"That's something you'll have to ask him about when we get to the valley."

Darra started. She didn't realize they were planning on going anywhere. Truth was, she had already arrived where she planned to go. "Get where?" she asked cautiously.

"The valley of course. Hasn't anyone told you about it?"

Now that she thought about it, she recalled all the times Cassey had spoken about going to the valley. She just never pictured herself going too. She didn't think to ask what valley they were talking about.

"I've heard the valley mentioned, but I don't know anything about it."

Nandin's eyes lit up as he leaned forward in his chair. With great fervour he explained the wall, the town and the hundreds of people that resided there. He then went on to explain the quarry and briefly touched on Mateo's castle, but he left out the detail that it was built on a floating rock — that was something he'd rather let her see for herself.

"I had no idea," she said then clamped her mouth shut as she hadn't meant to say that out loud. She assumed this would be common knowledge among the Kameil.

Nandin waved her comment aside. "You'd be surprised how many Kameil don't. There are a considerable number who have been out here in the wild for generations, completely unaware that there was a safe haven for them beyond these trees and rivers."

Darra's thoughts flipped back to her conversation with Cassey about Senda. She suddenly felt a glimmer of hope. "Will the Kameil living in the sewers in Senda go to the valley now that they know about it?"

Nandin sat back crossing his arms and spitting a seed onto the ground. "Maybe. The majority of people in the camp are from Senda, but it might take some time to convince more to come."

"But why? Don't they know they're not safe in Senda?"

"Why would you say that?"

"Well…I mean, really," she stammered, "they're living underneath an entire community who have threatened to hang them. And they're in the sewers — that can't be healthy."

Nandin shrugged. "I guess, but they've been doing it for decades. Besides, they don't trust Mateo yet."

"And you do?"

"Obviously. Why else would I be here helping him? It would be pretty careless to appoint a Commander who didn't trust you."

Darra wondered, if someone like Nandin trusted Mateo then surely he couldn't be that bad. Thinking of everything she had learned about the Kameil so far was proof enough how stories could get out of control. Maybe Mateo wasn't responsible for the tear that brought her here. Maybe it was the Addicts. Or perhaps the tears occurred all on their own.

She was uncertain how to proceed. Nandin had told her Mateo was making capsules, but she still had no idea how or whether there was any connection between what Mateo did and the tears. The whole thing was putting her on the edge; it was all she could do to stop from pulling out her hair in exasperation. She tensed; unaware the she was clenching and unclenching her fists.

"Darra, you've been through a lot," Nandin said obviously aware of her stress, "why don't you get some rest. We can talk again tomorrow if you want."

"Thanks," she replied, stood and turned to go when a thought struck her. "When do you plan to leave for the valley?" she asked hoping she sounded casual and unconcerned, instead of panicky, which was how she felt.

"I'm waiting for all the Yaru to join us first. It will be a few days before the Draka hunting party returns and there are a few others who haven't come back yet, so probably a week."

Darra nodded and waved as she numbly walked out the door. A week and the place would be teeming with Yaru. She needed to learn more and fast, otherwise how was she ever going to escape?

* * *

Nandin continued working on his report for Mateo, but was having trouble staying focused. He kept thinking back to the conversations he had with Darra. She was unlike anyone he had met. He chuckled as he recalled her inquisitive nature; he found it quite refreshing. Unprepared to accept information at face value, she constantly asked questions. Most people he knew, himself included, tended to accept what they were told. Jon was the only one who had the need to doubt the motives of others.

True the Kameil were not eager to trust anyone, but they shied away from confrontation and remained hidden more often than not. Darra's confidence grew daily. Nandin the Yaru, Mateo's Commander, didn't intimidate her. The majority of the girls he met rarely looked him in the eye, let alone treated him like an equal. He had only known her for a few short days, but already he looked forward to seeing her. The fact that she was a girl, and a pretty one at that, didn't really matter to him. What he did like was being able to share his knowledge and the chance to convince her of the good that Mateo was doing. He was positive he would be able to persuade her to move into the valley rather than continue her original plan of heading to Senda. In fact, he couldn't wait to show it to her. Having spent her whole life in the mountains in a cave with only her family for company, she was in for a shock. Nandin knew she would not regret this life changing experience.

He turned again to the scroll in front of him and sighed. He had to concentrate harder—the sooner he got it done, the sooner he could invite Darra back again.

* * *

It was late in the evening when a group of Yaru joined the camp. Darra had finished her meal and was just heading back to her tent for the night when she saw them enter the command tent. Being careful not to be observed, she snuck around to the back of the tent and pressed her ear up against it.

"Just set them down for now," she heard Nandin say, " Thank you gentlemen, you are excused."

She heard several different voices wish each other goodnight and was disappointed that she had arrived too late when Nandin spoke again.

"I have some news for you, Sim."

"Good news I hope. Mind if get settled?"

"By all means and yes, it's great news in fact. Jon is getting married."

"Sarah?"

"Of course."

"I'm glad his Jagare pride didn't hold him back. What did Mateo think about it?"

"He was in favour, after he had a moment to think on it. He was rather surprised by the news."

"No doubt. I'm sure the thought of Yaru wishing to settle down never crossed his mind. What makes you think he was okay about it?"

"He plans to give them a new suite at the castle as a gift. And he offered to give Sarah liquid Essence."

"He has enough left to cure her?"

"Apparently."

"That surprises me. I thought if he had more, he'd make more Yaru before curing a Kameil."

"Well, you know what Jon's like. I think Mateo's doing it to prove to him once and for all he actually does care about the Kameil."

"Either that or keeping a Yaru happy."

"Gee Sim, that sounded a bit like skepticism. Are you doubting Mateo's motives now?"

"Nah, you know me, I'm just here for the good times."

"Now you sound like Nean."

"Where is Nean anyway? I thought you came back from Senda together?"

"We did. He's out chasing a Draka right now."

"That should make him happy. You didn't want to join the hunt? I know how you love taking part in the kill."

"Funny. Chasing a Draka does sound a bit more exciting than stalking deer though, but—"

"Let me guess, you'd rather stay here and do paperwork."

"Hardly. But I do want to get it done before we break camp. I'd hate to be stuck working on it while every else is celebrating with the newlyweds. And on that note, what have you brought me?"

"Just a bunch of Gelei plants. The caves proved to be a waste of time."

"There were no crystals?"

"None that were useful. Some were clear and the rest were a few centuries short of being the pink gems Mateo needs."

"Too bad. Mark the map for me, would you? My eyes need a break. I think I'm going to go for a walk before I call it a night."

"No problem. I'll probably be sound asleep by the time you get back, it's been a long day."

Darra wasn't sure what she should do. If Nandin chose to go into the woods, there was a good chance he would see her. Moving from her current position would make noise and that could cause him to check it out. She carefully stretched out on the ground so she was as flat as could be. She listened intently. The sound of the tent flap being pushed aside was barely audible as were the sounds of his footsteps, especially over the noise the Yaru, Sim was making as he moved around inside the tent. Thankfully, she managed to discern by the diminishing sound of his footsteps, that Nandin had chosen to walk further into the camp and away from her.

Slowly, she got to her feet and made her way around the tent. When she was sure the coast was clear, she cautiously crept until she felt she was a safe enough distance away from the command tent and would not look suspicious if she was seen. At that point, she confidently strode to her tent and began to settle herself down for the night. As she undressed and got into bed she considered the conversation she had overheard, sifting through the pieces of information.

A Yaru was about to marry a Kameil — interesting, but most likely irrelevant to her cause. The fact that Mateo was treating the Kameil with something called *liquid Essence* was more pertinent. She tried to remember if she had heard the term before, but she had learned so much over the last year that some details had been lost. Using this liquid Essence to cure Kameil or create more Yaru was definitely something Master Juro would want to know about, even if it didn't relate to the tears. The other tidbit she had picked up was that the Yaru were collecting Essence. All in all, it had been a worthwhile conversation to listen in on. She still wasn't sure if it was helpful information. As much as she wished to get out of the camp before the rest of the Yaru arrived, she wanted to hear something that was connected to the tears. Perhaps she just needed a few more excursions to the back of the tent to eavesdrop — of course, she could only do that when it was dark so she decided to risk staying another night or two.

CHAPTER TWENTY-FIVE

Identity Crisis

DARRA WAS BAFFLED.

She paced around the command tent waving her hands in the air as she spoke. "I don't get it. If Mateo is such a great guy then why don't people trust him? Obviously my parents didn't and, from what I heard, most of the Kameil from Senda sure don't seem to. He must have done something to make people suspicious."

Darra had been part of the camp for three days. More and more often she had been slipping from the quiet, grieving Darra persona and into her more questioning, talkative Hanna. Fortunately for her, a similar transformation had been sweeping throughout the entire encampment. After spending their lives cowering in the shadows in fear, the campers finally had a sense of freedom and security. This liberation made for a tentative mirth that grew with confidence everyday. Even Nandin had a more relaxed air about him, or maybe she just thought that because he no longer wore his black ninja suit and opted for more casual apparel.

"In my humble opinion," Nandin explained, "people don't like it when things don't work out the way they want it to. It's easier to blame someone else for your misfortunes than to take responsibility."

"Wow, you're so wise for someone so young."

Nandin chuckled. "Well, it's true. He's considered a hero to anyone he's helped and those he couldn't, stormed away, like it was all his fault. It's not like he created the Kameil. He's just trying to help them, and he's doing it on his own, I might add. There's no Juro around trying to help him out. In fact, they just accuse him of everything that goes wrong. Crystal pockets being attacked? Mateo's fault. Kameil attempting to steal food? Mateo's fault. He just gets all the blame."

Essence being sucked out of the ground killing all the life around — Mateo's fault. So who was right? She could understand that the other races had a predetermined opinion of Mateo, anything to do with the Kameil caused them to close windows and lock doors, but if the Kameil themselves were skeptical of him, there had to be more to it.

"What did you mean about the people he couldn't help? What happened to them?"

"That's obvious, they became Kameil."

Obvious? She shook her head trying to clear it; it felt like she was chasing her tail.

"But you said he didn't make the Kameil."

Nandin leaned against the makeshift table, crossing his arms.

"He didn't, the Three did. Have you heard of them?"

She shook her head.

"They made the first Kameil and when Mateo came along he started looking for a cure — "

"Where did he come from?"

"He was their son." Nandin waited to see if Darra was going to ask another question. She motioned for him to continue. "He started working on a cure, and he needed volunteers to test it out. Sometimes it worked, sometimes not. I was fortunate because he had already created the cure when I came along."

"So you were Kameil before you became a Yaru?"

"Well…no, I was just an ordinary Jivan, but now I'm a Yaru," he added just to make sure she understood.

She stopped pacing and looked at Nandin. "That doesn't make any sense. Why would he give you a cure if you weren't sick?"

He shook his head at Darra's inability to follow along. "He wasn't curing me, he was improving me. The Kameil need the Yaru's help to survive. Surely you understand that the Kameil couldn't wander all over Galenia trying to save each other and defend off beasts, hunt and stuff all on their own."

"No," Darra conceded, "But a Jagare could."

Nandin sighed. "You remind me of my friend Jon. He was stubborn too. Listen, I have abilities no mere Jagare has."

Darra looked skeptical with her raised eyebrows; she wondered if this was the Jon who was about to be wed.

"Don't give me that look. It's true. I'm not bragging. It's just a fact. With hundreds of Kameil to look after, twenty-some Jagare are not going to make a difference, but twenty Yaru sure can."

She wasn't sure if she believed his logic, but she didn't think arguing about it with him would help her cause in any way, so she let it go.

"So you were Jivan and you let Mateo turn you into a Yaru. Right?"

Nandin grinned and nodded.

"How did you find out about this? Did you just decide to go to the valley one day and ask to be part of this great plan?"

Nandin wasn't sure if she was mocking him. "Not exactly. I talked to him first; right here in this camp actually, then I chose to go with him — me and a few others that is. There are those who do just that though...come to the valley I mean."

She was taken aback. "There are? Why would they do that?"

"The Kameil might be the most well-known outcasts, but they're not the only ones. People who've been banished eventually find their way to the valley."

"And then?"

"Then they decide what they want to do, and then do it. Some of them receive the treatment and become Yaru. Back before he had mastered the process, some of them became Kameil. Of course, they knew the risks going in and decided to take the chance, but those Kameil are the ones that tend to leave — they're angry it didn't work." He figured there was no harm in telling Darra any of this as the Kameil that were in the camp all knew it to be true. If Darra spent more time with them than with him they would have told her.

"Those that it worked on became Yaru?"

Nandin patted her on the shoulder. "You got it! In fact, he's made another two Yaru this year from people who just showed up to the valley after being exiled."

She began to pace again. She felt her stomach drop, and hoped Nandin didn't notice her increased anxiety. Over the last few days she had learned that banishment was the catchall punishment for pretty much every crime: thieves, brawlers, murderers. And Nandin just confirmed that these were the prime candidates for becoming Yaru. She didn't have to meet Mateo not to trust him; the company he chose said it all.

* * *

Kazi wished he had something to do. He spent his time at the empty campsite where Hanna, pretending to be Darra, had last snuck in to get food. The rest of his team was hiding in the trees surrounding the Kameil's camp and the Vaktare were an hour to the north. Kazi's job as messenger between the two groups meant he had to sit doing nothing until he received something to report or the emergency signal. At that time, he would have to sprint to the Vaktare. It was possible though, that there would be no signal and Hanna would just casually walk out of the woods and they would all head back to the Citadel together.

He tried to convince Karn to let him get closer to the action, but as he headed through the trees to find him, Tasha let loose an arrow that shot threw his hat and hit the tree behind him. Even he had enough sense to stay still at that moment. When Karn emerged, he pulled the arrow free and marched Kazi back to the campsite. Kazi was crestfallen by the lecture that followed. If Tasha, who was halfway around the clearing, could not only hear him, but

241

see him well enough to send an arrow safely his way, it meant he put the whole operation at risk.

Since then, he had stayed put as ordered. A couple times through the day his teammates would take turns visiting, give him an update of what was happening and share a meal before they left him on his own again. As soon as it started to get dark, he would climb the tree where he had hung a pico wrap. He had plenty of experience climbing at night from travelling with his father over the years, but he didn't want to do it in complete darkness nor did he want to do it while on the run from some sort of predator. He found it strange how unconcerned he had been when the fire was lit and he was accompanied by two Jagare. Alone, he felt vulnerable.

It was midday when he heard them. At first, he didn't know what the noise was, but he had been sitting in the calm and quiet long enough to notice additional sounds. Quickly he took cover in some bushes making sure to take his gear with him; just to be on the safe side. A short time passed before several Yaru on horseback emerged — and he was sure that's what they were due to the black-clad outfits they wore. He froze, barely daring to breath.

"What do you make of this?" he heard one say as he dismounted.

Another Yaru joined the first on the ground, knelt down and examined the ashes from the fire.

"Appears to be a few days old."

"Rather close to our camp. Look for tracks."

The rest of the Yaru hopped off their horses and began searching the area. Kazi had no idea how well he was hidden; every muscle tensed at the thought of being discovered.

It was only moments before one called out. "Over here. They lead further in."

"Are they fresh?"

"Can't really tell, the grounds pretty dry. It could have been made a few days or a few hours ago."

"What are you thinking, Blades?"

"Could be nothing. It's this campsite that has me concerned. Kameil don't stop here for the night when they're this close to base camp and the other races tend to stay clear of these woods. We'll follow the tracks and keep an eye out for anything unusual. Thanlin, you're our best tracker, you lead."

"Will do."

"The rest of you, give Captain Thanlin some room before you follow. I'll bring up the rear."

"Understood, Captain Blades."

"Sure thing Captain."

Kazi counted six Yaru in total as they all echoed their understanding and began making their way further into the trees. His mind raced. Karn, Tasha and Dylan were hidden from casual observers, but now the Yaru were tracking them. He wasn't sure if the tracks that were found were his, the teams or from the Kameil that led Hanna away. He just knew it put everyone at risk. What was more, six Yaru were about to join Hanna's camp and with them looking for *anything unusual* there was no way Kazi could alert Karn without drawing attention to himself. His team was greatly outnumbered. If trouble ensued, there was no way they would be able to get Hanna out.

Kazi waited until all sounds of the Yaru had faded before coming out of hiding. With one quick backward glance, he bolted for the road. An hour to reach the Vaktare was too long; he was determined to make it in less time.

* * *

After their morning discussion, Hanna was relieved when Nandin excused her so he could get some work done. The break in their discussion would allow time for her to calm herself and plan her next round of questions.

Nandin enjoyed their conversations, and invited her to return after lunch. She smiled and claimed she looked forward to it, which wasn't really a lie. She had been enjoying their banter, and if it wasn't for the imminent threat that the campsite would be crawling with homicidal, super-powered maniacs within the next few days, she might have felt relatively at ease.

Nandin's blasé attitude about the origins of the Yaru would have sent her running except that she was fairly certain he hadn't made the maniac-Yaru connection. The fact that he chose to return to the camp to do paperwork over hunting and killing a giant flying lizard said as much.

She needed to try and weed out what else he was conveniently overlooking. The more she learned, the more convinced she was that Mateo was responsible for causing the tears; he was doing enough unnatural experiments to warrant her suspicion. Alone in her tent, she spent the next hour going over possible causes. The thought crossed her mind that the capsules may have something to do with it, so she devised a way to get her hands on one: she was going to ask. Having witnessed Nandin liberally distributing them to the Kameil, she figured it would be reasonable to ask to try one. Mateo wanted all forms of Essence he could get his hands on and she would wager that Nandin was hoping to convince her to give up her little pouch in exchange for the pills. She hoped it wouldn't come to that.

The other possibility she considered had to do with the so-called *liquid Essence*. She had listened in on the conversations for the last two nights, but there had been no new information she had learned. She desperately wanted to know more about the liquid. It seemed the only option was to get Nandin to tell her about it. After she ate, she made her way back to the command tent, hoping she could get him to talk.

With no way to knock on the door, she poked her head around the tent flap.

"Are you decent?" she asked.

Nandin greeted her with his easy-going laugh.

"Come on in, Darra. Care to take a look at this?" He waved to a map laid out in front of him.

She walked over and glanced at the upside down map on the table.

"This here is Senda, where you were heading."

She cocked her head to view the map right side up. Nandin took hold of her arm and led her around to the other side of the table.

"What do these markings here mean?" she asked.

"Those indicate where Essence has been located. It's not much of a help though, as we knew there was Essence there — we still have no idea where it is in the sewers and we don't know our way around to go looking."

She was tempted to hand over her map of the sewers to help him out, but she made Cassey a promise, which she meant to keep. Plus, she didn't know what would happen if Mateo did know how to navigate the sewers and found the Essence or what would happen to the Kameil that lived there.

"Do you think you can locate approximately where your family's cave was?" he asked cautiously, not wishing to be indelicate.

She squinted as she tried to figure out the landmarks. He pointed to a distinctive feature on the map.

"This is the Citadel, if that helps."

Leaning in, she used her fingers to draw the road from Senda up towards the Citadel and veered into the woods. When her finger hovered on the location of the cave, she hesitated. She didn't know if she should show him the cave or not. Neither Karn nor Master Jagare had instructed her on this particular point.

"It's okay," he said softly, "I'm taking you to a new, safer home now. You don't need to protect the cave; you won't ever have to go back there, if you don't want. In fact, I can send someone there to pick up anything you left behind that you wish to keep."

She took his pen and made an 'X' on the map where the cave was before responding.

"It's alright, I brought the things that were important with me."

Subconsciously, she reached up and placed her hand on the pouch tucked under her shirt. His widening eyes and slight nod told her this was the perfect moment to ask.

"Nandin, do you think I could have one of those pills? I just thought maybe — "

Before she even finished her sentence, he opened the box on the table, took out three, grabbed her hand, placed the pills in her palm and closed her fingers around them.

"You can have as many as you wish. Just remember, you'll need to remove your pouch when you take them. You don't want to overdose."

"Take off my pouch?"

"I would be willing to hold onto your pouch for safekeeping. I promise you, I will give it back." He leaned in closer and whispered, "It will be our little secret."

Darra was touched. She doubted very much Mateo would have approved. Perhaps it was just a ploy to remove the gems from her, yet she couldn't help but trust him. Maybe she was naive, but he just didn't seem the type to lie.

She smiled, suddenly at a loss for words.

"So, what would you like to argue about now?" His words were light and cheerful.

"Uh," she choked, "I haven't been arguing. I've been questioning."

"And?" he said raising one eyebrow.

"They're not the same thing!" she argued.

He grinned at her response.

"Fine. I do have another *question* for you."

"Alright, let's hear it."

"How did he do it? I mean make you a Yaru. Was it a pill like these?"

Nandin sat down in his chair and rubbed his chin, his eyes staring off into space.

"No, not as simple as that." He paused a moment then explained, "He used a different type of Essence. It's all a little fuzzy."

She waited patiently while he gathered his thoughts.

"I don't know that I really understand. He...put it in me somehow. I remember it hurt."

"Like with a needle or something?"

A confused look came over Nandin's face, his eyes shifting to focus on her. *Uh-oh, what did I say now?*

At that moment, sunlight burst through the door as the flap was pulled back and two men entered.

"Oh, excuse us, Commander. Didn't realize you had company."

Nandin stood, gesturing for the men to come in. As the hulking figures entered, Darra's attention was drawn to the swords dangling from their belts.

"I'm glad you're here, there's someone I want to introduce you to. Darra, I'd like you to meet two of my fellow Yaru. This is Thanlin and this here is Mayon — we all call him Blades."

The Yaru dipped their heads in greeting and she returned their partial smiles with a tentative one of her own—until her eyes locked with Blades. She froze as she recognized the Yaru she had seen on her way to the Citadel. A thousand thoughts raced through her head; none of them registered other than the one that screamed, *RUN!*

She stuffed the pills that were still in her hand into her ever-present bag, slung it over her shoulder and turned to Nandin.

"I'll leave you to catch up with your friends. Perhaps I could go get a pot of tea?"

"Thanks Darra, that would be great," Nandin said, oblivious to the mounting tension.

"I could sure use some," Thanlin mumbled as he walked to a cot where he began kicking off his boots.

Blades turned to Nandin. "Surely she doesn't have to leave on our account."

"Tea sounds good, Blades," Thanlin protested not the least bit concerned if the girl stayed or left.

Darra nodded and made her way to the door, resisting the urge to bolt. As she passed Blades, he turned, watching her as she went. Just before she reached the door he snatched out and grabbed her wrist.

"Stay. I insist," he commanded tightening his grip as she made an attempt to pull away.

"*Ow*, you're hurting me!" she cried.

Nandin stepped forward. "Blades, what — "

"It's her! This is the girl that was with Biatach."

Pain mounting, her only thought was of escape. Her self-defence skills kicked in. Without hesitation she stomped on Blade's foot and then sent a sideways kick to his shin. Heat coursed through her arm as his grip tightened. That was until her knee met his groin. He cried out in pain, releasing her wrist, doubled over and shaking his hand that had held her. The skin was red and parts of the flesh had melted away.

Nandin didn't have time to react in the thirty seconds it took Darra to free herself from Blades. As the regrettable truth sunk in, she had already run out the door casting one last glance back at Nandin. Seeing the shock and look of betrayal on his face, she wished she hadn't.

CHAPTER TWENTY-SIX

Duplicity Disposed

HANNA BOLTED.

As she darted through the clearing, she shed all traces of Darra. The place was more crowded than she had last seen. Assuming that there were more Yaru that came back with Thanlin and Blades, she feared that getting out of the camp would be impossible — how could she ever outrun a Yaru?

She ducked between two tents and headed straight for the trees. It was the opposite direction from where she had first entered the camp and from the road to the Citadel, but she knew she couldn't make it through the group of Kameil that surrounded that route. Shouts of alarm went out to stop her and she thought she heard a bird call.

A Yaru jumped out from behind one of the tents and tried to block her path. Thanks to the months of training, she instinctively grabbed the man's wrist as he reached for her, pulled him closer causing him to stumble and allowing her the precious extra time to escape. Moments later, another Yaru darted out from ahead and ran towards her. Just before they collided, Hanna bent like a football player and shouldered him in the stomach, flipping him over her back as she went. It was fortunate that they kept underestimating her.

She thought she was free, but the fallen Yaru reached out and snatched hold of her ankle causing her to fall forward.

"Hold her!" hollered Blades as he bore down on her. Frantically she tried to break free, kicking at the Yaru without success. She twisted around so she could try pushing away using Essence, but as she raised her hands Blades pounced on her. He grabbed her by the hair and painfully dragged her to her feet. She screamed, trying to claw free and was rewarded by a fist to the face.

"Blades, what are you doing!" Nandin yelled as he caught up.

Before Blades could answer, he released her as he collapsed, clutching his shoulder and howling in pain from the gash left by an arrow that had grazed it. If he hadn't turned at the last second to answer Nandin, it would have gone through his arm.

Nandin, and the other Yaru, dove behind a tent as arrow after arrow sailed through the air.

"I've got to grab Darra," Nandin yelled, "give me some cover."

The Yaru pulled out several metal throwing pieces and flung them in rapid succession towards their assailant who was hidden somewhere in the trees. As the *thunk, thunk, thunk* of the metal dug into the tree, Nandin quickly pulled Darra back before she regained her feet. Blades dragged himself to safety.

Shouts deeper in the trees alerted them to the approach of others.

"Yaru, to me!" Nandin cried out as he made his way further into the clearing, one arm wrapped around a struggling Hanna. "The camp is under attack! You two," he said to the closest Yaru, "gather the Kameil in the centre of the clearing. The rest of you spread out around them."

Before they could carry out his orders, Jagare on horses came crashing into the clearing. Nandin barely had time to notice that they were not dressed like typical hunters. They wore heavy, steel-studded leather, metal helmets and carried round, wooden shields. He released Hanna and pulled out his sword that he had strapped on before pursuing Darra.

"Vaktare," shouted the Jagare that first entered the clearing, "Kill them all, save the Seer!

"No!" Hanna screamed.

Blades backhanded her, knocking her to the ground. "Stay down if you know what's good for you," he snapped. He pulled out a knife and threw it at a charging Vaktare. His aim was perfect. The Jagare clutched at the knife that was now embedded in his throat as he fell from his horse.

"Blades!" Nandin shouted above the noise of clashing metal, the trampling of feet, hooves and battle cries, "disarm them, don't kill them."

Blades pulled out his sword and eagerly sought out a new foe, despite his injured arm.

Hanna watched as Nandin easily dismounted a Vaktare and knocked him across the head with the flat of his blade. Before the man had collapsed to the ground, Nandin had swung up onto the horse and headed towards another Vaktare.

253

The Kameil were panicking, screaming and running in all directions in spite of the efforts the appointed Yaru made to round them up. The Vaktare quickly fanned out to attack from all sides and everyone was a target. Hanna watched helplessly as an unarmed Kameil was killed. When another rider charged towards Cassey, Hanna leapt to her feet and began gathering Essence. Before she could release it to knock the Vaktare down, someone grabbed her and pulled her up onto a horse.

"No!" she cried as she saw Cassey fall to the ground.

"Momma! Momma!"

"Oh my god! Oh my god!" Hanna watched in horror as Cassey's daughter ran towards her fallen mother and was trampled by the horseman.

"It's okay Hanna. I've got you," Karn said as he turned the horse away from the fighting.

"No Karn, go back! We have to stop them!"

"The Vaktare will stop them."

"We have to stop the Vaktare, they're killing everyone! Go back!"

She fought to get off the horse, but Karn held tight. Hanna twisted to see what was happening. More horses were without riders, and the Yaru were forming a protective wall around the remaining Kameil. The Yaru's numbers had increased in the last few minutes as those hunting the Draka stampeded into the fray—the Vaktare were now out numbered. A Vaktare saw Hanna just before she disappeared into the woods and hollered for the others to retreat. Their numbers were dwindling, the Seer was safe, it was time to get out of there.

* * *

Once the clearing was free of Vaktare, Nandin ordered for the Yaru and Kameil to start breaking camp, dismounted his horse and strode towards the command tent along with the other captains.

"Shall we begin pursuit?" Blades asked.

"No," Nandin replied. "I want the Yaru to get the Kameil safely back to the valley."

Barely containing his rage, Blades growled, "Why would we do that Commander? You know Mateo wants that girl. And now we know she's not just a Seer. Look what she did to my hand."

"We don't know if there are any more of those Vaktare out there," Nean said attempting to support Nandin who was busy packing his bag. Sim and Plyral started collapsing the beds, but were intently listening to every word.

"So? We'll kill them. We can't let her get away." Blades protested. Thanlin, arms crossed, nodded in agreement.

"Yes, you can," Nandin said. "I'm not about to risk the Yaru and all the other Kameil in this camp. Load the dead into a wagon and get the rest out of here as soon as possible."

"But — "

Nandin finished with his bag and then began stripping off his clothes.

"Uh, Commander?" Nean questioned as Nandin's clothes hit the floor. Something about their Commander standing with nothing but his underclothes on while enemies were so close by was not overly reassuring.

Once Nandin pulled on his black pants and slipped his tunic over his head, he said with determination, "You five have to make sure everyone gets back to the valley safely. I'm going after the Seer."

* * *

As they escaped through the woods, dodging trees and crashing through the bramble, Hanna desperately tried to get in sync with the horse's movements. It proved rather difficult as she was squashed in the saddle in front of Karn. With the Vaktare in full retreat, she was now more concerned with the lives of her friends than the safety of the Kameil, but she could hardly think straight. Every time the horse's hooves clomped down on the ground, a painful vibration rushed through her body and into her head. She could feel her face swelling where Blades had hit her and she was having trouble keeping one of her eyes open.

When they reached the road, she was given a horse of her own. They only stopped long enough to give her time to remount and then were off again. Now, with more space to move and a relatively smooth path of the dirt road, they were able to send the horses into a gallop. Once they put some distance between themselves and the Yaru, they slowed the horses back down to a trot. The hooves hit the ground in rhythm with the pounding in her head.

She replayed the events in her mind, desperately trying to figure out how things could have gone differently, but it was all in vain; it had happened and there was nothing she could do about it now. It had been a disaster and now Cassey and her little girl were dead. She had been so focused on getting information about the tears, that she carelessly stayed too long. Nandin even told her more Yaru were coming. It had slipped her mind that she had seen a Yaru before. The moment she saw Blades, her error had been so clear, and now, guilt plagued her.

They finally stopped to rest the horses and address the wounds of the injured. Once she slid off her horse, she discovered she could barely stand; between the physical and emotional stress of the last hour, she was utterly spent. Karn materialized beside her as she stumbled and he helped her over to a tree to lean against. She slid to the ground as he fumbled with his pack. As knelt down beside her, he poured water onto a clean cloth and pressed it to her head.

"The cut isn't as bad as it looks," he said. She didn't even know she had been bleeding. "I'm not sure there is much we can do about the swelling at this point. You're probably going to have a black-eye."

Kazi ran over to them followed by Tasha and Dylan.

"Are you okay, Hanna?" Kazi asked.

"No," Hanna replied, "I am *so* far from okay. It went wrong, just incredibly wrong."

"You did very well," Tasha said, "not many people can claim to take on two Yaru and survive to tell the tale."

"You took on two Yaru?!" Kazi said incredulously.

Hanna shook her head. "Not really. I only got past one, but I didn't get away from the second. And thanks to whoever it was for shooting the arrows, I'm sure Blades would have given me a few more bruises if you hadn't."

"You're welcome," Tasha replied, "but you're being modest. I saw you knock down two Yaru. My arrows were only a distraction after you did that. I doubt I could have taken out two Yaru without a weapon."

Kazi grinned. "You tackled two Yaru, without a weapon even? You're...you're amazing!"

"Oh yeah, I rock."

"You're a rock?"

"Never mind."

* * *

The return trip to the Citadel was frantic with few rest stops and, therefore, they made better time than the trip to the woods. There had been no sign of the Yaru pursuing them, but they kept a brisk pace just to be on the safe side. Half of the Vaktare guarded the campsites when they slept and even then, the others tossed and turned. They would not rest easy until the Seer was back behind the castle walls.

The weary travellers arrived at the Citadel in the evening on the second day. Hanna longed to collapse on her lovely bed, but she was ushered to Master Jagare's meeting room. She was hardly surprised to discover Master Jagare and the Tahtay were waiting for them; the road leading to the castle was clearly visible from the watchtower and their arrival was highly anticipated. The presence of Master Juro and Tahtay Biatach did catch her off guard. She was glad when Kazi brashly inquired as to what they were doing there.

"When word reached us that you had left on your mission, we left Kokoroe immediately. As it so happens, we only arrived this afternoon." Master Juro explained seemingly unaffected by Kazi's rudeness. Both Karn and Biatach's stern expressions showed they felt otherwise.

Hanna sat down heavily. "How serendipitous. I guess you are eager to hear what I've learned." Her tone was less than enthusiastic.

Master Jagare nodded. "That we are, but first, I would like to hear Karn's report. Judging by the injuries and the missing Vaktare upon your arrival, I'm sure we can assume you found trouble."

It took Karn half an hour to discuss his view of the mission. Hanna was taken aback when she heard how Kazi had hidden from the Yaru and then ran to alert the Vaktare. She knew that they had been hiding over an hour away, but she hadn't thought about how they had arrived so quickly or how Karn rode in on a horse. He explained how he had waited for the Yaru to enter the camp before he left his lookout spot and returned to where Kazi was suppose to be waiting. When there was no Kazi, he was concerned, but then he heard the sound of running horses in the distance. He went to the road and saw the Vaktare approaching and Kazi was among them.

He left Kazi to wait by the road with the spare horses; one for each member of his team. Karn joined the Vaktare on the charge of the Yaru's clearing where he sought out Hanna, grabbed her and escaped. She realized, she had yet to thank him for his heroism; she had been too distraught over the bloodshed around her at the time. As he explained the scene, she felt the need to interrupt.

Duplicity Disposed

"Why did the Vaktare attack the Kameil? They were harmless. They didn't even have weapons."

The leader of the Vaktare who had issued the order currently stood at the back of the room and now stepped forward to respond.

"We had no way of knowing who the Yaru were at the time. Everyone posed a threat."

"The women and children were a threat?"

"That's enough, Hanna," Master Jagare ordered. "Karn, please continue."

Hanna barely had the patience to listen to the rest of Karn's account. No one seemed to be bothered by the massacre of the Kameil except her. She couldn't understand how they could be so cold. How could they kill little kids and not be bothered by it? Her indignation must have been written on her face as Tasha reached under the table to place a hand on her knee. When Hanna looked at her, Tasha gave her a knowing nod and mouthed the words 'not now'. She knew that Hanna was on the verge of speaking out again. But Tasha was right — this was hardly the time or place for a debate on the unfair treatment of the Kameil.

When it finally came to her turn to debrief, she was not very forthcoming. The others had to keep asking questions to get the information from her. It wasn't that she was trying to be difficult; she was just overwhelmed and was no longer able to think straight. Unfortunately, because of her inability to articulate, the meeting dragged on.

It was late by the time they were finally dismissed. She had managed to reveal most of what she learnt. Mateo

260

was making liquid Essence and was collecting Essence in various forms. He had made Essence pills, which the Kameil could take and they would appear healthy. He was also on the verge of creating a cure for the Kameil.

She entered her quarters, relieved to be alone. The lanterns were lit and a hot bath had been prepared, but the water was only lukewarm by the time she arrived. Regardless, she stripped off her travel-worn clothes and sunk in the tub; it had been some time since she had felt clean.

Although there was no trace of grime on her after the bath, she still felt dirty. Wrapped in her robe, she opened the shutters to her room to get some fresh air; she felt like she was suffocating. She leaned out and stared at the woods beyond. Again she saw the look of betrayal on Nandin's face. She felt forever stained.

CHAPTER TWENTY-SEVEN

Seizing Shadows

NANDIN SMILED SMUGLY.

The confrontation with the Vaktare had given Darra a sufficient head start, but he had been fairly certain what her destination would be. On a hunch, he took a shortcut through the forest to the Citadel that he was sure only the Yaru knew. Sitting in a tree at the base of the cliff observing the castle, he spied her leaning out a window.

The window in question was high up, at least twelve storeys, which made it difficult to see details; nevertheless, the room was one of the few that was lit up and outlined her clearly. From his days at the Citadel, a lifetime ago, he knew students did not reside on any of the upper floors. This fact, coupled with the girl's slight stature, and long hair convinced him it could only be Darra.

Now that he knew where she was, he just had to figure out how to get there. Going through the main gate was not an option, and neither was the back gate, as both required someone from the inside to open them, not to mention the guards on duty. Once again he came to the conclusion he would need to climb the wall. Somewhat of a daunting task, he figured he could climb from one windowsill to the next, resting on the ledge if required. The trick was not to be seen by someone inside.

Of course, reaching her room would only be half the battle — once he was there he would need to then lower her down the wall with a rope. If she resisted, and he figured that she would, it would be even more challenging to leave unobserved. The deeper into the night it was, the greater chance of their escape. He decided to wait until the majority of the occupants would be asleep before he started his ascent.

After counting the windows to confirm which one he needed to reach, he found a rather safe, if not altogether comfortable, place to rest for the next few hours.

* * *

Halfway up the wall, Nandin's arms started to shake. As luck would have it, a strong wind had picked up and was making the climb more difficult and dangerous than he had anticipated. Too obsessed with reaching his goal, he didn't even consider postponing his climb for more favourable conditions.

Pulling himself up, he peeked above the sill to ensure the shutters were closed before sitting on the window ledge. He thought about resting there for a bit to see if the wind would calm down, but being battered against the rough stone wall as he sat cost him energy too. He would just have to continue on. After a short stop, he began climbing once again. Each time he placed a foot or hand he paused to make sure he had a firm hold and a momentary break in the wind before moving up.

By the time he'd finally reached the desired window, he was exhausted. The shutters were closed so he risked an extended break, sitting on the ledge to give himself a chance to catch his breath and attempt to relax his stiffened muscles. When he was ready to enter the room, he removed a knife from his belt, slid it between the shutters and carefully lifted the latch. It stuck a little at first. When it popped up it made a barely audible clicking sound.

He waited. There was no sound from within. Gently he pushed one of the shutters open just enough for him to slide into the room. Heavy curtains had been pulled across the window. Careful to disturb the curtains as little as possible, he closed the shutter and latched it again to prevent the wind from blowing them open.

Again he stopped, waiting for any sound of alarm. When none came, he parted the curtains a crack to look into the room. A small table and chairs sat just to the left of where he stood. In the darkness of the space, the only other shape he could make out was a large, four-poster bed across the room with closed curtains shielding it. He stepped out of the drapes, being mindful of the furniture, and glided towards the bed like a shadow. As he pulled back the curtains near the foot of the bed, he could discern a lump under the duvet and the outline of a head protruding out the top. He knew the first thing he had to do was ensure she didn't scream and alert anyone. In one hand he still had the knife. With the other he reached out to cover her mouth.

* * *

Hanna couldn't sleep. She was exhausted, sore and weary, but no matter how hard she tried she just couldn't drift off. Attempts to block out all the darkness in her mind with thoughts of beaches or star-lit skies were completely ineffectual. People she was trying not to think about intruded upon her peaceful images. It would start innocently enough with Kazi's friendly smile and morph into Karn laughing, then Biatach shouting for her to do laps. And that meant running. Running led to the woods, the clearing and into Nandin's tent where she was greeted with anger.

She tried to think of numbers. Math always put her to sleep. Searching for something to add, she counted the number of tents in the clearing and how many people could sleep in each one. This in turn had her thinking of the number of Kameil that lived in the sewers and how long it would take to hang them all if they used five nooses at a time.

Lying on her back, she stared at the canopy of her bed, resisting the temptation to get up and go get something to eat from the kitchen many floors below. As she contemplated whether she should leave her warm cozy bed for the cold dark hallways, she heard a click. At first she thought it was the wind, rapping at her window as it was whistling and rattling the shutters. She waited. The rattling eased up a little, she thought perhaps the wind was dying down. Moments later they rattled again. *Odd*. And then, there was something else. The curtains momentary billowed and a cool breeze touched her face, then everything was still. She had the distinct feeling she was no longer alone.

265

It was a ridiculous thought, how could anyone come through her window? Her room was, of course, way too high up. Even the Yaru would be hard-pressed to scale the castles walls. But her gut told her differently. Confirming her suspicions, she watched as her drapes moved aside. She made a conscious effort to keep her breathing calm, practicing one of the many techniques she had learned at Kokoroe. As the dark shape of a man leaned towards her, she could also make out the shape of a blade.

Waiting for her would-be attacker to get within reach, Hanna prepared her own attack. As the figure reached out his hand, lowering it toward her, she swatted it with her right arm, knocking it aside. With her left she struck out. Using her hand like the edge of a knife, she whacked her attacker hard, right behind his ear. He collapsed in a heap on top of her.

CHAPTER TWENTY-EIGHT

Cell Out

THE ROOM SPUN.

As Nandin regained consciousness his head lulled from side to side. Groaning, he finally managed to lift it. He blinked several times trying to adjust his eyes to the now-lit room. When he saw her sitting in a chair in front of him, wrapped in her robe, arms and legs crossed and his black mask in her hands, he smirked.

"Hello Darra, or should I call you the Seer?"

"It's Hanna, preferably."

Looking down he discovered he was now securely tied to a chair with his own rope. He chortled. "Is this really necessary?"

"I should think so," she replied curtly, "you were about to attack me with a knife."

He looked wounded. "I would never!"

Hanna reached down to the small table beside her and held up his knife to make her point.

"That was just to convince you to be quiet. I wasn't planning on using it," he said in his defence and then added sharply, "not like I was shooting arrows at you."

Hanna would have pointed out that it was Tasha and not her that had sent the arrows, but her pretence of anger gave way to concern.

"You didn't get hit, did you?"

He grunted. "I'd hardly be able to climb the wall if I just had an arrow tear through me. I might be good, but that's pushing it."

She sat back, relieved.

"So," he sighed, "can you untie me please? I promise to behave. I mean, where am I going to go? No way I could get back down the wall before you called for help. You'd have twenty Jagare waiting at the bottom to greet me."

"Sorry, I'm not taking any chances. What are you doing here Nandin?"

"Saving you, of course."

"Saving me?" she chortled, "Why would I need saving?"

"You're not one of them. It's only a matter of time before — "

The door burst open and Master Juro entered followed by a handful of Jagare.

"What's going on?" Hanna asked.

Master Juro said, "I heard a commotion, a great deal of thumping around."

"Oh, that was me dragging Nandin off the bed and then trying to get him in the chair."

"Well, I sent Tahtay Biatach to alert the castle guards." He motioned to the Jagare and commanded, "Take him to the dungeons."

"He didn't really attack me," she rushed to explain, "we're just talking. Wait!" she yelled as one of the guards pulled back and punched Nandin in the head causing his chair to rock, and his head to fall back. He went unconscious again.

They untied him from the chair and then bound his hands and feet together. Two guards grabbed him from under his arms and dragged him from the room.

"What are they going to do to him?" she asked Master Juro and Biatach as they all left the room.

"It is not your concern. Go back to bed," Biatach said sternly.

"No, I'll come."

Master Juro cast her a steely glare, an expression she had never seen on him and it made her recoil.

"The Yaru needs to answer our questions. You need to get some rest."

"Of...of course," she said crossing the room and crawling back into her bed, "After all, I am extremely tired."

Master Juro relaxed a little.

"You have been through much. Rest will do you some good."

He extinguished the lamp she had lit when Nandin was unconscious sending her into darkness as he closed the door. She lay still and waited. When she felt they were truly gone, she slipped back out of bed and grabbed the clothes she had thrown in a heap on the floor. It was more than curiosity that got her out of bed. She believed Nandin was a decent person; he was truly trying to help people. She saw how he refused to kill any of the Vaktare in the camp. Maybe they were just going to talk to him, but if they did something more she would never be able to live with herself if she just rolled over and let it happen. Once she was dressed, she carefully opened her door to make sure the hallway was clear.

* * *

There was no way she would be able to find the dungeons on her own, so she needed someone who could. She made her way down to the student's quarters in search of Kazi. Her biggest challenge, as she wound her way between the beds, was to get him out of the dormitory without waking up anyone else. Fortunately, her time at the Citadel had included many stops in the room so even in the dark she was able to find him without issue.

She knelt beside him, placed a hand over his mouth and whispered his name in his ear. His eyes flew open and he began to speak when he saw her, but she shushed him.

"I need your help. Come with me."

She grabbed him by the hand and pulled him out of bed. Between his sleepiness and usual clumsiness, she was particularly careful to ensure he didn't run into anything as she led him from the room. Once in the hall, he stretched and rubbed his eyes.

"Where we going?" he asked.

"Do you know where the dungeons are?"

He smiled. "Of course."

"Good. Can you take me there?"

"Sure, it's this way." He took his first right and began leading her through the castle. "What's with the midnight tour?"

"They took Nandin there."

"Really? How did they manage to catch him? I thought they weren't pursuing any of the Yaru."

"They weren't. I caught him. He climb the outside wall and came into my room."

"No way! That's incredible! He actually climbed the walls? And you really captured a Yaru on your own?"

"Perhaps we can talk about this later, I'd prefer not to wake up the whole castle."

"Oh, right."

He led her quietly the rest of the way down to the lower levels. They didn't encounter anyone on the way.

"Where is everyone?" Hanna whispered.

"In bed, I'd guess. No one's ever down here."

"But they brought Nandin."

"I'm guessing that means they're all with him."

They descended down the last staircase. The air was musty and smelt of old straw mixed with a hint of rodents. She wondered if there were rats on Galenia. When they finally came to a closed door at the end of a dark hallway Kazi, proudly, and loudly, announced, "Here we are, so what's the plan?"

Hanna rolled her eyes as she heard footsteps approach.

"Thanks for making our presence known."

The door creaked open letting light into the corridor.

"Sorry miss, I don't think you're allowed in here," the Jagare who opened the door said.

"Yes I am," she said and she motioned to Kazi to help her push the door open.

The unexpected move caused the Jagare to stumbled back. Hanna quickly closed the door behind her to prevent anyone from shoving her back out. Master Jagare, Master Juro, Biatach, the Jagare who opened the door and two Vaktare turned to look at her. Her face went pale as she saw Nandin strapped to a chair in a cell with another Vaktare who had clearly been beating him.

"This is your idea of questioning him?!" she hollered.

"Hanna," Biatach said sternly, "you shouldn't be here. Go back to your room. Kazi you too."

Hanna ran to the cell and grabbed onto the bars.

"He wouldn't be here if it wasn't for me! I can't believe your doing this! What do you think he'll tell you?"

"It is imperative that we find out what is causing the tears. This Yaru knows and is not cooperating," Master Jagare said.

"Let me talk to him, please!" she pleaded. The others in the room were at a loss for words. It was highly unusual for students to speak so boldly to any of the Masters, but to be pleading for a prisoner was unheard of. When they didn't appear to be moved by her request, she tried another approach.

"Can't I at least try? What have you got to lose?"

It was Biatach who finally relented. "She'll just keep at it if we don't let her have her moment."

Master Jagare suppressed annoyance as he indicated to one of the Vaktare to open the cell.

"Erac, stay in there with them."

Hanna entered the cell. Before the door was shut she reached out and used Erac's Essence to fling him through the door, then slammed the door shut.

"Open that door!" Master Jagare ordered, not the least bit amused.

Erac got to his feet and pulled at the door.

"I can't! It's stuck."

Another Vaktare joined Erac, but the door wasn't budging.

"Hanna is keeping it shut," Master Juro stated. "The hour is late for this sort of nonsense. Let us resume our questioning in the morning. Come Hanna, we will all get some rest."

"I'm not going anywhere. I'll just settle down here for the night, thank you very much."

"With the Yaru?" Erac asked incredulously.

"Yes. With Nandin."

"Don't be absurd, Hanna." Biatach scolded. This was no way for his student to behave; he'd had about enough. "Many Vaktare died to rescue you from the Yaru. I'm not about to let you risk your life by sleeping alone in a cell with one."

"Oh, I doubt I'll be alone. I'm sure you'll leave Erac and another Vaktare or two to keep us company. Besides, why would he bother hurting me? I seem to be the only one interested in keeping him in one piece." She turned to Nandin. "You'll behave, won't you?"

He tried to smiled, but his lip was puffing up and caused more of a grimace. "I'll be a perfect gentleman."

They watched as she undid Nandin's restraints and then, she flopped herself down on one of the three cots and kicked up her feet — it was clear she wasn't going anywhere.

"Kazi, would you mind getting some ice?"

Kazi slipped out of the room while the Masters and Biatach quietly consulted in the far corner of the room. After a few minutes, Master Jagare turned to the Vaktare.

"You three stay here. If that Yaru so much as twitches the wrong way I want you to get in there."

Hanna smirked at the threat, *as if they could.*

CHAPTER TWENTY-NINE

Captive Audience

MASTER JURO APPROACHED.

Everyone but the three Vaktare, left the room. Hanna stood up and joined Master Juro at the iron bars, somewhat concerned and embarrassed by her brash behaviour; she didn't know what had come over her. Master Juro was looking intently at Nandin.

"Hanna, is he typical for a Yaru?" he asked calmly.

"You mean the Essence?"

He nodded.

"For the most part, yes," she said. "but it does seem more, I don't know…active I guess."

Nandin approached Hanna and whispered, "You can see my Essence?"

She nodded, but didn't turn to look at him; instead she continued facing Master Juro.

"He's running hot," Master Juro said. "Do you know what you've sacrificed to become Yaru?"

"I gave up my home, my family. I've become an outcast."

"That…and more."

Hanna rolled her eyes. Master Juro seemed to thrive on being obscure. Nandin just crossed his arms, waiting for an explanation.

"You are dying."

"What?" she choked.

Nandin's face fell. "I'm…I'm what?"

"There is no need to panic. You are not dying right this second. I suppose, in a manner of speaking, we are all dying, slowly, but surely. In your case, it is just happening faster."

"That isn't very reassuring," Hanna complained. "Could you expand on that?"

"Essence, in a way, is like food. It is fuel for your body. Imagine a big log on fire. Slowly the fire consumes the log, at which point the flame goes out. Now if you add oil to the flame it burns hotter and therefore, consumes the log quicker. The Essence running through Nandin's veins is not natural. He is burning hotter and will burn out sooner. I would guess his life span has been cut in half."

Nandin was stunned. He suddenly couldn't remember what he was doing there.

"Can something be done?" she asked.

"Ask Mateo. He is the only one who is foolish enough to tamper with Essence like this." He stared at Nandin a bit longer. Hanna was sure there was more he wished to say, but he finally turned and walked away. When he had reached the door he paused and said, "I hope tomorrow our discussion will go smoother Nandin — for your sake."

Hanna was relieved, and a little surprised, that Master Juro didn't have sharp words for her; she was certain Tahtay Biatach would. The three Jagare watched them from a table on the other side of the room as Nandin placed a hand on her shoulder.

"So Hanna, what are you doing here?"

She cocked her head and with a sly smile said, "Saving you, of course."

He laughed, ending in a cough. "Thanks for that, but why did you save me?"

"Why did you order your men not to kill anyone?"

"Because it's not my mission to kill people."

"What is your mission?"

"I told you in the clearing. I'm trying to save people. Initially, I'm out to help the Kameil, because they need it the most."

Hanna nodded as she used her sleeve to wipe away the blood that was running down his face from a cut above his eye. "And that's why I saved you. You're not killing people. Besides, it was the right thing to do. What do they hope to accomplish by beating you to a bloody pulp?"

Before he could answer, Kazi returned with a chunk of ice wrapped in a cloth.

"Where did everyone go?" he asked with a yawn as he handed the cloth to Hanna.

"Bed," she replied, "and you should go back to bed too."

"What about you?"

"I'm guarding Nandin."

"Guarding him so he doesn't get away or guarding him as in protecting him?"

"Take your pick. Thanks for the ice."

"You sure you don't want me to stay with you?" he asked with another yawn.

"I'll be fine. No offence, but I'm not sure what you would offer that the three Vaktare can't."

"An uplifting limerick?"

She motioned for him to lean closer. "Thanks, Kazi. I think one martyr today will do."

"Alright. I hope you manage to get some sleep."

"Me too."

She returned to Nandin who had stumbled over to one of the cots.

She knelt down and held the ice onto his face.

"Looks like we're going to have matching bruises." She carefully wiped the blood that continued to drip.

"I am sorry about that. Blades should never have hurt you."

"I guess I made him mad. I bet his hand hurt."

"How *did* you do that?"

"I focused all my Essence into his hand, which seemed to cause him something like a chemical burn — I didn't know that would happen. I was just reacting."

"And you used Essence on Erac."

"Yes."

"But how? You're not a Juro and you're strong like a Jagare…did they give you something?"

"You mean like liquid Essence?"

"How did you know?"

"I overheard you talking. That's why I came as Darra. I was gathering information. But to answer your question, no they didn't give me something. I'm not from here. I came through a tear."

"Aside from how I became a Yaru, that's what they kept asking me about, in-between punches that is. They wanted to know how Mateo was causing the tears."

"What did you say?"

"Nothing."

"Hence the punching," she said shaking her head.

"Doesn't matter. I've no idea what they were talking about, I've never heard of these tears."

Hanna pulled up the chair from the middle of the room so she could sit closer to him. They kept their voices hushed. Neither of them were sure they wanted the others to hear their conversation. Hanna's trust in her own companions, and that of the Vaktare, had been called into question as of late.

"So you really don't know anything about the tears?"

"No. What are they?"

"No one really knows. I came from a different world. I was running through the woods back home and the next thing I knew, I was on Galenia and I can't get back. It's like I went through a portal. We've checked out a few tear sights — they stand out because, unlike anything else on Galenia, they are devoid of Essence, which means everything in the area is dead or dying. Master Juro is really worried about it. Whatever is causing the tears is destroying the planet."

"And they think Mateo has something to do with them?"

"Apparently they've ruled out everything else and, from what I understand, Mateo is the only one who messes around with Essence. I mean, he made the Yaru and now this liquid Essence stuff. It makes sense there would be a connection. But we don't know, so again, that's why I went to your camp."

"It's like I said before, they blame Mateo for everything. Now he's making these tears — some kind of portals to another world? I think I'd know if he was doing that."

"So does everyone else. But maybe he doesn't know he's doing it or if he does, he hasn't told anyone."

Nandin sighed as he rubbed his arms that were sore from being tied up and from his climb. He tried to get comfortable on the cot, which was little more than a bunch of straw thrown on a wooden frame.

"No offence or anything, but it sounds a little far-fetched. You came from another world? I just don't believe it."

Hanna shrugged and started to yawn. "You don't have to, Nandin. But there is one thing you can believe."

"What's that?"

"It's not my mission to kill or hurt anyone either. I'm just trying to figure out what's going on and hopefully, one day, find a way home. For now though, I'd be happy just to get some sleep."

As she stood up to go to the other bed, he reached out to grab her hand. One of the Vaktare lurched to his feet at the sudden movement. Hanna paid the Vaktare no attention.

"Thank you Hanna, even if they resume their beatings tomorrow, I'm glad you stopped them today."

She squeezed his hand then lay down on her own cot. She wasn't sure how, but she would make sure they didn't start hurting him again. It just wasn't right.

CHAPTER THIRTY

Divergent Delegation

THEY HAD A RESTLESS NIGHT.

The guards had tossed them thin blankets after making a final attempt to convince Hanna to return to the comfort of her room. She conceded, with the stipulation that Nandin be allowed to accompany her. They denied her request. After that, they accepted she would be staying in the cell for the night. The beds were hard, the blankets insufficient and the current circumstances all made it difficult to get much sleep.

Tahtay Biatach returned in the morning accompanied by another three Vaktare. He relieved the night watch as he entered the room.

"Okay you two. It's time to resume our questioning."

"Is this really necessary?" Hanna asked. "You could beat him all day, but if he doesn't know anything — "

"We won't be doing that today. We are going to the meeting room to have a more...civilized discussion."

"Oh, good. Let's go then."

"Wait," he said holding the cell door closed, "tie up the Yaru first."

"Gee Nandin, the Yaru must be pretty impressive if you have to be tied up while being escorted by three Vaktare and a Tahtay."

Nandin held out his hands for her to bind.

"Well if that's impressive, imagine how honoured I must feel being in the presence of someone who protected me from those Vaktare and Tahtay."

She grinned mischievously. "If they really wanted in this cell last night they could have gotten in and Master Juro knows it. My hold on the door was temporary, but I was making a statement. I was hoping it would help them see reason."

They marched through the castle with Nandin surrounded by Vaktare and followed by Biatach and Hanna. Biatach explained it was easier to keep an eye on him if he walked behind Nandin. When they entered the meeting room, Nandin was ushered to a chair at the end of the large table, seated and tied in place. Again, Hanna was left to wonder at the necessity of the precautions they were taking. She thought that maybe it had less to do with ensuring he didn't get away and more to do with reminding him that he was not welcome.

She took a seat kitty-corner to his, still feeling rather protective of him. *Strange to be protecting a Yaru, but he's the only one interested in a peaceful resolution, aside from me.*

Master Jagare and Master Juro sat at the far end of the table. Several Tahtay, as well as her team, were also in attendance. The Vaktare remained standing a short distance behind Nandin.

The silence in the room was oppressive. It seemed unlikely that anything had been decided or resolved overnight. What they possibly hoped to achieve was beyond her capacity to comprehend, especially since she was sleep deprived.

Master Jagare's booming voice finally broke the silence.

"Do you have anything new to share with us, Yaru?"

"His name is Nandin." Hanna stated. It was beginning to irritate her how they only saw the uniform; they refused to see the man.

Biatach shot her a warning look. The tension in the air was palpable. She would need to remember her manners; she was in presence of kings — or as close to kings as they got on Galenia. Nandin needed no such cautionary glances.

"I'm sorry sir, I have nothing to tell you."

"You still claim to have no knowledge of these tears?"

Nandin nodded.

"Pardon me," Hanna said treading softly this time, "maybe Mateo is causing the tears, but doesn't know it."

Master Jagare and Master Juro conversed quietly for a few moments before Master Juro spoke.

"Nandin, what can you tell us about the quarry?"

"There's not much to tell. The Kameil are removing rocks out of the ground."

"Of course. And why do they do that? What is the point of the quarry?"

Nandin thought a moment. He had already told Hanna that when the Kameil chipped away at the stones, Essence was released in the air. He saw no harm in repeating that point here; they probably already knew. He watched Master Juro's expression as he explained.

Master Juro asked, "And it is enough Essence to allow them to survive?"

"Yes."

Master Juro considered for a moment.

"Yet he makes Essence pills so they can leave the valley." It wasn't a question. "Tell me, are you familiar with how he makes these pills?"

Nandin shrugged. He would have preferred if he had never told Hanna, or Darra as it were, about the pills, but there was nothing he could do about that now.

"We crush the rocks and then Mateo takes the powder away and does...whatever he does with it."

"Do you have any more of those pills on you now?"

Nandin smirked. "If I had any sir, you would have found them when you had me searched and disarmed." The pills Hanna had been given were crushed in her bag as she attempted to escape. The remnants she gave to Master Juro the previous night were hardly enough to study.

Again the Masters put their heads together and also conferred with Tahtay Puto.

"Is this quarry deep?" Master Juro finally asked.

"I guess it's pretty deep." In reality it was incredibly deep, but he preferred to be as vague as possible.

"And does the so-called *liquid Essence* come from the quarry?"

Nandin felt cornered. He didn't want to talk about liquid Essence. He didn't know much about how it was made, but he did know what it was used for and he had no desire to tell anyone how Mateo had made the Yaru. He wondered what would happen today when he didn't answer their questions. Quickly, he determined what he *would* tell them.

"No, Mateo created liquid Essence, but I don't know how. The liquid from the quarry is something else, but again, I don't know what — "

"Other liquid? Is it clear? Does it have any odour?"

"Yes, it's clear. No odour that I can recall."

Master Juro sat back fingering his pencil-like beard. Hanna looked around at the others in the room. Kazi barely seemed awake, Karn was tense and was watching Nandin out of the corner of his eye, and the rest of her team as well as the Tahtays patiently listened to Master Juro's questions and Nandin's answers, their heads moving back and forth as if they were watching a tennis match.

"Master Juro," Master Jagare said, "any idea what this other liquid would be?"

"I have a theory, but no evidence to support it. For sometime I have considered that a substance I call Qual is the key component to survival. It allows Essence to bind. If I am correct, it would mean the Kameil have no Qual."

"Do you think it's possible that it could be linked to the tears?"

"Possible? Yes. Without seeing it for myself I do not know."

While she was relieved that the discussion had been less violent, Hanna was still crestfallen. For months and months she had trained so she could infiltrate the Kameil and speak to the Yaru to determine what Mateo was up to. Not only did she succeed, she had spoken with the Commander of the Yaru and because of her, he was sitting in this room being interrogated by some of the most powerful and knowledgeable people on Galenia. And yet, they were still no further ahead. They still didn't know what caused the tears. They didn't know how to stop them. They didn't know how to send her back home. She closed her eyes and flashed back to the violence in the clearing where both Jagare and Kameil had died. Was it really all for nothing?

"There is someone who knows," she said finally. All eyes turned to look at her. "Mateo. He's probably been analyzing this liquid for years. There's only way to determine if this liquid or the quarry has anything to do with the tears. We need to go to the valley."

Murmuring rippled along the table as everyone began discussing at once the implications of what Hanna had said.

"It would take a great force to get passed that outer wall."

"We don't have the manpower."

"Is it worth the lives it would cost us?"

"Silence!" Master Jagare stood and pounded his fist on the table as he shouted above the noise. As he resumed his seat he muttered, "It would take years to prepare for that sort of undertaking."

"We don't have years," Master Juro responded. "But Mateo is not likely to share his knowledge and would never let any Juro into the valley to investigate. There has to be another way."

Hanna's pulse quickened. The answer was obvious — to her at least. She cleared her throat and rose to her feet as if steeling herself for what she was about to propose.

"There is another way. I will go."

* * *

The room fell silent once again as they stared at her. She was afraid to go into the valley, but judging by the determined faces around her, she knew they planned to see this through with or without her help. She hoped, with her involvement, a peaceful resolution could be obtained.

"Listen, only a Juro, or someone with Juro-like abilities, has a chance of understanding what effect the quarry is having or what this liquid is. If I saw it, I would know what's going on with the Essence or at least I'd have a better chance of knowing than any Jagare or Jivan. There is so much bad blood between everyone that the only way to have a chance at a nonviolent solution, is if there was a neutral party going in and that's me. If I can't figure out what's going on myself, I will talk with Mateo. He wants to meet me anyway. The Yaru said as much back at the clearing, so it's really a no brainer."

"I don't like it," Biatach said. "It's too risky. There's no way we could protect you once you went past that wall."

Nandin sat up a little straighter trying to ignore the ropes that dug into his arms. He put as much authority into his voice as possible, determined to make his case. "Pardon me sir, I would protect her."

"Well pardon me if I don't trust you," Karn countered. "I'm not letting her go in there alone with just the promise of a Yaru to keep her safe. Besides, after the incident in the woods, I'm sure she will not be considered a *neutral party*. It wouldn't be any different than a Juro going."

"That's not true, Hanna didn't attack anyone. We all saw her get swept up on that horse against her will. Besides, that's the reason I came here: to bring her back."

Karn was not ready to concede. "Let's say she discovers what this liquid is, how does that even help us? If Mateo doesn't know he's creating the tears, her going in there could be a complete waste of time."

Master Juro said, "I need to know if the Qual exists and if it is what he is mining. If I am correct, the Qual courses through the ground, rather than Essence, which many Juro believe. It flows through the world like blood flows through the body. Digging deep into the ground could have an effect like cutting open a vein, if you will. A leak at the quarry could be causing a drain elsewhere on Galenia, depleting the area and making it unable to retain Essence. If Hanna could confirm any of this it would answer what it is we need to do."

"And that would be?" Master Jagare asked.

"Plug the vein — fill in the quarry." Master Juro sighed. Guesses and theory's: it did not sound very reassuring, even to his ears.

Tahtay Magnus, who had been listening to the conversation so far, felt the need to contribute. It sounded to him like they had come to a possible action part of the plan and this was more his department; he had been a key player in forming the Vaktare. If there was a need to get into the valley, it would be his men that would take on that challenge.

"How are we going to get anywhere near this quarry to do anything? There is no way we will get past that wall if Mateo doesn't want us to."

"Let us cross that bridge when we come to it," Master Juro responded.

"Hold on," Karn said, "are we actually considering this? Doesn't anyone care about Hanna's safety? We have no idea what Mateo would do to her."

"Maybe I won't even need to go to Mateo, Karn. It's possible I just need to get a good look at the quarry, get a sample of that liquid and bring it back." She sat down hoping she sounded more convincing than she felt.

"Mateo just wants to meet her, but I can get her out of the valley without anyone knowing if needs be," Nandin said.

Karn scoffed. "You can get her out without anyone knowing? Couldn't someone just stand on top of the wall and see you leaving for miles?"

"There's another way," Nandin replied.

Magnus cast Master Jagare a meaningful look. This was information they had longed to have. While they had never attempted to get into the valley before, it was an issue they discussed many times. They had both felt unsettled not knowing what went on behind that wall and apparently for good reason. It seemed almost too good to be true that this young Commander was about to reveal such crucial information.

When Nandin was not more forthcoming, Master Juro subtly prodded, "And how might you do that?"

Nandin considered a moment. He needed to gain their trust without betraying Mateo's. Again, he decided being vague was the way to go. "Through the mountains. It's not an easy passage and few know the way, but I have a trusted friend who does."

Most of those in attendance were anxious to pursue this latest development. Not that they weren't concerned for Hanna's safety, it was just that remote possibilities were suddenly being made available to them. The opportunity was too important to turn down. Biatach looked doubtful, but he had already expressed his concern; Karn wasn't ready to send Hanna into a potentially hostile situation.

"I still don't like it. How do we know Nandin won't just turn Hanna over to Mateo once he's on the other side of that wall? He could be saying all this just so we let him go."

Nandin cringed at Karn's words. It may have been subtle, but he felt the threat in the statement *let him go*.

Master Juro nodded. "That is a valid point Karn. I suggest your team accompanies Hanna as far as possible, and perhaps we could arrange for you to rendezvous with her in the mountains. When it comes down to it though, her fate will be in Nandin's hands. It is up to Hanna if she wishes to pursue this, she is the only one who can make the decision to go with him for it is her life that is at risk."

"Can't my team go with her into the valley? If he can get her in and out, surely he can do the same for us."

"Getting into the valley with Hanna is easy. The Yaru know I went after her, they will have alerted those at the gate to expect our arrival. If I show up with a bunch of Jagare, they will be suspicious. I can't guarantee your safety. Your men killed the Kameil and attacked the Yaru.

My injuries will also not go unnoticed. If you were discovered, there is little I could do for you."

"I thought you said you knew a way through the mountains. Can't you get us in unseen?"

"I can get her out that way with the help of Jon, but even I don't know the path that leads into the valley. We could be wandering through the forest for weeks if we went the wrong way."

"But — "

"Karn," Hanna cleared her voice trying to keep it steady, "I've made my choice. I don't want there to be a chance of anyone else getting killed over this. I'm looking for answers, not trying to lead a crusade. I'm going with Nandin and I'm going alone."

CHAPTER THIRTY-ONE

Excessive Plans

THE STUDY WAS COZY.

Master Jagare and Master Juro retired to the smaller, more private room. The glow from the fire was the only light source and the shadows cast, danced on the wall. The two chairs in front of the hearth sat close together. Master Jagare's legs stretched out onto the animal skin that covered the floor; Master Juro sat with his legs tucked under himself and his arms folded into his sleeves.

"This excursion is incredibly risky. The chance of success is slim," Master Jagare said.

"Hanna has not let us down yet."

"I don't argue that the girl has resilience. I'd still prefer if we sent her with the Vaktare."

"Agreed. Send them."

"The Yaru will hardly go along with it. The Vaktare will have to follow at a distance, like they did last time. Still, we barely got her out of the camp in the middle of the woods. Now we are sending her into a fortified city. I'm not sure what good it will do. If the Yaru betrays us —"

"I believe he will protect her. She may not understand the significance of her actions, but Nandin knows that in